Tennessee Rain

A Novel in Three Parts

Based on true events

Tennessee Rain

emylee bishop sturk

Edited by Laura D. Christian

BALBOA.
PRESS
A DIVISION OF HAY HOUSE

Balboa Press books may be ordered through booksellers or by contacting:

Balboa Press
A Division of Hay House
1663 Liberty Drive
Bloomington, IN 47403
www.balboapress.com
1-(877) 407-4847

ISBN: 978-1-4525-5758-8 (sc)
ISBN: 978-1-4525-5759-5 (e)

Printed in the United States of America

Balboa Press rev. date: 08/24/2012

for dear granny up above
for you and your sister's unfailing love
for grandma and her wildwood flower
for mama with her strength and power
for the best husband there's ever been
for all good, faithful family and friends
for my daughter that's strong and true
this book i give to all of you

PROLOGUE

Sitting in the car staring at the large, red brick hospital in front of me, my mind wandered as I waited. I was wondering what it would be like to leave the country. I knew I shouldn't be jealous, but I couldn't help it. *I* wanted to be the one going. Not that I would miss them. They had been on trips before - granted, never as far as England, but that wasn't the point. The point was that I wanted to go. The point was that I *was* jealous.

I wanted it to be me that needed proof of who I was in order to have a passport to leave the country. It all seemed so top secret, so daring, so mysterious, and oh so fabulous. Besides that, he was my father. It was my family over there across the Atlantic also. Why shouldn't I be going, too?

My racing mind came to a screeching halt when I saw them exit the building. She was holding the paper, and he was holding her. My first initial seconds of thought were, *Thank goodness, they finally got it.* This had been our third stop in two states for that piece of paper.

In the next second my 9-year-old brain registered the fact that something was very wrong. My mother was crying. They were still far away from the car, but I had seen her cry enough to know that she was crying uncontrollably. Surprisingly, her crying didn't alarm me. What alarmed me was that Daddy was holding her, actually holding her, as if she may fall if he released his grip. The closer they came to the car, the more apparent the red puffiness under her eyes became, and the streaks of makeup that ran down her otherwise perfectly made-up face and neck seemed out of place.

Daddy opened her car door, placed her as gently inside as he would a priceless china doll, closed the door, walked around the front of the car, slid behind the wheel, and started the engine. For a moment we all sat in silence. Mama and Daddy stared out the window at the looming red brick building. I stared at the both of them.

After what seemed an eternity, suddenly and without warning, my mother flew into a rage that caused us all to jump back and send our hearts thumping through our throats.

"How could she have done this? After all this time? Why did no one tell me about this? And to think I had to walk in there and be humiliated like that!" She was screaming so loudly that people walking through the parking lot started to stare in our direction.

My father slid closer to her and tried to put his arm around her, but she could not be consoled. She raged on and on. With each word, I felt the blood drain from my small face.

"I can't believe this is happening!" she continued. "The whole time she knew, and she never told me! No one told me! She could have spared me this embarrassment! Just look at this, Emery! LOOK AT IT!" She held the now crumpled paper up in her hand. I tried to read the words, but her hand was trembling so violently that I couldn't make it out.

My father held her shaking hand in his own. "I know, Mae." It seemed to be all he could muster.

She hung her head and studied the paper that had undoubtedly devastated her. In a small voice I did not recognize as my mother's, she murmured, "The trip is less than three weeks away. How will I prove that I am me with no birth certificate; only a registrar paper that reads 'No Name Baby Girl'?"

There was a long moment of silence.

"We'll find a way," my father said in an even smaller voice.

Aunt Mabel, who sat beside me in the back seat, picked up my small hand and stroked it. She remained eerily silent throughout the entire encounter.

As we drove out of the hospital lot, in a mere instant, my head was bombarded by a million facts that had been at my grasp my entire life, but I had never been able to explain; my mind began to race.

I had a small but complicated family in Tennessee. I had two aunts, both of whom were married, but only one had a child. Burke and Stella Crane were referred to as Mama and Daddy by my aunts and uncles. My cousin called them Grandma and Papaw. My immediate family called them by name and nothing more. I was never quite sure how they were related to me.

My parents referred to my mother's parents, Evelyn and Charles, as Mama and Daddy, even though my father had been born and raised in England; his parents had passed on long before. Burke and Stella called Evelyn and Charles Mama and Daddy as well. My aunts, uncles, cousin, brothers, sister, and myself called them Granny and Grandpa.

Granny and Grandpa's last name had been Resenger, and that was my mother's maiden name. There was no reason I could imagine for Mama's records to read "No Name Baby Girl", especially without even a birth certificate. Mama even had an older brother named John Henry, or JH for short, who had been raised with her by Evelyn and Charles. The kids liked to call him Burr-Head because of a haircut. The nickname stuck even after the hair grew out.

My aunts, Rose and Catherine, did not seem to be of any relation to Burr-Head. They were definitely sisters with Mama, and he was definitely Mama's brother, but somehow, Rose, Catherine, and JH weren't brother and sisters.

None of the pieces had ever fit, but up until that day, I didn't seem to mind. I was young. Confusion in my family seemed to be the norm, so I never questioned it.

"I'm so sorry, honey, are you OK?" Mama snapped back to reality and finally realized I was there. I had no choice but to snap back to the situation with her.

"I'm OK, Mama. Are you OK?"

She looked straight at me, but straight through me, and smiled an icy smile with tears remaining in her eyes. "Sure, honey. I'm just fine. How about we go and do some shopping and maybe get an ice cream?" And just like that, she turned off all emotions, to be turned back on again later behind closed doors when she thought no one was looking or listening.

At 9, it became my mission to solve the hidden secrets of my mother's sordid past before they haunted me as much as they haunted her. This is her story. This is an account of my mother's life as it should be told. It is not happy, not by any means. Neither is it particularly tragic; certainly others have suffered greater trials. Nonetheless, it is her story. It is one that has been gathered over the years through countless tales on good days and badgering questioning on bad. It is a story that should be told and should be heard because it is a shocking reality, and because it is hers.

GENERATION ONE
CHARLES

CHAPTER ONE

Through the early sunlight comes the fog surrounding the mountains that give them their name: the Smokies. Tucked neatly on the edge is a tiny town called Newport. In 1923, at the age of 22, Charles sat silently on the mountainside, watching the sunrise, pleased at how he had finally worked life out - well, mostly.

There weren't many options for a farm boy on a small tobacco farm in a small town nestled in the mountains. Charles knew that. School wasn't for him; it confused him, didn't make sense, and he felt it was a waste of time. He hated the farm, and he never wanted to become a farmer. He only worked hard at it to help Poppie. Poppie understood his son. Convincing Mommie of how he felt is what scared him. That was the hard part.

He had made up his mind. Moving to Knoxville for work was the best thing he could do.

He remembered seeing that big city as a young man of about 13. He and Poppie had ridden the train to gather materials for planting that had not been available in Newport that year. The entire trip had fascinated him: the changing scenery as they left the mountainside and made their way into the lower valleys, the buildings, massive in size compared to his tiny town, and carriages, shops, and people lining the streets creating the glamour of 5th Avenue and downtown.

The entire experience had enlightened him to a whole new world that he could conquer. Even then, he knew there must have been plenty of work, and it was at that time that he began to explore new options. He was young and could learn a trade. Only, Mommie felt that Knoxville was a city of sin and shame, although she had never been herself. She would be disgraced when she learned Charles would be moving there.

Poppie and Charles had already spoken about his big decision.

"How'm I gonna tell her, Poppie?"

"Ain't much else ya can do but come right out 'n say it, son. Yer mommie's bark is worse 'n her bite, anyhow."

"I'm guessin' ya ain't been bit as much as I have, Poppie."

They both laughed, but Charles had felt a sinking feeling in the pit of his stomach after their conversation. Poppie sensed his anguish, for he had felt it many times himself when it came to dealing with Mommie.

Charles walked the trail on the hillside from the creek, carrying two large pails of water. He kicked a rock in the woods and studied a squirrel nestled in a tree, nibbling on an acorn. *If only I had my gun*, he thought, *we could have us a fine supper.*

The thought of it filled his mind again with the wonders of the lush, lavish restaurants he had seen in Knoxville; he was positive that squirrel was not on the menu. Newport had only one small diner, and most of its business came in the mornings when old men gathered to drink coffee and chat, away from their wives.

A million thoughts paced back and forth through Charles's head. The small cut out section of newspaper carried in his pocket wallet, wrapped in the cash he had been saving up for quite some time now, tucked away secretly so that Mommie couldn't find it, stated that the factory job started in three weeks. That wasn't much time. There was no guarantee he would even get the job. Trying to stay optimistic, he was sure that there would be other jobs, maybe even better jobs, if this one didn't work out.

Suddenly, like an unexpected slap to the face, water buckets almost spilled as his thoughts turned to Ella. He hadn't told her yet. How could he not have thought of this earlier? She was a big part of this decision. She was the biggest part of his life.

They had become so close recently. There was no explanation for his feelings other than love. He knew for certain that he loved her, but what could he do? There was no future here for them. He had seen what the tobacco farm had done to his father and mother, how they had suffered over the years.

And what would be the alternative to farming? Only a week prior one cousin had been shot to death while running moonshine, and another had been caught and sent to jail. He didn't want to end up like that. What choice was there? Things just weren't the same in Newport as other places. At least, that's what Charles had hoped. Ella would have to understand. He would get a job in Knoxville, find a nice place, and send for her. That was the only way.

By the time Charles made it home, the sun was full up. Mommie was fuming mad and screaming from inside the small box house.

"Where ya been, boy? Off daydreamin', I 'pose. Git in here and wash up so ya can help wit' what's left of fixin' breakfast. 'Tis good thang we had water left from last night, or we'd a died a thirst waitin' fer ya to drag it up from the crick."

Charles rushed out back to the wash bin to clean up. He did all he could not to agitate his mother any further; he knew the blow that was coming was going to be hard enough to last a lifetime.

According to Mommie's plan, Charles was to take over the farm that had been handed down for many generations. The only problem was that the farm was failing and had been for some time. Charles couldn't imagine his life worse off than the life his mother and father had spent. He couldn't see himself turning as bitter and sour as Mommie.

He vaguely remembered a soft, kindhearted woman in his younger years. He could see the small, white, box house with the large stone columns creating a cover for the porch and beautiful snowball bushes in between. She was sitting in a rocker on the stone porch rocking, knitting, and laughing as he played in the lush yard as a boy. He would run through the barn with his arms scraping the hanging tobacco and eat apples from the tree until she would fuss gently that he would get a tummy ache if he ate more.

Mommie glanced out the window at her handsome, young son with a slight smile. She, too, remembered softer times and longed for them as well, but *Don't look back, never look back* was her life long standing motto, though she never spoke the words.

Charles also remembered several harsh, bitter winters where snow covered the windows and doors and they all faced death. He remembered hard seasons with no help where Mommie worked the fields with Poppie until her fingers bled. With each passing season, Mommie became the hard woman she was now. The thought of this farm doing that to Ella made Charles's heart shudder. *No*, he thought, *there is no choice.*

He walked back inside and did everything Mommie asked and most things she didn't before she had to ask. He shoveled more coal into the potbelly stove Mommie was cooking on in the parlor, straightened up the cushions, folded the handmade afghans neatly, and swept the entire parlor before setting the table, which was in the brightest part of the tiny main room, near the window. His stomach did flip flops at breakfast. He didn't know how or when he could bring up the subject with her.

Mommie sensed something was strange. She kept glancing at him with a suspicious eye.

"What's gotten inta ya, boy? Yer off daydreamin', late fer breakfast, and ya been squirmin' in yer seat all mornin'." She studied his face intently looking for some clue that would tell her what was happening.

She knew her only son as well as Poppie did, or so she thought.

"Nuthin', Mommie. Just daydreamin'. Just like ya said."

She studied him harder, positive something was on his mind. "Well, git yer head together, boy. Ya gots a big day of work ahead of ya."

"Yes'm."

After breakfast, Charles helped Mommie clear the dishes and take them out back to be washed up. Washing was women's work according to Mommie, so after clearing, he fed the chickens and slipped on his boots to help Poppie run the small acreage field. Mommie watched him, knowing that something was on his mind. She thought about a good whipping to get his head straight, but she imagined what things a boy of his age could be going through, so she decided to leave the matter alone.

The day dragged for all of them. Poppie was tired, hot, and dehydrated from the sweltering heat coupled with unbelievable humidity, but just as Poppie always did, he ignored everything else and focused on his work. Mommie finished up the housework and started on the ends of the fields Charles and Poppie hadn't gotten to. They were all aware of the fact that, in many ways, Mommie was tougher than either of them.

Charles's mind couldn't help but run wild with thoughts of leaving Newport, of leaving Ella, during his work. After much debating, he decided that he needed to talk to Ella before he said anything to Mommie. Talking to Ella would be hard, but not as hard as his conversation with Mommie. Ella's heart would be broken, but it would soon heal, especially with his promise to come for her. Mommie would feel betrayed, and her heart might never heal. Charles had never done anything that would cause his mother anguish - not just for the sake of a tanned hide, but for her sake as well. As tough as she was, she was his mother, and he loved her dearly. He only wished he could foresee the future. He didn't want to hurt either of them.

As soon as dusk settled in, Charles helped Mommie and Poppie clean up the tools and mess from the fields. Before Mommie had a chance to protest, he announced that he wouldn't be home for supper, opened the gate to the yard, and set down the dirt road on his way to Ella's house. He hadn't even had a chance to wash up and was covered in dust and grime.

Both Mommie and Poppie stood confused and speechless. Mommie was sure something was going on and could tell by the look in Poppie's eyes that whatever it was, he knew. Speaking to him about the subject would be useless. Poppie was not a man of many words, especially when it came to Mommie.

During the three-mile walk to Ella's home, Charles practiced over and over again what he would say to her. The moon glimmered softly through rolling clouds, darkness covered the land, and the only lights were those of the scattered porch lanterns and the extremely occasional vehicle passing by slowly with dimly lit headlamps. The long trek up the wooded hill to Ella's cabin in the dark was an effort compared to climbing it in the light of day, especially after a day of back breaking work in the tobacco field.

Standing in front of the dark, clapboard house with the dilapidated wrap around porch, he wondered if she was home. The hunting dogs, gathered under the porch woodwork, knew Charles well and didn't even raise their heads. An owl hooted in the distance, breaking the silence and startling Charles.

Having seen his moonlit figure climbing the hillside, a puzzled Ella pulled back the tattered window curtain with a crooked smile and motioned for him to come up the walk. She came to the front porch and lit the lamp, wondering what he was doing there. He reached the porch to see her smiling face, which gleamed in the glow of the lamp. Her green eyes sparkled. Her dark curls shone. With each passing day she became more beautiful in his eyes. She noticed his admiration, blushed, and then she asked why he was there.

"Din' know if ya'd be home. House was dark n' all."

"Pa went out drinkin' again, and Ma went after him. Same ol', same ol'. I like it dark when they ain't here. Makes it seem quieter, ya know, without the arguin' an' all."

Charles instantly became quite nervous, not knowing what to say or how to start. A rush of horrible memories of Ella's past in this shack shuddered over him. He immediately realized he was planning on leaving her in a bigger mess than he had thought himself to be in.

Again, Ella, still puzzled, started with her questioning. "Whatcha doin' here, Charles? I din' think you'd come a callin' tonight. It's purty late 'n all."

"Well, there's somethin' I been meanin' ta talk ta ya 'bout," he said, growing quiet again, not knowing how to begin.

Ella just smiled and looked deeply into his eyes. She had thought for a while that he may be ready for marriage. After all, they were growing up quickly and some of the married couples in Newport were younger than they. Still, he hadn't spoken with her pa yet. She knew that for sure, so in second thinking, she became inquisitive again.

Charles rubbed the skin on the back of his neck while staring at the ratty shoes on his feet. Ella's feet were bare, as they usually were except in harsh winters. Unexpected to him, Charles's thought at that moment was, *I even love her toes. How can I leave her?*

His precious thought was shattered by the roaring, bickering voices of Ella's parents coming up the hillside. They were screaming with such force it echoed through the mountainsides. Ella's face drained of all color, startlingly visible in the darkness of night.

"I tole ya ta stay away from that house of whores!" Ma Milner was speaking very harshly in an extremely loud tone. "Ya done gone and embarrassed yerself 'n this here family 'gain!"

The closer they came to the small house, the louder and clearer their voices became. Charles and Ella stood frozen in silence, staring, watching, waiting.

"Why'nt ya go on 'n call me a disgrace again liken' ya did las' time!" Old Man Milner was breathless and hoarse from the argumentative climb. "Ya high 'n mighty bitch!"

Ella sucked in her breath. They had reached the front walkway and were less than 10 yards away from the house when Old Man Milner's backhand came down so hard onto Ma Milner's face that they all heard a loud crack. She fell to the ground. Charles jumped up to go to her aide. Astonished, Ella stiffened, and in an action that seemed slow motion to her, she tried to grab at Charles's shirt as she yelled, "NO!"

Old Man Milner's surprisingly quick hand came in fast on Charles, giving him an instant cramping stomach ache that caused him to lean straight over and vomit. On his hands and knees heaving, a steel toed boot ripped into his ribcage where there was another loud crack. More vomit spewed forward, this time joined with blood, and a jolt of pain seared through every inch of his body.

Old Man Milner's back was to Ella. Her rage caused her to run towards her father as soon as she was able to breathe. With all her might, she shoved the overpowering man to the ground, just as he was about to kick Charles in the side again.

She didn't do him any harm, and when he rose, he was furious, gutting out a deep, sinister laugh. His dark eyes flashed red, reaching for his daughter who was now at Charles's side. Grabbing her by the left arm, he picked her tiny, malnourished body up off the ground as if she were a rag doll. Slinging her body with the brute force of one giant hand he screamed, "What's a matta, girl? Daddy not good 'nuf fer ya no more? Are ya mad at me fer hurtin' yer poor little beau? Don' see ya too worried 'bout yer ma layin' ova there."

In one swift movement, Ella was tossed to the side, nearly landing on top of her ma. She had hit her head on a rock and was bleeding from a gash in her forehead.

Charles regained his composure and rose while Old Man Milner drank white lightning from a flask he had kept in his rear pocket. The old man laughed an evil laugh again, staring at his battered wife and child. Charles stood upright slowly, walked to Ella's pa, and punched him in the jaw as soon as he had turned Charles's way. Old Man Milner's head only jolted to the side as he laughed.

Before he could move, the hard metal flask came down on Charles's face. Through a ringing ear and an already swollen eye, he watched Old Man Milner enter the house and slam the door behind him.

"Ella!" Charles rushed to her side and gently cradled her in his arms. He stroked her hair, wet from blood. Blood from his split cheek and dripping, broken nose trickled down, coinciding with hers, entangling their souls in a moment of deep distress.

Ella's eyes fluttered open, and quickly jumping to her feet, she ran to her mother. "Ma, Ma!" She shook her shoulder, to which Ma Milner responded with a loud, drunken moan. Ella hung her head and sobbed with Charles at her side. Suddenly gluing the pieces of the clouded puzzle together, she asked Charles frantically where her father had gone.

"He's inside. Don' 'spect he be comin' back out. Come on. Help me least get yer ma up on ta th' porch."

He moved closer towards them, and Ella could clearly see the swollen, red and black puffiness that surrounded most of Charles's face.

"Wha'd he do t'ya?" she gasped.

"Nuthin'. Don' ya worry 'bout nuthin' now. I be just fine."

He scooped his arms under Ma Milner and tried to lift. Weight crushed on his chest and side, causing him to fall back from the pain of trying to lift the small woman.

Ella's faced changed as Charles had never seen it before. A dark anger raged in her eyes that turned her usual sparkle into blackness. She jumped to her feet.

"Pa! Pa!" She was running up the stairs of the dilapidated porch, screaming frantically, and disappeared inside the shack before Charles could catch his breath. Seconds later, screams and crashes could be heard from inside.

A voice that pierced Charles's heart howled, "PA, NO!"

Charles, now feeling no pain, bounded up the rickety steps and into the front door where he saw Ella crouched in the corner, protecting herself with her arms by covering her head and face. The sight of Old Man Milner's sheer brute force heading towards Charles's delicate flower gave him the full, fierce force of his strength. Forgetting pain and broken bones, Charles overpowered the old man.

"Get out th' house!" Charles screamed back at Ella. "GET OUT!"

Wild eyes glaring at the horrific sight froze her momentarily before her legs rattled enough to retreat from the shack.

The battle ensued as, one by one and hit by hit, each man tried to drive the other down. One last, loud thunderous crack in the face finally knocked Old Man Milner to the floor. Charles stared down at the pitiful drunken excuse of a man lying before him. As he turned to leave, he flipped his head back and spat on him where he lay bleeding. Exiting, with a confidence he had never felt before, he spied Ella at the end of the walk comforting her ma.

Charles strolled her way with a strange sort of smile - a sinister smile of complete satisfaction. It was a smile Ella had never before seen across his face.

"How's she?" he asked, still smirking in spite of the situation.

"She be OK, I think." After a moment she whispered, "And Pa?" She stared into Charles's eyes with uncertainty.

Charles's crooked smile broadened. "Like I said, they's 'nuthin ta worry 'bout." He draped his arm over her shoulder and said, "Let's get on outta here."

Hours later, the frogs still croaked and the crickets still chirped, undisturbed by the cruelty of life. Ella and Charles sat at the creek, silently watching and listening. Here they had come and here they had sat, not speaking a word, each lost in their own thoughts.

Charles stood and reached for Ella's hand. Without question, she allowed him to lead the way.

Chapter Two

*D*aylight rising through the early morning mists found Charles and Ella walking hand in hand towards the main road out of town. Charles's mind was reeling from the series of events suddenly thrust in obstacle of his plans. He had wanted everything to be perfect. He had wanted to have a job, a home, to be the kind of man that Ella deserved before sending for her.

Ella was only filled with the horror that had, up until this moment, been her life.

A loud, slow moving motor vehicle puttered up behind them and stopped. It was a sound they knew well. Turning, they saw Foster driving his fairly new, but battered, International truck, used for his masonry business, with Poppie at his side. The truck came to a slow, squealing stop, and the two emerged.

"Oh, Foster, t'was horrible. Have ya been there? Is she alright?" Ella's panic made her voice shrill and terrified as she ran to her brother, embracing him tightly.

Foster pulled her arms length away and examined the large gash, swollenness, and blue bruising that had risen in her face and forehead. Her dark, beautiful curls were frumpy and stained red, having only been rinsed in the creek.

Infuriated, Foster calmly stated, "Yeah, hun. Ma's OK. She be jus' fine." The wicked thoughts in his head said, *Pa ain't gonna be for long.*

Poppie exited the truck and stepped to his son. "Ya took ya a beatin', din' ya, son?"

"Guess so, Poppie. But I be fine."

Charles was silent for a moment before continuing, glancing at Ella with tears in his eyes. "I gotta take 'er now, Poppie. She can't stay now. I can't leave her behind."

"I know it, son. Pieced it all together when yer mommie 'n me got up 'n ya wern' home. Walked myself down there ta Foster, 'n we drove over ta th' house 'n found their ma in th' yard with 'er face all bashed up 'n ya two nowheres ta be foun'."

"Din' mean ta worry ya, Poppie. Kinda' a bad night, I 'pose. Head ain't quite clear." He paused before continuing, "But, we got ta go, Poppie. I got ta take 'er now before he comes fer her."

Poppie hung his head, knowing his son was right. When Old Man Milner woke from his drunken stupor, he would be out to kill Charles, for sure. And Ella, poor Ella, he would lock her away, never to be found again. Or worse.

He was an ornery, mean, nasty drunk, whose drinking had become more and more severe as new stills arose throughout the mountain range. Although he was not quite "old" as one would assume, years of drinking mountain moonshine and living hard had traced deep lines into his face, giving him the forever name of Old Man.

Foster came to Charles and shook his hand firm. "I wanna thank ya fer what ya did."

"I din' do nuthin' any decent man wouldn't a done. Tried ta a' least pull yer ma onto th' porch, but I'm a thinkin' yer pa done cracked my rib. Couldn't lift her."

"Yep, he sure did a number on ya alright." Foster contemplated the situation for a moment before proceeding.

Poppie had told Foster, on the way to find Charles and Ella, that they might be headed out of town. Through his sleepiness and lack of any further gained knowledge, his first thought had been that there was no way in hell Charles was taking his baby sister away. He didn't care if he was married into the Resenger family. There was nothing Poppie, Charles, Ella, or even his wife, Bessie could say to convince him otherwise.

That was until he found his ma laying in the front yard, bloody and swollen; his pa, equally bloody and swollen, sleeping off the previous night's lightning, upright in the parlor, guarding the door with a shotgun. Then, and only then, did he begin to realize that Charles may be right in taking Ella away.

Foster finally continued. "First, we need to git yas both to th' doc. He got to fix y'all up."

Charles began to protest, thinking Old Man Milner would soon be after them. Foster read his mind and held up his hand to finish. "Pa'll be sleepin' off that drunk fer awhile. After th' doc takes a look at ya, I kin take yer poppie home an' then I'll take yas both wherever it is y'all are goin'." He glanced at Ella, saw her battered face, and turned away, focusing on the fields and forcing back stinging tears.

A small smile formed across Ella's delicate face. She wasn't questioning. She only knew that Charles was taking her from this awful place. She didn't care where they were going. They were going.

All four climbed into Foster's work truck as he started the rumbling engine. The roosters crowed at the light of day, and the dim front lights had just been fired at the home of Doc Murphy in town. With a small rap at the door, the good doctor was faced with a minor injury on a beautiful face and the more severe injuries of her protector. He knew the Milner family well and accepted all in with open arms. The Resenger family was a strong breed who had never had need for a doctor, so he politely introduced himself before beginning his work, without question.

Poppie and Foster waited in the large parlor, fidgeting impatiently. After nearly an hour and a few cries of pain, Ella was cleaned up and stitched. Charles was stitched, had a broken nose set, and had two cracked ribs wrapped tightly to prevent further injury and restrict movement.

As they exited the back room, Foster stood, shook the good doctor's hand, and pulled out his pocket wallet. Poppie hung his head, knowing there was no wallet in his pocket and no money to gather had he owned one. Observing all of this, Charles reached for his own money.

Foster grabbed his arm and squeezed gently. "T'was my fight." He continued thoughtfully, "I should'a been there for 'em. It be my bill."

Charles knew not to argue with Foster. He was shrewd. Rarely anyone, excepting Bessie, could outwit him, much less win a debate. Bessie would often joke that the only reason Foster married her was because she was the only one who could keep him in line. Charles secretly smiled and thought, with a slight blush, *I know Ella could keep me in line.*

They departed the doctor's home, climbing back into the large, sea-green International. Turning onto the dirt road out of town, they headed toward the hillsides and the path to the Milner house became visible. They all sat in silence, every eye turned toward the path as they slowly passed. There was no movement - no signs of life. Once out of sight, Ella let out the breath of air that she had been holding in deeply.

Breaking the silence and changing the subject to what he knew was on all of their minds, Poppie asked Charles if he was going to talk to Mommie.

"Tell ya th' truth, Poppie, hadn't even thought 'bout it till now. Come dawn, th' only thin' on my mind was gettin' away."

Ella's heart jumped in her chest. Was he changing his mind?

Charles stared out the window for a long moment before continuing. "I can't leave without a goodbye ta 'er, Poppie. She'd always be a wonderin' an' a worryin'." His voice trailed off. More to himself than anyone else, he said, "She'll just have to understand."

Ella calmed herself before becoming nervous at the realization that they were passing Foster and Bessie's house on the old dirt road and would soon be at the Resenger farm. Charles's mother would surely be there, waiting, wondering, and boiling mad. Ella was afraid and intimidated by Mommie Resenger, and it seemed that this situation would be the worst she was ever to encounter with her.

"Wait!" she cried out. "Stop the truck!" Foster brought the truck to a slow stop. Before he could ask why, Ella was out and running toward Bessie and Foster's. Banging on the back screen door, she found Bessie welcoming her with open arms.

"Oh, dear God, chil'. What's he gone an' done ta ya now?" Bessie's concerned face turned to worry as Ella recalled all the events of the past night and early morning in a fountain of flowing frenzy.

Without another word, Bessie had Ella's hand in her own and was climbing into the back of the truck to break the news to Mommie with them. Bessie knew that this was going to take an intervention. With Mommie's temper, she felt being there could help calm matters; at least that's what she hoped for.

Past the creek and up the hill, the spitting, sputtering truck made its slow climb. Around the bend, the white box house and small farm, sprawling up the hillside, became visible. Slowly, the porch came into view with a very worried, angry, wrinkled-faced Mommie standing and waiting. Foster pulled between the gated yard and the tobacco barn, cutting the engine. One by one, they piled out of the vehicle, the two that were battered exiting last. Mommie saw her son's face and bruised body and began to sprint towards him with the force of a young girl.

Shouting hysterically in an inaudible voice, Mommie ran to her son, holding and rocking him as much as his tall body and fractured ribs would allow. Poppie came over and carefully pried her from Charles, walking her slowly back to the porch and sitting her down. Crying was not her way, but tears streamed down her face as she continued to shriek, still inaudible, staring at Charles.

Poppie stood behind Mommie, gripping her shoulders steadily. Charles sat at her side, holding her hand; Ella was at his side with a gentle hand placed over his own shoulder. Mommie rocked back and forth, mumbling under her breath.

At the truck, Bessie held Foster back for a moment before joining the others.

"This the right thin', darlin'?" she inquired sensitively.

"Got ta be. Only way I see. Damn no good low life might go on an' kill her if'n she stays," he grunted gruffly, strolling slowly toward the porch.

Bessie stood behind and watched the plight of horror taking place in front of her, affecting such a very close part of all of their personal lives, as well as their hearts. Foster had always protected his sister with every fiber of his being. Letting her go, no matter who it was to be with, would be as hard for him as it would be for Mommie to watch her baby boy walk away.

Bessie joined the others as the evening, as well as morning, events were unfolded before Mommie. She crouched in front of her, placed her hands on Mommie's knees, and listened as intently as Mommie to see if she had missed anything from Ella's breathless revelation. When Foster reached the point where he and Poppie had found them heading out of town, Bessie interrupted quickly, talking over him. She didn't want Mommie knowing that Charles was going to leave without speaking with her first.

"Ya know him, Mommie. That old man ain't never been no good. Ya know what he can do. If'n she stays, we can't hide her forever. And he *will* get to her."

There was a long pause.

"She has to go, Mommie." Bessie took a deep breath and lowered her head, focusing on the stone floor of the porch. After a moment she looked up, straight into Mommie's eyes. "*They* have to go," she whispered, almost silently.

Mommie's face lost all expression as she stared at Bessie blankly. All were mute, waiting for the words to sink in.

Suddenly, Mommie's eyes opened wide. "Oh! No!" She jumped straight up and paced the yard. Red faced and full of fire she spat out, "My boy ain't a goin' nowheres!" Tears streamed down her face as she continued furiously. "That's *my* boy! He gonna take on th' farm. His future already been set! Thinkin' he gon' take off with a girl t'ain't even his wife." Her voice trailed, "No sir. No son o' mine."

"Mommie?" Charles spoke softly. "I been thinkin' 'bout goin' ta Knoxville fer a while now. They got plenty of jobs there. I could send you and Poppie money to help yas get by."

Mommie instantly became indignant. "We don' need no money from that Devil's town." She became quiet, full of fury. In a wicked voice she winced and spat the words, "Sounds like yas made yer mind up already. Get yer thin's 'n go. An' yas better be married as soon as yas get there, or you will be no son o' mine. I raised ya better 'n this, boy."

Charles walked to his mother and embraced her. She stood frozen, refusing to clutch his embrace. "Thank ya, Mommie, fer yer blessins."

She shoved him away. "Ya ain't got my blessin', boy. Y'all better mark my words, y'all be back, believe you me, y'all be back." With that, she pivoted indignantly and walked inside, slamming the screen door loudly behind her.

Charles bowed his head, praying that she would understand, would turn, embrace him, and wish him the best and her love. His heart ached from her anger and defiance to understand.

Poppie's hand touched Charles's shoulder. "Pack yer thin's. I can calm yer mommie. Ya got to go. Don' worry 'bout us, just make sure to always write."

They embraced momentarily before Charles entered the house. Mommie was sitting in a corner chair, staring out the window, silent and still.

Charles packed a burlap sack full of tattered clothing and memories. Pulling open a dresser drawer, he delicately opened a folded tissue that had been tucked neatly into the corner. He examined its contents, carefully folded it again, and placed it gently into his front pocket. Looking around his tiny bedroom, he departed with harsh, but fond reminiscence. Walking into the parlor, Mommie was still seated, staring glassy-eyed.

"Mommie?" There was no response. "I love ya, Mommie. Always will. Hope ya can understan'."

She didn't look his direction, didn't say a word, didn't acknowledge he was there. She didn't want to lose her son; to look at him would confirm that. He could have changed it all. He would've turned the farm around. He would've made it work. Why, oh why, would he leave for that sinful city? And with a girl that was yet to be his wife.

With a sigh and a sinking feeling in his heart, Charles said goodbye one last time accompanied by a gentle kiss to her cheek. The screen door closed, and Mommie heard the rumbling engine start and drive away. She touched the cheek where his lips had grazed; quiet tears streamed constant down her weathered, wrinkled face.

As the truck tugged along the old dirt road away from the house, God Himself felt Mommie's pain, opened the sky, and allowed the Smoky Mountain Tennessee rain to fall.

The truck slowly descended the mountain and turned. "They's a quick stop I got ta make," ordered Foster.

"Whatcha gonna do now? Foster?" Bessie's question received no response.

Foster stopped the truck in front of the path leading to Foster and Ella's former home. As he grabbed the shotgun that hung in the back window, an eerie glow shone in his brilliant green eyes.

"Foster, NO!" Ella screamed hysterically, but he was out the door and headed up the path regardless. Ella jumped out of the truck and stopped inches short of the path, frozen, realizing that she would never be physically able to walk that path again. It was a pathway into a glimpse of hell.

The remaining passengers watched as he walked upwards until he disappeared into the woods. They listened as rain pounded on the roof of the truck; each knew what Foster's mission was, but none spoke of it.

Ella returned, soaked wet from the pouring rain. She shivered, not from the cold, but from fear and uncertainty. Charles took a jacket from his burlap sack, placed it around her shoulders, and held her tight.

Once at the wooden shack, Foster kicked open the door to add dramatic surprise, only to find his pa still passed out cold, shotgun gripped in his hand. He checked his ma, whom he had placed in the bed earlier. She was still sleeping off a drunk, and was battered, beaten and blood stained with what he was certain was a broken nose. Foster walked back to his pa and cocked the shotgun directly into his face, which woke him, groggily, but instantly.

Slurred words tried to pronounce, "Go on if yer such a man, shoot me! Ya ain't got the guts."

"Maybe not," Foster thought out loud with a smile, "but, I will fight ya man ta man, no guns."

"Oh! I see! Thinkin' ya can take yer old man, now, huh?"

Hard blows immediately ensued from both men. For a drunk, the old man could fight the fight of a champion. Foster knew this well. He remembered many instances of his pa beating men half to death over issues that did not matter. He had once cracked a man's skull for bumping into him on the street and not saying excuse me. Regardless, he was still drunk from the previous night, and Foster's force of energy was his rage. Blow after blow the old man took until he fell to the floor, bleeding, gripping his stomach, and trying to catch his breath. Begrudgingly, he told his only son to get out. Foster knew he had won the battle. *Once and for all*, he thought.

"Ya've lost it all, old man! Lettin' that bottle take ev'ry bit away from ya! Ya was happy once, but neva' again. NEVA' AGAIN!"

His pa was speechless, breathless, and most of all, non-inquisitive, realizing in a moment of clarity that he had forever lost any love either of his children had ever held in their hearts for him.

Foster raised his shoulders straight, held his head high, and with dignity that was his own, not instilled, walked past the withered, bloodied, broken old man and into the small cubby Ella had called her bedroom for years. He gathered what little she owned, saddened by how little there actually was.

Back at the truck, Foster handed Ella a small sack holding her belongings with a strange smile. No one asked questions, but Charles noticed the bloody knuckles on Foster's hands, recognized the similarity to his own, and knew words were not needed. Bessie and Ella sat silently staring, neither looking at the other, knowing in their heart of hearts what had taken place, but not wanting to imagine, much less have details.

Despite their trepidation of what lie ahead, driving through the hillside, rain pounding, Charles and Ella truly witnessed the lush beauty that had surrounded them their entire lives for the first time. Sadness as well as excitement filled them both. Ella's eyes became wider and wider as she witnessed land she had never seen. Newport had been her prison for many years, having never left. The long, slow drive through dirt and gravel roads, as well as the occasional gravel paved streets allowed Ella to truly soak up God's beautiful creations. As unsure as she was of what may come, she was certain in her mind that whatever it was would lead to a better place.

At first glance of that big city, all of them had their breath taken away. None of them had been there more than once, and Ella had never been at all. Charles's last visit had been nearly 10 years ago; so much had changed. The city seemed larger, more buildings had risen, streets had been laid and there were more motor vehicles than any of them had seen in a lifetime. Only an elite few in Newport had owned a vehicle. Bessie and Foster noticed the changes as well, all three commenting as they gawked out the windows of the International. Ella only sat in silent amazement.

Excepting the occasional general conversation required for a long trip, no one had mentioned any plans upon arrival, although different thoughts were drifting through all of their heads. Bessie changed all that; she always knew how to take charge and manage any situation.

"T'is Friday. It's early enough. The first thin' we gonna do is go on down to th' courthouse an' get yas hitched. Ya promised Mommie, Charles."

Everyone shifted a bit uncomfortably. Ella's heart did pitter patters, even under these circumstances.

Bessie continued. "Th' next thin' we gonna do is take ya 'round ta some places where ya can maybe get ya a good paying job. After that, we start looking fer a place fer yens ta stay."

"I got some money saved up, sis."

Bessie turned his direction with a thoughtful gaze. "Ya been plannin' on leavin' for a while now, ain't ya? I knew somethin' was goin' on. Mommie did, too. Done talked to me 'bout it."

Charles instantly flipped his head in Ella's direction. Her shocked face revealed her immediate pain. "That's what ya wanted ta tell me, wat'n it? Las' night." She spoke softy through teary eyes, "Ya was gon' leave me, weren' ya?"

"I'm sorry, Ella. That was what I came fer. I was plannin' to go git a job 'n send fer ya. I wanted it ta be done right. I wanted ta do right by ya. I'm sorry I din' tell ya sooner."

Ella turned her head away from him as a small tear trickled down her face. Silence passed for what seemed hours for all of them until Foster spoke up.

"What's done's done. Ya was plannin' to go and send fer 'er anyways, now y'all can tough it out together. Make yas stronger."

Ella dried her tears, understanding her brother's advice, as she always had. Charles was also given insight by this revelation, as he had admitted in his mind that he secretly had doubts. Charles held Ella's hand firmly and squeezed. She turned to him, not smiling, but eyes filled with love. Bessie's plan would work, and they knew that.

Finding the courthouse with ease, Bessie noticed that there were shops all around. "Y'all two keep yerselves busy. Me 'n Ella be back directly." In a flash they were gone, Bessie tugging Ella along by the elbow.

An hour had passed when they returned to find the boys sitting on the courthouse steps. Charles was wearing one of his best shirts, taken from his burlap sack, and had picked up a beautiful flower bouquet during their wait.

The gorgeous woman standing at Bessie's side hardly looked like the girl Charles had fallen in love with. As they drew closer, his heart pounded in his chest at the special splendor standing before him. Her simple, but new white dress was dazzling. Her tiny, pale blue earrings and necklace made her green eyes glow. The embroidered pocket book and shoes made her more beautiful than Cinderella herself. A hair pin, passed down for generations in the Resenger family, had been holding Bessie's hair; it was now enlaced in Ella's dark flowing locks. She carried a pale blue Bible that Charles knew well. He had given it to Bessie as a birthday present the past year. Something old, something new, something borrowed, something blue.

Charles, as well as Foster, was speechless.

"Well don' just stand there an' look at me! Say somethin'! I ain't never had no new clothes on 'fore and it's my weddin' day!" She giggled giddily after her words, blushing slightly.

Charles stepped close to her and gathered her in his arms. "Ya're the most amazin'ly beautiful bride I ever did lay my eyes on."

Tears welled in both of their eyes before they let go of their loving embrace. This is what they wanted. They both knew. This is what had been missing. This was their destiny, as well as their wedding day.

As they walked up the stairs to the courthouse, with her arm slipped through his and his hand on hers, all was right with the world. At the top of the stairs, Charles stopped, turned toward her, pulled out the tissue he had placed in his pocket, and unfolded it. He bent on one knee, with his hand still embracing hers and, again with tears in his eyes, held up the dainty engagement ring that had also been passed down throughout the years, although it had never had another owner to be worn for this purpose.

"Ya th' one I wanna be wit' foreva', Ella. Ya're the girl that took my heart, and it can neva' belong to another. Will ya marry me?"

Through uncontrollable tears, she smiled, shook her head, and said yes.

Charles jumped up, grabbed her and spun her around as they both laughed.

Foster and Bessie looked on and smiled. *They're going to be fine*, they simultaneously thought. *Just fine.*

After countless papers to fill out, they were soon standing in front of the Justice of the Peace. The love in their hearts sparkled in their eyes. The ceremony was short, but it meant the world to both of them. Foster and Bessie witnessed, both choking back tears, Bessie dabbing her eyes with a handkerchief now and then. When asked for the rings to exchange, they grasped the fact that neither had a band for their exchange. Foster smiled, knowing they wouldn't, and pulled two small gold bands from his pocket.

"These were Grandma and Grandpa's, li'l sis. Been saving 'em fer ya."

Tears welled in her eyes as simple, perfectly fitting, beautiful golden bands were placed on their fingers as symbols of a never ending love and connection.

"I now pronounce you man and wife."

Neither of them had ever been happier than at that single moment.

CHAPTER THREE

---

*S*ome say all things take time to adjust. This was not the case for
Ella.

Foster and Bessie stayed in Knoxville with their newly wed siblings
that day, the rest of the evening, and well into the next day before
heading back to the sleepy, but sly, town of Newport. Ella was positive
that they were only sticking around to make sure that their young
brother and sister would be all right in that big city that was so new to
all of them.

Charles found a job almost immediately at the railroad yard. It was
hard work, lifting and unloading freight cars, work he was not fully
capable of doing for the first month due to his cracked ribs, but he
kept moving for the sake of his new wife and their new life together.
Upon arrival, he realized that the position for the job he had carried in
his pocket wallet had already been filled. In all actuality, Charles was
happy to have found work at all, having come to this city blindly, on a
whim that should have been better planned. He had decided long ago
that even in the best of circumstances, much less the worst, plans can
go awry.

Ella refused to let the city or the situation overwhelm her. They had
quickly found a boarding house close to the rail yard. It had a shared
kitchen with a giant potbelly stove and a shared indoor bathroom with
running water. That in itself was more than she ever had. She prided

herself, feeling like a queen in a 10' x 10' castle with a window. She was fascinated with each passing car. She gawked at the large city buildings in amazement. The people, the markets, the excitement, the hurried pace; she soaked in every last detail.

She did her best to make their one small room a home. Delicate curtains let in the light, causing a cozy feel. A moving neighbor, saddened by their lack of furniture and such, had donated a worn, sunken couch. Ella had quickly sewn and stuffed pillows for added comfort. She had found odds and ends at the markets, only things they could afford, adorning the small room with precious, treasured knick-knacks. She diligently worked - cleaning, sweeping, dusting, fluffing pillows, folding hand-knitted afghans and doing the wash - until their tiny room actually took on the feel of a real home.

She took what little money Charles brought home each week and she, along with some other wives in the row of boarding houses, would walk the street to the markets and do their shopping. Many complained about being too poor to own an automobile, that the trek was long and strenuous, especially on the way back, loaded with parcels. Ella's thoughts were that these women had no idea what poor was. She had walked much further to school or church and back each day of her life and even further hauling scrap materials for her father after school and on Saturdays.

Charles came home exhausted each night, his young body aching and famished. Ella always made sure to have dinner readily available as soon as he came home by cooking at the shared wood stove earlier than the other women in the house. Each day, Charles was showered with kisses, which he gladly returned, before settling in for a quiet evening with his beautiful wife. Ella alone, by his side, made all aches, pains, sorrows, and worry disappear.

"Yer hair looks real nice today. Jus' like the angels done came down and kissed it," he spoke quietly one evening, as his thought had somehow escaped.

Her flowing curls draped over her shoulders, glittering from the setting sun shining through the window. She smiled, blushed, and quickly looked at her plate.

"Them other women in th' house says I should pin it up. Says that's th' way ya's supposed ta do thin's when ya's married an' all."

Charles's face crinkled, and his eyes instantly flashed red as he pounded his fist on the table. Ella jumped along with the dishes, silver and place settings.

"Don't ya listen ta a damn thin' them women sayin'. Yer my wife an', I'll be damned if'n ya gonna get bullied by some old hags inta wearin' yer hair or anythin' else differt than the way I likes it."

Ella sat silent, unsteady, staring at her plate, at the corn thrown into the mashed potatoes from his hard blow to the table. She wasn't sure whether to cry or defend herself. Charles had never raged at her before, and he had never shown this wicked, angry side of him, other than that dreadful night at her father's house. She had dismissed his rage that night, feeling it had only occurred from the situation.

Charles's face faded, seeing the shock and fear in Ella's eyes. She had been raised by an abusive father, and he was horrified at his own terrible act of screaming and slamming his fist on the table. He wanted to take it all back - the pain he had just caused as well as all the pain she had ever felt.

Gently, quietly, almost whispering, he said, "I'm sorry, hun. I likes ya just how ya is, an' I don't want no one a changin' that."

He reached for her hand, which she held, holding his gaze with tears in her soft eyes.

"I be whatever ya want me ta be, Charles. I love ya, an' I's yer wife."

The rest of their dinner was eaten in silence.

On Friday, Charles came home at his usual time. It had become their custom for him to come home for lunch on those days. All other work days, Ella brought Charles's lunch to the yard and ate with him at his lunchtime. She always made sure to bring extra for Charles's single co-workers that had no women to care for them. But on Fridays, he would have lunch at home, giving his earnings for the week to Ella for shopping, chores, and whatnot. This particular Friday, she heard him walk through the door and turned with her usual happy smile, bearing a tray holding his sandwich and milk. The look on his face let her instantly know something was wrong. She sat the tray down and rushed to him as he collapsed onto the soft, tattered couch.

Her face was drained of all color as she asked, "Charles, what is it?"

Silence.

"Charles, honey, wha's wrong?"

Silence.

"Charles, ya're scaring me. Talk ta me! Wha's happened?"

With dark eyes full of what appeared to be anger, fear, or both, he turned to her. "He foun' us," was his short, distant reply.

Ella sat back in repose. Who had found them? Were they in danger? Was someone after them? As daybreak wakes the rooster, it dawned on her. With shock on her face and fear in her eyes, she whispered, "Pa?"

Charles stared blindly at the scratched wooden floor.

"Got a telegram from Poppie at the yard today. Said yer pa'd been a lookin' fer a while now, and he was purty sure he knew where we was. Weren't two minutes after I read the 'gram that two men from the yard I din' know were pushin' me 'round. Foreman saw it an' stopped 'em, but they's from yer pa, I know it. Jim and Dale jumped in ta git 'em offa me, too. They roughed 'em up some, but them boys be back. Ya know they gonna be back."

Ella sat silent beside Charles, hand in hand. They had both known in the back of their minds that this day may come, but it had never been discussed, and time had faded their fears.

Old Man Milner was a sick, drunken, sorry excuse for a father. Foster had protected Ella as much as he could, but their pa would beat her severely anyway, no matter who stood in the way. About three years earlier, Foster and their pa came to blows in an argument. His pa literally kicked him out of their small cabin and told him, by shotgun, that he was never to come back. Foster, in his anger and being happy to leave, had followed the trail down from the cabin, basically walking nowhere and trying to collect his thoughts.

As soon as Foster had left, Old Man Milner returned to the cabin to take his aggression out on his young daughter. By the time Foster came to his senses, knowing Ella was in grave danger, it was too late. He found her lying on the floor of their cabin in a pool of blood. Her face was beaten so severely he could not recognize her. Her arm was broken. Her ripped shirt and flimsy skirt revealed strap marks that had left large welts surrounded by bleeding wounds from her shoulders down onto her thighs. Foster had seen the old man beat her before, but this was worse than anything he had ever witnessed, or that he could have ever imagined his pa was capable of. Their ma had been sitting in a corner, staring off into space, rocking back and forth.

Foster took Ella from the cabin that day and took her to Bessie at the Resenger farm after he had taken her to the doctor. Of course, Mommie and Poppie took her in immediately and began to nurse her back to health.

This was the first time Charles and Ella had actually gotten to know one another and become close. They had been several years apart in school, and her pa had kept her locked away on their claim of the hillside. They knew one another through Foster and Bessie's romance; that was the extent of their relationship before that traumatic day.

Charles's bed was given to Ella, and he slept on the cold floor of the parlor in the box house, never once minding the sacrifice. For weeks, each morning while she was healing, he would check on her and see if she needed anything. Most days, after his chores were completed, he would help Mommie with supper and take a plate to Ella. They shared many meals together in the tiny bedroom as she regained her strength. They would talk for hours, until the sun had disappeared between the mountains, before they would say their goodnights. Morning would come to find Charles right at her side to get her what she needed before he had even tended to his own needs.

As her face healed, he began to realize how beautiful she was, but by that point, it would not have mattered. He was already in love.

A few weeks after her arrival, Old Man Milner showed up on the doorstep at the Resenger farm, wielding his shotgun, demanding to take his daughter. Poppie came to the door with his own shotgun and told the old man that Ella wasn't going anywhere. Poppie somehow managed to back him down, but the next day he returned with the sheriff who told Poppie that Ella would have to go with her pa.

Poppie begged and pleaded with the sheriff, explaining the situation and detailing the extent of Ella's injuries upon her arrival. After several harsh words exchanged between the three men, the sheriff explained to Poppie that it was law. Ella had to go with her pa.

During the outdoor confrontation, which could be heard clearly inside, Charles stayed with Ella, consoling a girl he knew he would love forever, who knew she was returning to a life of hell.

Charles was with Ella as much as Foster from that point forward. The two were inseparable, although their relationship had to be kept a secret because of her pa. Old Man Milner would never allow any boy to be near Ella. Foster and Bessie had made it easier for the two of them to see each other. Their relationship may not have been possible without the marriage of Charles's sister to Ella's brother.

Snapping back to the present situation, Charles heard Ella's shattered, shaking voice whimpering softly. "What if he finds us? What if he...."

Charles was brought out of his thoughts. His new wife was trembling from fear of what horrors the monster in her life could, and would, do to her again.

He squeezed her tight. "It's all gonna be alright, hun. You'll see. He ain't neva gonna hurt ya again. Neva no more," he stated firmly, but turning slightly, not wanting her to see the uncertainty in his own eyes.

Charles knew Old Man Milner would come again. He knew he would find them. He knew he would find Ella. His anguish began to show. He walked to the door and said, "I ain't hungry no more. I need some fresh air," before stepping into the brisk day. He would not return until the work day had ended.

Ella's determined outlook and strong will was crushed by the prospect of one human being. The one person in her life that could frighten her very soul had returned. She reached over her shoulder and touched a large raised scar caused by the hard blow of a belt buckle. She shuddered again, uncontrollably. How could he take this happiness away from her that she had so desperately wanted her whole life?

Her pa had never liked Charles, or any of the Resengers for that matter. He had shown up at Foster and Bessie's wedding, slobbering drunk, only to announce that he wasn't losing a son, but gaining a whore. When he had finally found out that Ella and Charles were a couple, he marched to the Resenger farm, shotgun in hand, and threatened to kill Charles; then he returned to the shack and beat Ella with a belt. Nonetheless, he knew how she felt about Charles; he had learned to accept the situation over time. He didn't plan on keeping her as his whipping post forever. Did he?

She cried hysterically - fearful of her pa's wrath, dreading being brought back to that dusty town in the Smokies, and horrified of losing the only man she would ever love. She sobbed until there were no more tears to cry.

Charles's lunch tray, still holding his food, sat on the table where she had placed it. The afternoon was spent guarding the window, peering endlessly. Each neighbor that knocked sent a jolt of fear through her entire body as she would sit quiet, motionless, chair propped under the door handle, waiting for the visitor to leave. She watched the streets up and down, as well as in the direction of the rail yard, impatiently waiting for the six o'clock whistle to blow.

Time slowed to a heartbeat as the *tick tock, tick tock* of the clock resonated inside her head. She began to pace the floor, but the dizziness of stress would set in, and she would slowly sit back down. *Tick tock, tick tock....*

Lights shining brighter than the sun filled Ella's eyes as she struggled to open her lids.

"She's comin' 'round," a strange, muffled voice murmured.

Ever so slowly she tried to focus. She felt what she knew to be Charles's hand in her own and turned in his direction. The blinding light faded, and she was able to open her eyes wider. As her eyes adjusted, she saw concern and worry covering Charles's face. Instantly frightened, she sat straight up, trying to ask what was wrong, but she was overwhelmed by exhaustion, laying her head back again. Voices she knew were all around her, speaking at once, not making sense through the haze in her mind.

Charles leaned over and kissed her softly on the cheek. "I'm jus' so glad ya alright. Had me scared half ta death."

"Wha' happened?" She spoke weakly, whispering.

"I shouldn't a left ya, darlin'. I'm so sorry."

"Wha' happened?" She inquired again softly, more frightened.

Bessie was quickly at her side, surprising Ella with her presence. "Charles came home from work an' foun' ya on the floor. Yer face was all white. Said he had ta bust th' door down ta git ta ya. Foster and I was already on our way down 'cause we knew y'all was in trouble with yer pa an' all." She paused, reflecting on her statement as the situation with Old Man Milner had obviously taken a back seat to the present situation. "We got here not long afta' Charles foun' ya."

Charles looked up at the strange man that had been holding the bright light in Ella's eyes when she had awakened. "This is the doc from over at the rail yard," Charles explained to Ella. "He came a runnin' when I sent fer help." Charles shook the doctor's hand, remembering the gesture Foster had taught him. "I really 'preciate ya comin' over as quick as ya did. T'was real good of ya."

The doctor smiled. "I was happy ta come. Glad she's alright." He was packing his items into a small, black leather bag with a clasp.

As the doctor headed for the door, Charles reached into his pocket wallet. Ella winced, not understanding what was happening, but knowing they could not afford another dollar taken from their tight budget.

The doctor noticed the gesture from Charles, a convention he had learned from Foster, and held his hand up. "It wasn't trouble fer me ta come over. There won't be a charge." He opened the door and stepped into the windy night. He looked back, smiled tenderly, and said, "Congratulations."

The door quietly closed behind him, taking with it the whistle of the spring wind.

The silence in the room was deafening.

"Wha'd that mean?" Ella inquired. "Congratulations? Why he sayin' that?"

Fog still not cleared from her head hung heavy as the three people closest to her in the world sat closely, watching, waiting, each smiling in an uneasy manner.

Charles's hand squeezed tighter. "Ya gonna have a baby, my darlin' Ella." He paused momentarily then added softly, "We gonna have a baby."

Ella sat silent and stunned, fog still filling each brain cell.

Bessie ran to Ella's side, opposite Charles, and squeezed her tight. "Oh, Ella, honey, a baby! We gonna have a baby!" Excitement began to fill the air, as it always had with Bessie's presence, just before a loud banging came to the door.

Ella jumped straight up, panic filling her to her core. "IT'S HIM! Pa's foun' us!"

Foster swung open the door with brute force. The two men on the opposite side of the door were no threat. They were friends from the rail yard who also lived in the boarding house coming to check on Charles and Ella.

Charles and Foster spoke with the men outside on the porch, while Bessie tried to calm Ella by speaking of the upcoming event. As the realization of having a baby came over Ella, she began to fret.

"Wha' we gonna do, Bess?" Ella's cry was shrill. "How'm I gonna take care of a baby? We can barely make our own way." Tears welled in her eyes.

"Come on, now, honey," Bessie comforted. "It's gonna be a wonderful thing. Ya've a wonderful life to look forward to. Ya know things have ways of workin' themselves out. Jus' keep it in yer prayers, honey. This really is a beautiful thing." Bessie held Ella's trembling hand. "God bless yer heart. We'll make it through this. All of us, together, honey. It'll all be fine."

Outside, the boys were discussing an entirely different topic: what to do about Old Man Milner.

"Seems like he's just gone plumb damn crazy, Charles." Foster stared at the grey sky, at nothing in particular, as his mind filled with thoughts of his father's erratic behavior worsening since Charles and Ella had left Newport. Foster was hesitant to tell Charles all of the details, but as Charles persisted, Foster gave in.

"Poppie sent me a 'gram, Foster. Talkin' 'bout yer pa and how he was comin' fer me." Charles reflected before continuing, "What's he done, Foster? He ain't threatenin' Mommie and Poppie, is he?"

Questions of that nature continued for several minutes before Foster broke down and told Charles about Old Man Milner heading to the Resengers' farm, wielding his shotgun and demanding they tell him where Charles and Ella were. Poppie wouldn't say a word, shotgun pointed straight at his chest. As Charles had expected, Mommie had run Mr. Milner off when her 12-gauge was shot into the air as a warning. Foster had not yet found out how he located Charles and Ella, but it was soon all over town that he did know where they were and was looking for people to band with him against the Resenger family in order to get his daughter back.

"Whatcha mean, Foster?" Charles was puzzled.

Foster hesitated. "Charles, he been sayin' awful stuff 'bout ya in town. He's tryin' ta git people to be on his side an' come fer ya."

Charles's mind was sent reeling. What things could he have been saying? He dare not ask Foster. He knew in his own mind that his anger was growing into a raging force that he could not control. To fully understand what Old Man Milner had concocted would surely set a fire in him that he would not be able to extinguish.

A long, thunderous crack descended from the heavens, so loud that it shook the foundation of the house. Charles stood bold, strong, unwavering. He looked through the screen door at his beautiful wife inside, so unsure and so afraid. Bolts of lightning lit the sky for a momentary glimpse of daylight. The thundering boom to follow set inside Charles something he could not describe. At that moment, he was more powerful than he had ever been; he knew he possessed the potential for destruction if caution was not used. The sky opened up and the rain began to pour once again, drowning any need for caution in Charles's mind. She was his wife, the only thing that had ever been worth having in his life, and no one was going to take that from him.

CHAPTER FOUR

*W*eeks passed slowly into months. Ella, ever fearful, grew weaker with each passing day. Pacing the floors and continually peering through the covered window had caused her to slip in her household duties. She no longer cared about making their small room a home. Charles's meals were now cold sandwiches or, possibly, a soup broth. While the springtime sun shone brightly outdoors, dust gathered in dingy, darkened corners. The once sunny, cheerful room was now drab and dark. Petrified of being seen outside, she had stopped walking with the other wives to the markets, if she even went at all. The women had all tried to help her in any way they could but eventually gave up when she refused to answer the door.

She watched for her pa continuously. Her heart thumped and pumped out fear in waking and in sleep. She incessantly wondered if Charles would make it home safely from the rail yard. If he was two minutes late in arrival, it would send her into a dark frenzy; dizziness surrounded each horrible thought until Charles would enter their small, dreary room. Each day that passed left her dreading horrible news, but if there had been any, Charles would not tell her.

Charles was happy that he did not have to lie to her. He was ready to fight at a moment's notice, but the opportunity never arose. An eerie feeling had come over him after not hearing any more of the situation with Old Man Milner. The only word he had received was a telegram from Foster saying that his pa had seemed to settle down, or had just gone off on another drinking binge. In other words, Old Man Milner was missing, which could have meant he was headed for Knoxville and Ella.

Bessie had stayed with Ella for the first few weeks after learning of the pregnancy. Ella had been a wonderful actress, fueled by hiding years of abuse, and convinced Bessie that she needed to be back in Newport. She assured Bessie repeatedly that she would be fine. Ella knew this wasn't true; she was not fine. She was frightened and sick in a way that she could not describe. Charles could see this, but Ella begged him not to say anything. The last thing she wanted was to be a burden to anyone.

As the months passed, Ella's emotional and physical health declined. She ached in places that didn't seem natural. Standing from a seated position was a chore. She spent most of her time in the shared washroom or out behind the house if the room was occupied. While her stomach grew slowly, the rest of her seemed to shrink. Her arms and legs were withering away to the point where she had no energy. She could hardly stand or lift anything. She could not remember a time when her face had any color at all, and she eventually stopped peering into the small looking glass that hung by the door.

The doctor from the rail yard came by often to check on Ella. He lived close by and had taken pity on her condition. He was, after all, only a doctor for a rail yard. He attended mostly to cuts, bruises, and the occasional broken bone. He could offer no medications, only advice, which consisted mostly of proclaiming that she was malnourished and needed to eat better. Ella knew these words to be true, but anything that went into her stomach came back out almost immediately.

Charles worried immensely about Ella, but he felt helpless. He knew she wasn't well, and he could not afford the care that she needed. There was a hospital in Knoxville - a very good hospital named Knoxville General - but they expected payment, money Charles knew he would never have. He had saved some, little by little, but the men at the rail yard had spoken to him of the outrageous expenses of the large hospital. It was clearly a place intended only for the well off. Foster could and would help, but Ella refused. She refused any help whatsoever.

Most of the money Charles had saved upon arriving in Knoxville had gone towards deposits and securities for the boarding room. Weekly pay seemed devoured by rent, meals, and necessities. When Charles had envisioned working in the city as a young man, he had thought that there would be plenty of money no matter what work he chose. The harsh truth had been that living in the city meant that you had to pay for your home. In the country, your home was where you had made it, and you worked the land hard for it. Either way, Charles was left bitter and cold for the life mapped out for him. His rage grew daily as he watched the finely dressed well-to-dos eating lavishly in public dining areas while his wife withered away in a 10' x 10' hole.

Charles wrote Mommie and Poppie often, although Mommie would never answer the letters. In his letters, he would describe Knoxville, his work, and Ella's condition. Many times he would lie about Ella, saying that she was growing strong and beautiful. Sadly, Charles knew that the beauty of a woman with child was not something that his wife possessed. She was weak and sickly. He hoped upon hope that he would make some reference in his letters that Mommie would pick up on, without breaking his promise to Ella.

He knew they needed Mommie. She would know what to do.

Mommie was well versed in handling sickness. In her mind, all illness was the work of the Devil, and only a Smokey Mountain Healing Exorcism would do. Amazingly, she was usually right. Many people had been healed by her words of scripture and the touch of her hand. It was a practice she had learned from years of attending the Church of God, a lifetime of constant prayer, and knowing the hand of The Lord. God's power and God's infinite wisdom always won over evil; Mommie knew that and felt that she had received the power to heal from The Lord Himself. Mommie felt that if her hand in prayer could not heal someone, then it was the Devil inside them that would not allow them to be healed.

Many people in Newport knew her to be a woman of great power, but they were also extremely frightened of her. Some felt her strengths were so great that she could easily be considered a witch. These words were never spoken in the light of day. There was a dark, bitter, almost sinister side to Mommie. None knew how deep the gift she had received stemmed, and many feared what afflictions she could bring upon them. People such as these did not understand the power of her faith in The Lord. It was her faith that gave her power and her faith that gave her wisdom. With that faith came what she described as keen insight of good and evil.

"Le's head on back up ta Newport, Ella." The words fell out of Charles's mouth one evening before he could catch them.

She sat motionless, lifeless, and non responsive.

He stared at her a moment and continued. "Ella? Honey? Ya ain't been a doin' too good. Ya know that's true, now. We could go on back up ta th' farm until afta th' baby's born. Then we can come on back down ta Knoxville. I'm sure I can git my job at the yard back. Won't be that much longer, now, 'fore the baby comes an' all." The leaves had all fallen, and the bare trees were starting to whip in the winter wind. The calculations would show that the baby was to be born sometime in late December or early January.

Ella saw no winter sky. She felt no crisp winds. She did not enjoy the colorful dance of the lifting leaves. She felt nothing, saw nothing, was nothing; and so she sat, staring into the nothingness that surrounded her.

Charles looked concerned, rubbing the back of his neck as he did in his most nervous states. "Foster says yer pa's off somewheres," he continued cautiously. "They ain't heard from him in months. It'll be safe for us ta go back fer a couple a months. It won't do no harm. 'Sides that, we got Foster and Poppie there if'n anythin' was ta happen." He glanced at her again, "Ella?"

Charles jumped up from the frumpy couch and paced the small room from end to end. Rage ran through every vein. He took a deep breath, wanting to shake her, wake her somehow, but he could not stand the thought of hurting her. In a harsher tone, but careful not to sound angry, he said, "Ella, I think we got ta go back. We ain't got no choice."

Still, Ella sat silent and made no movement.

"DAMN IT, ELLA! LISTEN TA ME!" His roar could be heard throughout the streets, breaking the night silences and stirring animals hidden in the darkness outside. Birds fluttered away from porch coverings. Squirrels in a close by thicket of trees jumped from limb to limb, tightly clenching food for winter storage, trembling at the disruption.

Charles stopped himself suddenly and fell at Ella's feet. Defeated, he said softly, "I can't take care of ya th' way ya need ta be taken care of. I don' know what ta do fer ya. We have ta go back."

A single tear drifted down Ella's delicate, colorless cheek. "I know," was her only reply.

That was that. No more was spoken of it between the two, and the very next day, Charles began making plans. Telegrams were sent out to Foster and Poppie. He spoke with his boss at the rail yard, who assured Charles there would be a job there for him when he returned. He spoke with the owner of the boarding house, who knew full well the situation and understood that they had to leave on very short notice. Each day after work he would pack up some of what little they had, speaking to neighbors and saying goodbyes for himself and his wife.

Ella sat and watched the buzzing around her, only moving to occasionally peer out the ever covered window, each time expecting to see her monster. When he did not appear, she would take her seat to again stare into nothingness or watch a buzz of activity she denied to take part in.

A few days after the decision was final, Charles came home from the rail yard with a telegram from Foster. It had said that he and Poppie would be coming for them early Saturday and that they still had not heard from Old Man Milner. He hurriedly opened the door and stepped into the small room, excited to give the news to Ella. He stopped dead in his tracks and stared at the sight before him.

Ella's frail body stood just inside the doorway. Her head was tilted downward. Her tiny arms clutched the small bulge protruding from her tummy. As Charles entered, she slowly looked up, revealing a sparkle in her green eyes and a slight glow in her cheeks. Charles stood gazing, unbelieving, as a tiny smile appeared on her frail lips.

"It moved," she whispered softly.

"What? What's moved?" Charles wasn't quite sure what she meant. His mind was trying to grasp hold and comprehend the situation.

"Th' baby. It been too long, and t'ain't been a movin'. I din' think…," she trailed off.

Charles rushed to her side. "Ella, why'nt ya tell me?"

Without saying a word she placed his hand flat on her tummy. The child inside jumped and turned, causing Charles to yank his hand away as his eyes grew wide.

"Ya see?" she said. "It's all alright now. Don' matta if'n he does fin' me. He won' hurt me if'n I got me a baby. I know it! And, 'sides that, I know now that the baby's gonna be well. I been awful scared, Charles."

Charles sat down slowly onto the sagging couch. He now fully understood the extent of her worries. It had been nearly seven months now. In his concern for his wife, he had never inquired about the child she was carrying.

Ella sat beside him on the couch and rested her head on his shoulder.

"I don' know why ya din' tell me, Ella." Charles sat staring at Ella, thoughts filling every crevice in his brain.

"Weren't nothin' ta tell ya. Ya had enough ta worry 'bout on yer own. I din' want ta make anythin' worse on ya."

"But, Ella, it's our baby."

A wide smile came across Ella's face - a wonderful, beautiful smile Charles had not seen since before Old Man Milner had sent his people after him. "Our baby," she repeated, "an' it's gonna be alright."

Charles smiled broadly and placed his arm around her skeletal shoulders. The evening was spent that way. They laughed and talked and felt the baby kick and squirm. It was a simple joy of togetherness that they had been without for far too long.

The next days passed quickly as they prepared for their trip back up to the Smokies. Ella had more energy and was able to keep some food in her stomach, but she was still very weak and would have to rest often. Almost immediately after the baby's movement, she had begun to clean and tidy up, but Charles argued and scolded, telling her she was doing too much. Even still, she would work until she could not, pushing herself at each turn. She felt that they were at a new beginning in their lives and somehow felt guilt for her health and state of mind from the prior months. In trying to compensate, she knew she was overdoing it.

Saturday morning came, and Ella was up before dawn making breakfast and last minute preparations. The distant, but familiar sound of Foster's masonry truck rumbling to a slow stop made her heart do a flip flop.

"They's here!" she cried.

Charles was still pulling on his boots as Ella made her slow descent to the street side. As he approached, he realized that Foster and Poppie were seeing for the first time what he had seen for months. A shell of a woman, all nourishment being fed to the child within her, stood weak, but excited before them. Foster and Poppie were mirror images as waves of shock and surprise passed their faces.

"Wha's happen' to ya? Charles says ya was doin' fine, sis!" Foster's face was turning a shade of crimson, climbing from his chest and neck.

Playfully smacking him on the arm without enough force to even capture a fly, she replied, "Oh, ya sound jus' like Charles. I's tired of hearin' 'bout how bad I look!" Elation filled her face, even through the shade of pale.

Charles stood back, unsure of Foster's next move. Poppie stood silently staring at the stranger before him. Foster looked from Charles to Ella, then back again.

"Why din' ya tell me?" His anger was apparent in his voice.

"She wouldn't let me, Foster. I tried, I swear I did, but she made me promise her. All I could do was talk her inta comin' back up th' mountain again." Charles stammered for words.

"T'ain't his fault, Foster. Don'cha go a actin' like that. Ain't no need in it. Wha's done's done. I wouldn'ta been no better off in Newport than I been here." She spoke wearily, weak from the excitement.

Foster calmed himself as he led Ella back into the room that she and Charles had called home for nearly a year. There were two small boxes stacked neatly in one corner. Aside from the donated couch, the room looked exactly as it had one year prior.

Ella began to realize that each new beginning had to start with an ending. It had been this way her whole life and would not change now. For her, to start anew was to completely destroy what had been. These were the thoughts that filled Ella's head on her last day in Knoxville, Tennessee.

Boxes were gently loaded onto a truck that was much too large for them. Women that Ella had not seen or spoken to in months came out to say goodbyes and give well wishes. In an instant, it was over…much more quickly than it had begun.

Ella watched the dark, grey clouds rolling above and waited for the rain to fall. She understood full well the irony of the Tennessee rain. It was always there. It served as a constant reminder of what was: of hearts broken, tears shed. Only, this was to be different for Ella, too. The cloud did open. A thundering crack did strike down. But, no rain fell. The *tink, tink, tink* on the tin porch cover told her that this was much worse.

Shivers went up and down Ella's spine, not from the bitter cold that had rolled in on the dark clouds, but from the dreadful worry rolling through her mind that they had brought with them. She waited for the rain. The rain was supposed to come. It always came. She needed it now. The rain could wash away your sorrow if you allowed it. Sleet only allows sorrow to stay stuck, frozen in time, making it hard to chip away the icy, saddened pieces of your heart.

Her arms slipped around her small tummy and squeezed gently - loving, caring, protecting the child that grew within her. Charles and Foster came to the small porch and led her to the large International truck. Her eyes gazed in horror as the icy shards sliced through the sky, scraping the streets and stinging the trees.

"We better git outta here quick, 'fore this gits any worse!" Foster shouted above the cracking of the icy pieces.

All Ella could think was, *It already has.*

CHAPTER FIVE

*I*t was a long trek in the International as the sleet slivered through the somber sky. Several times the men would have to stop the truck to get out and scrape the frozen particles from the front window because the wiper blades had frozen.

Ella could not shake the feeling of dread and continued to shiver uncontrollably. Charles wrapped a tattered old afghan around her shoulders, but it was of no use. Her fear stemmed from the inside, but only revealed itself on the out. To Ella, the slow, icy ride was an ominous descent into hell. In her mind it may as well have been fire falling from the sky, not ice.

Shapes of mountain ranges, seen in the distance, resembled iron bars, bringing her back to her life-long prison. As they drew nearer, the snowy peaks on the mountaintops cast a foreboding glow on the dank city.

She didn't want to return. There were too many demons to face: a drunken, abusive father, an uncaring mother, a new mother-in-law she was terrified of, and the thoughts and gossip of an entire town. Despite wanting to scream and run the opposite direction, she understood the pain and anguish that she had caused Charles and knew that this was the best decision he could have made.

As Charles pondered Ella's thoughts and facial expressions, he wondered how he could have brought her back here. He could have gotten a second job. He could have had someone to stay with her at all times. He could have saved more than $50 and taken her to that fancy Knoxville General hospital. Had he held the money, they would not turn her away. There was a sudden, unforeseen dread that he had just made the worst decision of his life.

Bessie and Mommie, despite the rigid temperature and side slanting sleet, were standing on the rock porch of the white, clapboard box house as they arrived. Bessie ran to the truck, thrusting open the door with such force it could have ripped from its hinges. Each passenger sat silent, gazing intently at the sight of Bessie's exuberant face instantly turning to cold steel as she set her eyes upon Ella and her shocking condition. Poppie, seated next to the door, stepped out and stated that they needed to get her inside.

Bessie stood solid, bold, strong, but speechless.

Foster and Charles gently lifted Ella from the International and set her on the ground, each holding her close as they led her inside as quickly as possible. Poppie walked swiftly behind them, but Bessie kept her position in the sleeting shards of ice, unwavering in her stance.

Ella, weak from the trip and her condition, could barely lift her head. Foster and Charles held most of what tiny weight she carried. As they neared the porch Mommie caught a better look at her.

"I knowed it. Ya done waited too late, and ya been a lyin' to me, boy. Ain't no hope for yuns now." She spat the words wickedly.

Charles was preoccupied with concern for his wife and unborn child. He knew Mommie had said something, and that it wasn't nice, but the words did not register in his mind. Ella, though weak, heard and soaked in every word.

"Bessie!" Mommie screamed from the porch as she followed the others inside the house. "Git yerself inside this house 'fore ya catches pneumonia! I can't be a handlin' two sick 'uns at once!"

Foster and Charles led Ella to Charles's small bedroom. She felt somewhat comforted in this room as it had been a safe haven for her once before.

"Leave me be with her!" Mommie shouted in a rage and rushed the men through the door, slamming it shut behind her. Turning to face her, Ella could see the rage and fire in Mommie's eyes, and she trembled with fear.

"How ya go 'n git yerself in this condition, girl?" Mommie's tone was harsh and brutal.

Ella was speechless and not sure how to respond.

"Ansa' me when I speak at ya, girl!" Mommie was bellowing at the top of her lungs now. Charles banged on the door, pleading for Mommie to calm down. There was no lock on the door, but even still, he knew he dare not enter.

"I, I..." Ella stammered for words. Mommie was sitting on the bed next to her, prodding her - lifting her arms, feeling her stomach, touching her in places that made her uncomfortable.

"I tell ya what's happened. Ya done gone ta that sinful city and ya got the Devil in ya. That's what ya got." Mommie's voice had dropped to a malicious whisper. "Ya done took my son from me. Ya take him off ta that God forsaken place, makin' him think he some sort of hero fer doin' it. Ya've done sinful deeds, married or not. Sinful, disgraceful thin's, an' now look at ya, look at what's become of ya. Ya got the Devil oozin' outta ya, chil'. I can feel him here."

Mommie bent down close to Ella's ear. With a whispering growl, she hissed, "Ya made my son lie to me. Ya did that. My boy wouldn't lie ta me. Tha's on you. Don' ya eva expect that I'd forgive such as that. Ya're here 'cause I love my son. That's all. I try an' help ya as best I can, but ya th' one gonna have ta fight them demons." With that, she stood, turned the door handle, and walked out of the room, leaving Ella drowning in her own darkness.

Charles rushed in and sat by her side. "Ya alright, honey?"

Ella had no tears left to cry. "I's fine," she smiled. She patted his hand. "Everythin's jus fine."

The next months were spent in an early, bitter cold winter. The wooden walls of the clapboard house streamed the cold air straight through, making the potbelly stove work overtime just to heat the small parlor; the two adjoining bedrooms felt little, if any, of this heat.

Ella was ordered to bed rest by Mommie, which meant she was cold most of the time, even with the numerous blankets piled on her. She felt stronger, healthier, and she felt that getting up and moving around would do her some good, but Mommie wouldn't hear of it. Mommie would bring her concoctions to drink, which stayed on her stomach, but they were either bitter, sour, or just unbearable all together.

The words spoken the day of her arrival were the last words spoken of that nature. From that day forward, Mommie was seemingly concerned with Ella's health only. Ella knew that most of Mommie's "doctoring" was some sort of punishment for taking Charles from her. All the family members knew that Ella had regained much of her strength, but Mommie was stubborn and insisted she follow her treatments, despite the pleadings of Charles, Bessie, Poppie, and Foster.

The months passed with no word of Old Man Milner. Ma Milner had become increasingly concerned, but Ella had felt a weight lifted from her shoulders. Pa was one cross that she would not have to bear for the moment.

Ella had been feeling increasing pain. She tried not to complain, but she was seen more than once by Charles or Mommie gripping her back in agony or doubling over, her stomach in aching pain.

"She's close," Mommie said to Charles and Poppie one morning at breakfast.

"Ya think so, Mommie? Think she gonna be alright?"

"Time will tell, son," was her only response.

They bowed their heads to pray as Poppie not only asked blessings for the food, but to give Ella strength, guidance, and wisdom. When the prayer was said, there was an evil glare in Mommie's eyes that would not subside.

Ella, eating alone in her cold room, heard Poppie's prayer and said one in silence for herself and her unborn child.

Charles slept in an uncomfortable chair beside Ella each night. Although she complained that he should sleep with her, he wanted to give her the space in the small enough bed. He slept lightly and checked on her constantly, but he did not hear her gasp as a gush of water spilled onto the covered mattress. What he did hear was the scream that followed. He jumped up quickly, lighting the kerosene lamp with the night candle. Not only had her water broken, but with it came a surge of blood. Mommie was in the room as soon as the lamp was lit.

"Git yer sista', boy."

Charles stood frozen, fixated on the dark, seeping blood that covered his beautiful wife.

Mommie slapped him hard on the face, leaving a mark. "I said git yer sista'! NOW!"

Charles scampered, putting on his boots, and he was out the door running down the hill to the main road where Foster and Bessie's fine house stood. He banged on the back door of the large house and screamed Bessie's name. It seemed an eternity to Charles before Foster and Bessie came to the back door clad in their bedclothes.

"It's a happenin'. Somethin's wrong." His breath was heavy and staggered from running the full distance. He tried to make his point quickly. "Mommie needs ya now!"

"God bless her heart. I got ta git me some clothes on. Git th' truck runnin', Foster. It be faster up th' hill." Bessie ran back inside as Charles and Foster started the rumbling engine of the International.

"Wha's happened?" Foster asked breathlessly as they ran for the truck.

"I jus' don' know, Foster! I woke up an' she was screaming an' they was blood everywhere!"

Foster's eyes grew wide with fright as he climbed inside the vehicle. The look on his face made Charles certain that something was definitely wrong. Bessie was out the door, wearing only a flimsy dress with an overcoat and no shoes, before they had the truck turned around to head up the hill to the farm.

Foster's masonry truck, the International, was tough and durable, but it did not like to climb hills of any kind. It stammered and sputtered as Charles felt like getting out and running up the hill, thinking it would be faster. He had to get back to Ella.

The ride seemed to last an eternity, and when it finally ended, the first passenger out of the vehicle was Bessie, running in bare feet to help her mother and sister-in-law. Charles was right on her heels and Foster right behind him, but they were stopped just inside the door of the parlor.

"Ya know ya cain't go in there. That's one thing that is woman's work an' always will be." Poppie flatly stated. Foster and Charles both protested, but to no avail. He was right. Men just weren't welcome at a birth in the hills.

Shrill cries of pain coming from Ella grew worse and more horrifying as the hours passed by. All three men paced the small room, waiting and wondering. Each time the door would open, their hearts would stop for a brief moment. There never seemed to be news; they only needed boiled water or linens, and that wasn't very often.

Ella's wails and howls of agony lasted for hours. Charles began to walk around the small room strangely as if he were drunk. He yanked off his hat and began simultaneously smacking his head and pulling his hair every so often.

Foster walked over to him and sat him down at a dining chair. "Charles?" He waited for a response before repeating, "Charles?"

His madness turned to fury as he bolted up from the chair. "WHY CAN'T I DO NUTHIN'? SHE'S A HURTIN' IN THERE AN' I CAN'T DO NARY A DAMN THING 'BOUT IT!"

Foster came over and gently touched his shoulder. "I know, Charles. She's my sista. I know."

Charles turned to his brother-in-law and grabbed him tight, burying his head in his shoulder as he sobbed. He couldn't remember the last time he had cried. Even the last time he had a switch taken to him, he had been tough and held back his tears. Now, they flowed like all the rivers of the earth combined.

Poppie sat staring out the side window of the box house, helpless to the situation and quiet as always. The sun had begun to rise through the hazy mist, revealing yet another dark, dreary, cold morning. The winter had been particularly harsh this year and showed no signs of letting up. He allowed himself to think of how it would affect his crops as the past years had not been too good for him anyway. Poppie's mind wandered from subject to subject as he watched the sun rise full up, oblivious to the screams of anguish. He knew that if he stayed focused on the situation at hand that it would be very easy for him to pick up the bottle again - something he had not done in nearly 10 years.

Slowly, the doors leading to the bedrooms creaked open, and Bessie's tortured face appeared. The spine shivering cries of pain had been replaced by the tiny cry of a newborn child. Charles's eyes lit up as he looked toward the rooms. He didn't see the child, Ella, or Mommie.

"We need you now, Charles." The tone of her voice made Charles's knees buckle. Foster steadied him as all the color drained from his face.

"What is it?" Charles asked.

Bessie lowered her head as a tear streamed down her face. "Jus' come." She turned and walked back into the room that held the tiny sound of infant cries.

As if in a dream, Charles floated across the parlor and into the first bedroom. He turned his head to the right and peered into the second room. Mommie was holding a tiny child in her arms, wrapped in clean linens. Blood covered the entire bed and most of the floor around it. Ella lay in the middle of it, gazing at her perfect creation. Charles entered the room cautiously and walked to Ella.

"She's beautiful," she whispered, all strength gone from her withered, tired body. Her grey pallor and lifeless movements told Charles what was to come.

Mommie crossed the floor with the child and placed her in Charles's arms. "Th' chil's a girl," she stated flatly before leaving the room, covered in Ella's crimson blood.

Tears streamed down Charles's face as he gazed at the beautiful baby girl he was holding. "She is beautiful." He looked back at Ella. "She looks jus' like ya."

Foster, Bessie, and Poppie stood in the corner of the small room. Charles gently lifted Ella's hand and placed it in his own. She smiled a gentle, sweet smile and looked at her child once more. Charles's tears continued to stream into the rivers of his life.

"It's alright, Charles. Everythin' gonna be alright now." Tears welled in her eyes. "Charles, ya be strong, now. An' ya make sure she knows how I love her so." With that, her eyes fluttered closed and her head tilted to the side. Her limp hand fell from Charles's.

"NO! NO! NO!" Charles's sobs broke free, aching through each vein. The tiny child lay in his arms, silent and still, as if she understood. He turned toward the onlookers. He could see Foster's deep anguish, Bessie's sorrowful pain, Poppie's undying love; it was all expressed in their faces, but all Charles could see were people watching during his darkest hour.

"GET OUT!" he bellowed.

The three left him alone with his dead wife and newborn daughter. He climbed onto the blood soaked bed beside her and cupped her lifeless arms, placing the baby inside them, holding steady that their child may not fall.

"I love ya, Ella. I've always loved ya." His voice was inconsolable and brokenhearted. "I neva meant for this ta happen!" He raised his head to the heavens and cursed God. "Why? Why would ya take her from me? She was all I ever needed, an' now she's gone!"

Some time later, Bessie came in to find Charles laying awake next to Ella, watching her, his head on her shoulder, his face tear streaked. The miraculously silent child was still cradled in her dead mother's arms, with Charles supporting her tiny weight.

"We got ta clean her up, Charles. Family an' th' townspeople be comin' soon." She touched his shoulder tenderly, which he jerked away from with force. "Charles," she continued, "I know yer a hurtin', but we can't jus' leave yuns like this. We have to clean ya up. All of ya."

Charles turned to his sister as he lifted his child into his own arms. "Why, Bessie? Why'd He take her?"

Bessie knew the 'He' that he was speaking of. "Don' ya dare let Mommie hear ya talkin' like that!"

"I don' care what Mommie says. If'n she had the power like she say she do, she'd a done somethin'."

"Charles, now, stop that. We did all we could. Weren't nothin' else we could'a done!"

"She could'a tried."

Mommie was standing in the doorway, and they both jumped when they heard her harsh voice. "Weren't nothin' ta do. She had the Devil in her, an' he wouldn't allow it. I tole her she had ta get rid of them demons. Wouldn't listen ta me. Surprisin' ta me that th' baby done lived." She said these words as if she were speaking of someone else - another family, a stranger.

"Mommie, stop it!" Bessie cried.

Charles handed the baby to Bessie and was immediately facing the woman that had terrified him for most of his life. His eyes flashed red as he spat out, "Ya din' even lay yer hands on her, did ya? DID YA?"

Mommie smirked at her son. "Weren't no need."

Charles bolted out of the room and the clapboard house. Foster was seated on the porch with his face in his hands. Poppie stood beside the stone columns and looked at the mountain peaks. Each man was in his own world and none meant anything to the other.

Charles, still covered in the crimson flow of death, marched to the back house and opened the door to the room that held the farm tools. Grabbing a shovel, he blocked out all thoughts except for his mission. He walked the sloping hill to Dunn's Cemetery, which sat just above the Resenger farm. He chose a nice spot next to a large shade tree and kicked the shovel into the ground. Kick after kick and toss after toss of dirt buried a small piece of his misery deeper into his heart. Hours passed before Charles realized that an ice cold rain had begun to fall and that Foster was by his side, trying to bury his sorrow as well.

Charles stopped digging. "What they doin' down there?"

Foster wiped the wetness from his face - some rain, mostly tears - and said, "They cleanin' her up, now. The funeral's already startin'. Today be the first day. Folks already showin' up from miles 'round. They's been askin' 'bout ya. I tole 'em ya was up on the cemetery hill, preparin' for Ella and ta leave ya alone."

"Thank ya, Foster."

They continued their work in silence as the cold rain beat down.

Down below, at the farm, people were arriving in droves to bring food, console, and give condolences. Ella's body had been cleaned up and dressed. She was laid in the middle of the parlor on a solid gurney covered with white ruffles. Her body was only a shell of what it had once been. Her once shining hair was now dull. Her once beautiful body had been twisted and tortured. Her joyous expression was gone. All that remained of her was a child in her exact likeness.

Bessie held onto the child, who quickly became the center of attention. A wet nurse had been quickly and easily found to suckle the child. Other than feedings, Bessie took over as the baby's caregiver. Each person arriving for the three day funeral wanted to see the child, wanting to envision the miraculous, devious cycle of life.

Ma Milner was hysterical. The fact that her husband was still missing, combined with the passing of her only daughter was too much for her to cope. A lifetime of neglectful, uncaring feelings had come back to haunt her. Foster had offered her no comfort as she had offered none to him.

Mommie stayed hidden in the background, speaking only when spoken to. She was trapped in her own thoughts and feelings. Her son was lost to her forever; she was certain of that. She may have been able to help the girl, but she didn't try, wouldn't try. She felt, *knew*, she would answer to God for her actions here on earth as well as in the after.

Foster and Charles dug the grave that would be the final resting place of their loved one. They left the shovels on the hill, standing upright in the mounds. The deep grave was already filling with water from the rain.

As they descended the hillside, soaked and covered in mud, Foster asked, "Whatcha gonna do now, Charles?"

"Ain't thought much 'bout nothin' past today."

"Thought 'bout whatcha gonna name the baby?"

"Stella. Her name is Stella."

Foster smiled to himself at the turmoil this would cause. Mommie would be furious, as would Old Man Milner as soon as he returned. Foster understood, though, and appreciated the gesture.

"I can buy her a nice casket, Charles. If'n that's what ya want."

"Nope. I'm a gonna build it, jus like I should."

"Mind if I help ya?"

"Nope."

The men continued their descent.

The house and porch were full of people from all over the mountains. Tables had been moved outdoors to house the massive amount of food brought from each family. Two young boys played marbles on the floor of the front porch while two older men played a game of checkers in the chairs above them. Women were buzzing about the house, preparing for this and that, gossiping, and inquiring.

It would stay this way for three days. On the third day, Ella would be buried.

Charles and Foster noticed the commotion, but avoided it, cleaning themselves up only enough to get in the truck and head for the lumber yard. When they returned, the rain had stopped, but the grounds were wet. Foster backed the International just inside the barn where they unloaded the fine pine wood and began to cut and saw.

"Foster?" Charles looked up from his diligent work.

"Yeah?"

"I think I's gonna be needin' a truck, or a car, or something. I can't stay here. Not now."

Foster stopped his sawing motion and looked deep into Charles's eyes. "Where ya gonna go?"

Charles started to saw again, avoiding Foster's gaze. "I don' know. Not Knoxville. I don' think I can go back there without her. I was thinkin' maybe the other side of the mountain, in North Carolina."

"Ya gonna take the baby?"

"Yep," was his only response; he continued his work.

When the coffin had been completed, Charles stood back and cried tears he did not know remained. He had hand engraved, "My Forever Love" on the pine lid.

Foster and Charles headed back to the house where they were shooed by numerous women and urged to change and clean themselves up because of germs to the baby. Charles, ignoring their scolding, went straight to his wife and fell to his knees. He buried his face in her bosom and sobbed uncontrollably. Bessie handed the baby to Mommie, who held her for the first time since she had been born. She looked at the child with disdain. Bessie ran to Charles's side and pulled him to his feet.

"C'mon 'lil brotha'. Let's get ya cleaned up. Ya got plenty of time for mournin'."

Charles knew that his mourning would never subside. He would feel this pain forever. No amount of rain could wash away this sorrow.

He abruptly stood and frantically looked for the baby. He spied Mommie holding her at arms length with obvious disgust for the child. "Git yer hands offa my baby, woman!"

Bessie ran to the child as the entire room fell silent. Mommie stood staring at her son with a smirk.

"That what that city done ta ya? Think ya can talk ta yer mommie like that?"

"That city din' do nothin' but bring me happiness with a woman I loved. I LOVED HER! I BROUGHT HER TA YA FER YA TA SAVE HER! I LAID HER LIFE IN YER HANDS, AN' SHE'S GONE, NOW, GONE!"

"T'weren't my fault." She was quiet, unlike herself, looking around at the family members and townspeople, embarrassed that she could not control her son's outrage.

"IT'S YER FAULT SHE DEAD, AN' I AIN'T NEVA GONNA FORGIVE YA FER IT! NEVA!"

Charles stormed to the bedroom he had called his own. It was the very room where his infant child was born and where his darling wife had died. He no longer felt the need to mourn. It seemed senseless as this pain would be with him for eternity. What he felt was anger against anger. His fury was larger than himself, and he was afraid of what he may do. He stayed in the room for hours, turning away each person that knocked. The bloody mattress had been removed, and, after changing his muddy clothes, he sat on the baseboards that had held the mattress.

When he emerged from the room, the house fell silent. He stood in the doorway to the bedrooms and looked at everyone gathered in the twilight glow of the moon combined with kerosene lamps.

"My daughter's name is Stella," he announced flatly. Several gasps were heard throughout the crowded room. "No one will call her any different. My wife gave her life ta bring my child into this world, and my child will carry on my wife's name." Not a sound was heard as he continued. "I thank all of ya fer comin' an' seein' her off with a proper burial. I know she'd a appreciated it, too." With that, he walked into the yard, leaving the room silent and speechless.

The next day was agonizing for Charles. He could not enter or leave the house without seeing the pitiful sight that was his wife lying in the parlor with people all around her who were eating, drinking, laughing, and talking. It was disgraceful to the dead to sleep during the three day period, and Charles knew in his rational mind that the activities were only there to keep the mourners awake and alert, but the irrational side that had surfaced raged inside at the sight of it all.

On the third day, Ella was placed in the pine coffin made by Charles and Foster, and the lid was nailed closed. A procession of mountain people, strict in their rituals, followed the coffin up the hill to Dunn Cemetery. The preacher from the Church of God said a few words, tears were shed, and the box was laid into the ground. Charles held young Stella, who seemed to understand the somber feeling of the day, never making a sound. As he held his child and watched the ceremony, he did not hear a word. He stayed and watched, waiting until each piece of dirt had been retuned to the ground, covering his heart.

Mommie did not attend the procession, but Charles did not notice, nor would he have cared. He noticed nothing around him. When Poppie spoke with Charles, using more words than Poppie had mustered before; Charles only nodded or just didn't respond at all.

Charles walked down the cemetery hill carrying his child. He walked past the farm and straight to Foster and Bessie's, who had already returned home to sleep as had most of the funeral goers.

"I'm a needin' that truck, Foster."

"I talked ta a fellow I work with that has an older Ford. It's been beat up and don't look like much, but it runs good. Says he'll sell it ta ya for $25."

Charles pulled the money he had been saving for Ella's treatment from his pocket. He took a twenty and a five-dollar bill and placed it back. Handing the money to Foster was like blood dripping from his hand - money that could have saved her, traded for a beat up truck.

"Can I git it tomorra?"

"Sure, I'll tell him to have it here in the mornin'."

Charles walked the dirt road back to the farm. Young Stella was starting to fuss, needing her wet nurse. He walked straight to Poppie who was seated at the table in the parlor with Mommie.

Without even glancing Mommie's direction, he said, "Poppie, I'm a leavin' in the mornin'. Not sure where I'm a goin', but I'm a goin'."

"What 'bout the baby?" Poppie asked cautiously.

"I'm gonna take her with me."

Fire sparked in Mommie's eyes as she spat out, "No, ya ain't. Ya can't take care of that chil' on yer own and ya know it!"

"I can do anythin' I damn well wanna do. I can take care of her. I know I can." They were the first words he had spoken to her since their argument at the funeral. He stood from the table and sat outside the bedroom door, where his young Stella suckled from a mother that was not her own.

Sleep came down hard as hammers on Charles's head. He kept the small infant in the bed with him while he slept. In waking, he realized the child was gone. Upon further investigation, so was Mommie. The sun was barely up, and Poppie was at the table with tears welling in his eyes.

"What's she done ta her, Poppie?"

"I don' know, son. She left with her 'fore the sun came up. I don' know where they gone."

Charles dressed quickly and filled his suitcase. He rushed out the door yelling a quick goodbye to Poppie and rushed down the hill to Foster and Bessie's. Banging on the door frantically, he heard young Stella's tiny cry. His heart jumped, knowing she was there. Foster opened the door.

"Th' truck's parked out back," he said somberly. "Yer Mommie's here with li'l Stella."

"I know, I heard her cryin'." He pushed his way into the house without Foster's permission, which was not his way, or it hadn't been. He walked past the large kitchen and into the parlor that could hold the entire farmhouse. There he found Mommie and Bessie, with young Stella in Bessie's arms.

Bessie looked up from the child with tears in her eyes. "Ya can't take her, Charles. Mommie's right. Ya don' know how ta take care of a baby.

We can take care of her here. I know why ya have ta leave, Charles, but ya jus' can't take the baby. This is where her home is."

Charles knew she was right. He had tossed and turned thinking about it the night before. He didn't know the first thing about taking care of a child, but to let go was a hard fact to face. He had lost so much already.

"All right." Charles was defeated and broken.

He took his beautiful child in his arms and cradled her close. He held her only a moment before kissing her gently on her small cheek and handing her back to Bessie. Without another word, he took the keys from Foster, loaded his suitcase in the back of the beat up, rusted, black Ford truck, and headed up the mountain - away from the farm, away from Newport, away from Knoxville, trying to escape the memories, all of the memories.

The only raindrops that fell during his trip were the tears that continued to flow through the rivers of his life. By this time, he felt he had created an ocean.

GENERATION TWO
STELLA

CHAPTER SIX

Stella crouched in a dark corner of the small, square room, held her knees close to her chest and tried to focus. Something crawled across the top of her bare foot, and not being able to see, she said a silent prayer that it was not a spider. She sat perfectly still, her legs pulled in as far to her chest as she could. Though she was terrified and wanted to howl out, she knew better than to cry. As afraid as she was of being locked in the dark room of the back house, she was more frightened of the switch or the leather strap Mommie would certainly have on the other side of the door if she were to wail.

She moved, just slightly and ever so slowly, to the only light that came into the room: a tiny, dry rotted hole in the clapboard. The hole was at the back of the room, where Mommie had thrown her and where she had stayed, so it faced the mountainside, not the house or the dusty, dirt road. Peering out with one eye closed, she could just barely make out the trail that led to Dunn's Cemetery.

She knew she wasn't allowed there. It was just one of a long line of strict rules Mommie doled out. At 6-years-old, Stella had seen more hard times and heard more harsh words than most people had absorbed in a lifetime. Her young mind understood that the woman she called Mommie was no mother at all, at least not to her, nor had she ever tried to be.

Stella had defiantly, although without thinking, walked the trail, only wanting to be close to her real mother - the one that shared her name and had been buried on the hill only three days after she had been born. Only, it had been Mommie working the tobacco fields that particular morning, and she had spied Stella walking toward the forbidden place.

Mommie's wrath had come down hard and swift on the small child. Stella had been surprised that she hadn't received the switch already, but judging from the heat of the day, she knew she had already been there for hours. Stella feared Mommie might have been planning to keep her there indefinitely. At any other time, Stella would be famished by now.

The back house was a small building with three separate rooms and three separate doors to the outside. None of the rooms were accessible to the others once inside. She was in the middle room, which held mostly storage and jarred foods for the winter months. The room to her left held tools for the farm. The room to her right was a smoke house.

The day prior had been what had been termed in Newport as "hog slaughtering day", which meant that Butcher Johnson drove to each farm and would slaughter one or more animals on site, for a fee and the farmers would then smoke the meat. On that particular day, Poppie had drunk too much moonshine; Stella could tell by the way he had walked and slurred his words. When Butcher Johnson came, Poppie had mistakenly chosen Beatrice, Stella's favorite pig, to be slaughtered. Mommie had been inside with Stella as they watched the entire incident take place. Stella had cried out and tried to stop Poppie, but Mommie held her back and let her scream, quietly smirking as Stella watched her beloved pet and friend squeal and writhe in terror, understanding full well what was to become of her.

Beatrice was now hanging in the room next to her, smoke from coals covering her now dissected body. The odor was horrific. The memory and the smell, coupled with the heat of the day and the long sleeved, burlap dress she was wearing made Stella feel that she had to vomit. Her head swam as dizziness and remembrance overwhelmed her.

When Poppie had realized what he had done, he felt horrible and went off to drink more. He had once told Stella in a drunken slur that the moonshine could sometimes "make the bad stuff go away". At age 5, she had tried a swig from his jug once on a day that Mommie had been extraordinarily cruel. The taste on her tongue twisted her face. Hot fire burned her throat, chest, and stomach until she thought it would never end. She had coughed, sputtered, and drunk numerous handfuls of water from the creek to wash away the trampling of her taste buds. She had decided that she would have to find another way to make the bad stuff go away.

Stella peered out the tiny hole again and looked for some sign of Poppie. She worried about him terribly when he would leave to drink.

Her real mother's father, the man the townspeople called Old Man Milner, had been found dead on one of the close by mountainsides the summer after she was born. She had eavesdropped on numerous occasions and had overheard many stories that recounted when he was found; he had been curled up, as if asleep, clutching an empty flask. He had been missing for months before his body was discovered. The sheriff had determined that he had gotten drunk, fallen asleep, and frozen to death during a particularly harsh winter, coupled with an ice storm that had barreled through the eastern parts that year. Stella often worried that something similar, if not the same, might happen to Poppie.

Poppie normally made sure never to be gone for long. He knew the irrational hatred that Mommie held in her heart for Stella. He would try to always be near in order to ward off any harm Mommie may cause. Stella had sustained several injuries at Mommie's hand in her young life. Stella had become the only reason that Poppie had been able to endure.

Poppie had become weak after his son had left the farm for a second time. He had picked up the bottle again, trying to escape a merciless, vindictive, and brutal existence.

Poppie was a gentle man - kind-hearted, quiet, caring, and loving.

The demented deterioration of the woman he once loved, the loss of contact with a son that had been a substantial part of his soul, and a farm that he could not seem to keep from ruin had made it much easier than he had thought possible to take another drink.

Bessie begged Mommie continuously to let Stella live with them at the Milner home. Bessie and Foster understood Stella's anguish as well and were also aware of the fact that Poppie was no match against anger and wrath such as Mommie's. Mommie would always refuse Bessie's offer, proclaiming that she needed Stella's help on the farm and that it was the least she could receive from a child such as Stella, a child that had taken her beloved son from her. Bessie protested constantly, but to no avail.

Stella had heard the conversations, the arguments, and the discussions-turned-debate her whole life. She was very aware of the fact that her father had left shortly after her birth, and that Mommie blamed Stella for losing Charles, Stella's father and Mommie's beloved son. She tried to be on her best behavior at all times for Mommie; she tried every way she knew to please her. Nothing would ever suffice, and even through all of the efforts made, Mommie was constantly cold and bitter.

She remembered a time that Mommie had called her worthless. When it had been spoken, she hadn't understood what the word had meant. A few months later, a work horse had busted a leg pulling a plow. While Stella stood outside the barn listening, Foster and Poppie had described the horse as worthless after the incident and said they would have to put it down. The sound of the shotgun resonated through Stella's mind, giving her a full sense of the word's meaning. It was a meaning she did not want to understand, for it forced her to realize that Mommie would never love her as she felt she should be loved, longed to be loved. She knew she would never be anything more to Mommie than a mere farm hand, or worse yet, a disposable animal to do with as she saw fit.

Coming back to her present situation and seeing no signs of Poppie, Stella slowly slid back into position, her back against the wall, legs tucked in tight. The longer she waited, the more her tummy tumbled and her head spun. She pulled up the sleeves of her burlap dress and considered removing it to help sustain the heat, but she knew she would certainly be beaten if she were to be found naked in the small room when, or if, she was finally released. There was no air flow into the room, and as the heat rose higher, Stella began to stagger her breathing, seemingly suffocating. There was no time for reaction as the small amount of breakfast on her stomach screamed out of her body, covering her dress in vomit and bile. She continued to heave uncontrollably through air restricted gasps of breath. She heaved once more, so violently it caused her to urinate in the thick, heavy, sack dress.

Death had not occurred to Stella and was not occurring to her now. Her only thoughts were that she had soiled her dress and would definitely be receiving Mommie's switch. Tears streamed down her face as the already horrendous smells in the small room were now coupled with the smell of vomit and urine. The room began to spin as Stella's eyes fluttered.

The door was flung open to find Stella on her hands and knees, head tucked to her chin, covered in vomit and urine.

"MOMMIE!"

Stella was swooped up and cradled into a set of strong arms that brought her out of the storage room. She tried to focus in the bright sun, but dizziness still filled her head, making it hard for her to understand what was happening and impossible to focus. She wasn't sure if she should be relieved or frightened.

"Where's that vile woman at?"

It was a woman's voice speaking, and Stella soon recognized it as Bessie.

"MOMMIE!"

Her screams caused Stella's head to pound and she moaned slightly. Bessie rushed to her side and stroked her sweat-soaked hair.

"She burnin' up, Foster. We gotta git her ta th' house quick!"

Bessie was furious, but tried to calm herself for Stella's sake. Foster ran with Stella to the beat up International work truck and gently placed her inside. Bessie climbed in beside her and slammed the heavy door, shut hard in an act of anger, causing Stella to jump at the loud bang. She fluttered in and out of consciousness on the short descent to Foster and Bessie's home. Once there, Foster had to fill the large wash basin that sat on the back porch with water from the well as Bessie stripped Stella of the burlap sack and wiped her down with a cool cloth.

As Stella stepped into the tub, the cool water touching hot, sweat-soaked, tender skin made her scream out in pain. Bessie lowered her in slowly and gently, explaining that she had to be cooled down and that the pain would subside shortly. After a few moments, she was full in, resting her small head on the back of the tub wall, but still in excruciating pain.

Normally for Stella, a bath at Bessie's was a sheer delight and a luxury she did not posses at the farm. At that particular moment, however, it was a strange form of torture, her skin prickling like needles throughout every inch of her body. Bessie sat close to her side, wiping her face and wetting her long, dark hair. Stella tried not to cry out, as this had become habit in her young life, but she could not disguise the whimpering noises that escaped her mouth.

The sounds Stella emitted reminded Bessie of a tiny, un-weaned puppy that had lost its mother too soon, searching for warmth and a place to suckle. The thought brought tears to her eyes as she realized how close her thoughts were to the actual truth. She held the small child tight, but tenderly, as tears streamed down both of their faces.

Just as Bessie had promised, the prickling pain soon subsided, and Stella began to feel slightly more comfortable. When Bessie saw that she was feeling better and that her body temperature had almost returned to normal, she lifted her frail niece from the tub and wrapped her in thin linen, drying her skin softly.

"Wha'd ya do, chil'?" Bessie whispered, as if Mommie could hear.

Tears began to fill Stella's eyes again as she said, "I jus' wanted to see my mama."

Bessie's heart ached tremendously for the small child.

"Ya walked up ta th' hill?"

Stella nodded her head. "I din't know she was workin' the fields, Aunt Bessie. I din't see her." Tears began to stream, although they fell in silence.

Bessie held her close and patted her back.

"There, there, chil'. No need to cry, now. It gonna be alright. Don' ya worry."

"I really done made her mad, Aunt Bessie. Ya should'a seen her." Stella's small face was contorted out of fear and anguish.

Bessie smiled at her when she said, "I've seen it, chil'. I know. It's scary!"

The statement made them both giggle as Bessie led Stella inside the house.

Foster and Bessie's large house had always amazed Stella. Although it was at least 90 degrees outside, the house was nice and cool. The house was built of rock, and for some reason that Stella did not understand, this made the house cooler than any other she knew of. There were many windows in each room, always open in the summertime. The beautiful windows were even open during the rain, as there were so many trees on the land that they covered and sheltered most of the house. The winds floating down the mountainside into the small valley seemed to flow directly through the house, drastically cooling it in its shady spot with its majestic rock walls, even on the hottest of days.

The old, clapboard farmhouse had only one tree: an apple tree that sat nearer to the barn than the house and offered no shade to the home, yard or porch. There were only two small windows in the parlor, but they sat on different corners of the square room, making air flow almost impossible. The back two walls of the parlor were solid, one holding the black, belching, potbelly stove and the other holding the door leading to the two small, connected bedrooms.

Stella could feel and act like a princess in Bessie's home and did so each time she was there. Bessie escorted Stella into the main floor bedroom, which was the room she slept in when she stayed over. Bessie referred to it as the guest room; she had heard a room such as this described in a magazine she had once read.

Bessie walked to the wardrobe with a smile on her face and pulled out a blue and white short sleeved dress that came below the knees, but far above the ankles - the type of dress Stella had seen other girls wear at church meetings or in town what few times she was allowed to leave the farm. It was the type of dress that Mommie would *never* approve of, but the type of dress Stella had always dreamed of wearing.

Stella couldn't hold back her gasp, and this made Bessie beam at her excitement.

"I saw the pattern at th' store and picked up th' material ta make it fer ya. Thought ya'd look purty in it."

Stella stared at the dress, half of her thrilled, the other half terrified.

Silence caused Bessie to continue, which was her way.

"I was a savin' it fer ya fer the church picnic, but I thought I'd go on and give it ta ya. Thought it might'n cheer ya up a bit."

"Mommie ain't never gonna let me wear that, Aunt Bessie."

"Oh, go on, now. She'll know I made it fer ya, and she'll like it." She smiled her broad, bright smile. "Go on an' try it on. See if it fits ya."

Stella held the dainty material in her arms and immediately loved the feel of its touch on her skin. Slipping the dress over her head made her feel like Cinderella, a character in a book Bessie had read to her recently, which was still very vivid in her mind. With her arms slipped through and the dress fully on, Bessie buttoned up the back and tied the waist sash into a bow. Bessie brushed Stella's long, dark, wavy hair and tied it back with a matching ribbon.

They both faced the looking glass as Bessie smiled, and Stella marveled at the sight of herself, looking like a doll, or a child model in a rarely seen magazine.

"Does ya like it?"

"I love it, Aunt Bessie, I really do. It's th' most beautiful dress I ever saw, but I still don' think Mommie will let me…."

Bessie cut her off. "Now ya jus' let me handle Mommie."

"How she doin', Bess?" Foster was calling from the front door where he had just come in.

"Oh, she gonna be alright," Bessie called back. "We're in th' guest room."

Stella continued to look at herself in the looking glass; a look of joy sparkled in her eyes. Foster walked through the door and stopped immediately once inside. Seeing Little Stella, as he called her, in her beautiful new dress made his face beam.

"Well, don' ya look jus' gorgeous!" he proclaimed.

Stella blushed. "Oh, stop it, Uncle Foster."

"No, I mean it, Little Stella. Ya look just so darn purty. I don' 'spect I ever seen ya look so purty."

"Aunt Bessie made it fer me."

"I know she did. She's been a workin' hard on it. Fine job she did, too. Fine job." He glanced at his beloved wife with pride and joy filling his eyes as he focused on her love of this child. "Fits ya jus' darn near perfect, too, don' it?"

Stella completely forgot her inhibitions and for a moment became the 6-year-old child she should have been. She spun around in the dress, truly feeling like a princess. Foster smiled at her, happy that he and Bessie could offer at least some escape from the horrible life she led - a life almost as bad as his sister's had been. He pushed the thought out of his mind and focused again on Little Stella and Bessie.

"I do believe that y'all are two of the purtiest girls I ever seen in my life."

Bessie playfully slapped Foster on the arm.

"Ya stop that, ya big flirt and help me with fixin' supper. It's late and I bet Stella's starvin' ta death!"

"I'm really not that hungry, Aunt Bessie."

"Nonsense, chil'. Ya got ta eat ya somethin'. How long was ya in there for, anyway?" She spoke as she walked to the kitchen and began preparing food for a light supper. Foster and Stella followed along, as had to be done with Bessie to be able to keep up and listen. She was always on the move with this or that.

"How long Mommie have ya in there for, Little Stella?" Foster asked again, curiously and cautiously, when Stella didn't respond. In his mind, he was furious.

"I walked up the hill at early mornin'. I din't see her around nowhere. I jus' figured she was a lookin' for Poppie. He left again after what happened with...." Tears welled in her eyes, and Foster took her hand.

"We heard 'bout Beatrice. I'm jus' so sorry, Little Stella."

She sucked up her tears and continued.

"She was a workin' the fields and saw me. She grabbed me up almost as quick as I saw her and threw me in ta the back house. I don' know how long I was there."

Foster mumbled something under his breath to Bessie, but Stella could only make out the words "more than 4 hours". What she didn't hear was Foster proclaiming that he felt like killing Mommie for what she'd done.

As they sat down to supper, they said grace and began with usual family supper-table conversation. Stella sat silent, playing with her food and hardly eating a bite.

"Why ain't my daddy ever wrote ta me?" Stella's question came unexpectedly, interrupting a sentence Foster had been speaking about an event that had taken place at work that day.

Silence deafened the room as Bessie and Foster stared at each other blankly. They had both had conversations of why Charles never wrote. He seemed to love the child so much when he had left that it seemed impossible that he would never contact her. They both wondered if his hatred for Mommie had any effect on his decision, but it had been more than six years. He had to wonder how the child was.

"Why won't ya answer me? Is it my fault? Did I do somethin' wrong?"

"Of course not, sweetheart." Bessie's hand covered Stella's. "Ya ain't neva done nothin' to cause no harm ta no one."

"I killed my mama." Stella whispered this in a voice hardly audible.

Bessie tossed down her fork onto the plate, raising her voice furiously and said, "Don' ya ever say that again, chil'! It jus the way things are. Din' have nothing ta do with ya! Weren't yer fault at all! When the Lord calls you is when ya gonna go and that's that!"

"But Mommie blames me for takin' her son away, why wouldn't my daddy blame me for takin' his wife away?"

The fury growing inside Bessie was so strong that it could be seen in her face. Her own anguish knew that it was devastatingly wrong for a child so small to carry such guilt and heartache. Foster saw the anger Bessie possessed and jumped up quickly, embracing Stella.

"Ain't none of this yer fault, Little Stella. Ya was a gift ta yer mama. She loved ya so much. I wish ya could remember the look in her eyes when she saw ya fer the first time. T'were beautiful. Neva seen her look so happy."

Bessie stood back and watched Foster's gentleness with the child that so desperately needed someone.

"An' yer daddy," Foster continued. "Whew, yer daddy, boy, did he love you. Ya made a light shine in his eyes like I ain't neva seen before." He paused before continuing, becoming somber. "What yer daddy did, he had ta do. Yer too young ta understand now, but one day ya will."

Stella pushed Foster away with unbelievable force for such a small girl.

"Everybody always sayin' I'm too young, I'm too young. It don' matter why he did it! He left me here! He ain't never comin' back fer me, and it ain't fair! It just ain't fair!" She burst out into a crying fit that was completely unlike her. She screamed and cried until her eyes were red and her face puffed up. Bessie and Foster allowed her to let it out, knowing that, at that moment, she was so distraught that there would be no way to console her.

Loud, intense bangs at the back door made all three tense up from the unexpected interruption. Stella dried her tears quickly, knowing with fierce fear what was standing on the other side of the door.

"I know ya got her in there, Bessie! Ya better let me in!" She continued to bang, louder and harder, jiggling the door handle violently.

"I locked th' door when I came in," Foster explained to Bessie.

"What should we do, Foster?"

There was no response. Terror was flashing through Stella's eyes, but Bessie did not notice. Foster stood speechless, staring at the door as if the booming knocks would break it down.

"Well, I got ta answer th' door, Foster. I can't jus' leave her out there. She be even more mad than she is now, an' she sounds awful mad as things are."

In their own ways, Bessie and Foster were just as afraid of Mommie as Stella, Poppie, and most of the people in and surrounding Newport. She was a powerful woman, and her mind had deteriorated to the brink of insanity when Charles had left the farm after Stella's birth.

Bessie walked to the door as Foster stood close to Little Stella. Stella's heart thumped in her chest so loudly, she was sure Foster could hear it. Foster took Stella back into the guest room. He stared at the door out of the corner of the room, dreading the worst and knowing it was coming. Bessie flung the door open wide; a look as bitter as Mommie's was plastered across her face.

Mommie walked right in, uninvited, and looked around the house in her investigative, judging way. Stella and Foster stayed in the guest bedroom, listening intently.

"Where's she, Bessie? I know ya got her."

"Ya durn right, I got her. She safe with me. Ya almost killed her today. Lockin' her in that room with no air to breath. How long was she in there for, Mommie?"

Mommie gave no response.

"How long?" Bessie spat out her words with fire.

"How dare ya talk ta yer mommie that a way. Ya should be ashamed of yerself. That girl done disobeyed my rules again, and I jus' won't stand fer it. I can tell ya she weren't in there long enough, since ya came an' got her out."

"Mommie, she was close ta death when we foun' her. Any longer an' she would a died."

"Then it'd a been God's will."

"Like it was with Ella, Mommie?" Bessie's words fell like icicles off of her tongue, stabbing Mommie with each syllable. Mommie knew she had done nothing to save young Stella's mother during her birth; they all knew that. She knew in her mind that it was her own fault that Ella was dead and Charles was gone, but she had pushed the thought so far back into her corroded mind that she no longer believed it to be the truth. Words such as Bessie's forced her remembrance and fueled her fury.

Foster kept Stella behind the door where she could not see, but he could. He saw the look in Bessie's eyes, the flash of hatred and the cold, bitter, heartless stare.

Mommie stood silent, her smirk replaced by a look of nothingness, her eyes a dark void.

"Ya know what I mean, Mommie. Ain't no denying it."

Mommie stood silent still, glaring through her darkness.

"It ain't God's will when it's at yer hands, Mommie!" Bessie was furious and screaming now.

Mommie now had reason to stand with a bold, stern, cold smirk. She had won the small battle by breaking her daughter and causing her to rage.

Stella could feel her heart thumping through every vein as she heard every word. Had Mommie had something to do with her mother's death? There were so many questions unanswered in her young mind. Foster held her close and tried to ease her tensions.

"She stayin' with me, Mommie." Bessie was cold and convincing.

Mommie only smirked.

"Think ya can take her from me?" Mommie's tone was bitter and brandishing.

Foster's mind wandered back to a time when his father had come once for his sister.

Mommie whispered something close into Bessie's ear, turned abruptly, and walked out the door, slamming it shut behind her so hard that it rattled. Bessie stood motionless for a moment, staring at the closed door, desperately collecting her thoughts.

Bessie returned to the guest room with a reluctant, but reserved smile.

"Guess you'll be staying here tonight."

Stella ran across the room and hugged Bessie who pulled her into the air and swung her around while Foster laughed.

This is what Stella longed for: a mother, a father, a family. At that specific moment, it felt almost attainable, but later that night, the feeling of being a princess became what it was: a fairy tale. Soon, the clock would strike midnight.

She tossed and turned in the night, not sleeping well. She woke every so often thinking she heard noises or felt a presence. Seeing nothing, she would fall back into a restless sleep filled with unpleasant dreams that quickly turned into nightmares.

As the roosters crowed, Stella awoke immediately to the misty morning daybreak. She wiped her sleep filled eyes, sat up in the comfortable, cozy bed, and looked out the window into the haze of a new day. She glanced around the room.

When it caught her eye, it made her blink and rub her eyes again, disbelief causing her to think it was her mind playing tricks on her. After staring at the unimaginable sight for a moment, she let out a loud, painful wail full of sadness and despair.

CHAPTER SEVEN

*B*essie and Foster came running frantically into the guest room to see what had caused Stella's outburst. Bessie saw the sight almost immediately as tears began to well in her own eyes. Foster looked in the direction of their stares, at the wardrobe, and gasped.

The beautiful new dress that Bessie had made for Stella was destroyed. It had been shredded from top to bottom, shards of beautiful blue material now littering the floor. Bessie was at Stella's side immediately, placing her arm around her, offering some comfort, but Stella knew as well as Bessie that the devious act had hurt them both.

Stella's heart was shattered as she wept silently. A slow, deep thunder rolled through the hills, and Stella knew that the rain would arrive shortly. It always seemed to come when her heart felt its worst.

Foster paced the room, back and forth, mumbling under his breath, anger seeping from every vein. "How could she? She done some bad thin's, Bessie, but this. This takes the cake!" The more he spoke, the louder he became. "Damn it! Bessie, ya worked so hard on that dress, an' Stella jus' loved it! What the hell is wrong with that woman? How could she do this?"

A thunderous crack coupled with bright lightning lit up the dim room and shook the solid house.

Her eerie figure stood in the shadows of the doorway, as if she had appeared along with the thundering boom. "T'ain't nothin' wrong wit' me! It be yuns that got somethin' wrong wit' yas!" Her scream was loud and shrill, rising high above the sound of the rolling thunder.

All three jumped at the dramatic sight.

"Guess'n that how ya talk ta th' chil' when I ain't around? Usin' them devil words and poisonin' her 'gainst me?"

"Mommie! How'd ya git here?" Bessie's voice was high pitched, as well as obviously terrified. Calming herself, she added, "Why'd ya go an' do such a thing?"

"Ain't neva left, girl, I's been here all night, jus' a waitin'. That chil' is comin' back ta th' farm wit' me one way or another. I cut up that thing ya was callin' a dress 'cause it was despicable and ungodly. That chil' won't be a wearin' no dress such as that!"

"Her name is Stella, Mommie." Bessie sat close to Stella, protecting her.

"I know what th' chil's name is. Is th' name she shares with th' woman that took my son from me th' first time. They's jus' alike, an' that name be a name I'll hate till th' day I die."

Foster had never hit a woman before in his life; still, his fists were balled in fury. Ella had been his sister. He had controlled his rage at her death for Charles's sake, but this was too much. He had failed in protecting his sister from this woman. He feared he was making the same mistakes with her child. At that moment, he could have murdered Mommie and never given it a second thought, just as she had murdered his sister. Bessie read the rage in his eyes and quickly stood between them. This act put her directly in front of Mommie, face to face. Her entire body trembled, but her voice was calm and sure.

"She ain't a goin' wit' ya, Mommie."

"Yes'n she is, even if I got ta take her."

"I'll go," said a tiny whisper.

A small smirk came across Mommie's face, knowing she had successfully intimidated them and won the situation.

Bessie stared at Stella in disbelief. "Ya ain't got ta go, Stella. Ya can stay here wit us!"

"Aunt Bessie, she'll jus' call the sheriff or do somethin' even worse," she was whispering quietly, so unsure of her words, but somehow knowing they were true.

Bessie lowered her head in defeat as Stella stood from the cozy bed and began to gather her burlap dress to wash up and change.

"Bessie, no! Ya jus' can't let her go!" The despair in Foster's voice clung in the air.

In a beaten down voice, completely unlike Bessie, she said, "T'ain't nothin' we can do," because she, too, knew Stella's words were true. Mommie would not stop until she had attained what she wanted. Bessie had known her temper and fury for far too long to say otherwise.

Mommie stood in the parlor and waited for Stella, not speaking a word.

Stella walked weakly into the small room that Bessie called the wash room. The room contained a wash bowl, cloths and a small looking glass. She washed her tear-soaked face and stared at her tiny reflection in the glass. Her long, dark hair had curled from the heat and humidity. Her eyes were glassy and distant. Her look made her wonder if her mother had carried this same look of void and despair.

She exited the small room wearing her burlap dress, saying a silent prayer of thankfulness that Bessie had washed the dress the night before so that Mommie would not see the vomit and urine that had covered it.

When Stella emerged, Foster came out into the parlor and told Mommie he would take them up the hill in the truck.

Mommie was aggressive in her tone when she spat out, "Don' need no help from th' likes of ya. We can make do." She shoved Stella out the back door and slammed the screen shut behind them.

A million thoughts ran through Stella's head on the long incline back to the farm. She was in terrible fear of what awaited her when she arrived. Mommie was relentless, making her walk faster and swifter and pushing her much more sternly than a child of 6 could keep pace with.

Stella's fast trot had quickly turned into a run. Still weak from exhaustion from the day before and with no food on her stomach, Stella fell to the hard ground, barely alert. Mommie quickly swept her up by one arm, pulling her tiny body fully off of the ground.

Flinging her around like a rag doll, Mommie screamed, "Wha's a matta, chil'? Ya can run off, but ya can't run home where ya belong?"

"Mommie, I didn't run off, Aunt Bessie came." She was weak in her voice, gasping for breath.

Mommie cut her off quickly. "Ya gonna argue wit' me, too, chil'? That how it gonna be?"

Mommie drug Stella by the arm she was squeezing to a nearby tree stump. Still clutching her arm so tight that it turned red and burned, Mommie stood next to a sagging willow and clipped off a thick switch. She sat down on the stump and bent Stella over her legs. Stella had tears in her eyes, knowing the pain she was about to receive, but she knew better than to fight back. Mommie lifted her burlap dress up to her waist, revealing her legs and bare bottom.

This was the part of being switched that humiliated Stella most. She was fully exposed to a woman that felt that exposure of any kind was ungodly and sinful. Stella felt that Mommie enjoyed her humiliation; she was correct in thinking so.

Mommie beat Stella severely, causing open gashes across her legs and bottom, some so deep that they were already welting, seeping, and oozing blood. Silent tears ran down Stella's face, but she never cried out. Mommie continued to thrust the switch at Stella, over and over, until she herself was exhausted.

"Git yerself up and cover up your nasty nakedness, ya sinful chil'."

Stella stood and lowered her dress, trying to quickly but gently cover the open wounds with the sandpaper material. Another boom of thunder rattled the ground as the sky opened up and poured. The rain only caused her more pain as it instantly soaked her burlap dress, making it heavy and causing it to stick to the fresh wounds.

The rest of the walk up the hill was excruciating for Stella. Agony ran through her body as the dress rubbed against the painful wounds. Mommie had worn herself out during her outrage and no longer pushed Stella to climb the hill faster. Even during Mommie's hiatus, Stella feared that this was only the beginning.

They came around the bend where the farm was in sight, but still much farther away. Stella could barely make out Poppie, standing on the porch and looking their direction. When he saw them, he started a steady trot towards them.

"Wha's happen to y'all? Yas had me worried sick!" Poppie looked at Mommie first for an explanation before noticing Stella. Once he laid eyes on her, he knew positively that his suspicions were true; something had gone horribly wrong in his drunken absence.

"Wha's it matta ta ya? Ya been out to who knows where doin' who knows what! Ya comes back here and I's got ta explain everythin' that been goin' on?" Mommie was harsh and bitter, her words crashing and cutting, sharp-edged as glass. "If ya got ta know, she done run off an' went ova ta Bessie's house. I had ta walk myself down there an' get her back."

Poppie saw that Stella cringed at the lie, but she dared not speak; this they were both aware of. Poppie's despair could not be hidden in his eyes. He felt fully responsible for what horrors had taken place to his dear, precious granddaughter - the only link that remained to his son.

Almost afraid to ask, he squeaked out, "Did ya punish her?"

"Well, o'course I punished her, ya fool. How else'm I gonna teach her a lesson?" Words again stabbed at both Poppie and Stella.

"Wha'd ya do ta her?" Poppie's voice was small and insignificant as he stared at the tiny, vulnerable child.

"I punished her. I thought we done talked 'bout that." Mommie smiled at her terms, satisfied with herself and her wit. She felt she had no need to explain herself to anyone when it came to the task of raising a forgotten young girl.

"Come on over here, chil'." Poppie's open arms were welcoming and inviting to Stella. Still, she glanced at Mommie for approval before proceeding. Seeing no signs of protest, Stella practically fell into Poppie's frail arms as the rain pounded down in buckets.

"Ya two stay outside if'n ya want. I got sense enough ta get outta th' rain." With that, she pivoted her heel toward the direction of the house and started walking slowly through thick sheets of rain. Stella and Poppie watched her slither through the water as if she were a snake until she was fully inside.

"Wha' happen, girl?" Poppie asked softly.

"I don' wanna talk 'bout it jus' yet, Poppie."

The events seemed only a distant dream, excepting the stinging sensations on her legs and behind that she had become accustomed to over the years. Being locked in the storage shed was only a nightmare - one of many she had starred in. She had not been to Bessie's glamorous home. She had not touched and modeled the most beautiful dress anyone had laid eyes on, made especially for her. That had only been a tiny glimmer of hope in her eyes. Things such as these were never dreamt at night; they were only vivid daydreams in waking.

Mommie had not come, cut the dress to pieces, and drug her away from Bessie's home. This had never occurred because she had never been there and had never seen such a dress. She slowly took her mind back to the morning before, convincing herself that she had only been caught sneaking up to Dunn's Cemetery and switched harshly.

Stella looked back at Poppie's pained face and quickly added, "If that's alright with you, Poppie."

He held her tight in the middle of the dirt road as the rain began to let up, but not cease. She captured his embrace, clinging tightly, and stared at the small house and sloping tobacco fields.

The green plants, some of them starting to yellow, waiting to be cropped and placed in the drying barn, danced and bowed in the heavy rain. She watched their dance and listened intently, hoping to find the music they heard that made them want to rejoice. There was not a time that she had heard anything other than the persistent pounding the rain caused. It came so often that she ached for the sun. There was no need for dancing or rejoicing or laughing or singing; there was only need to survive, to be swept away and drown down below in the floods, or to climb to the peak of the misty mountains where the clouds dare not tread.

Suddenly, the harsh winds began to blow and the rain flew sideways, stinging everything in its path. Poppie and Stella had no choice but to retreat into the house.

The field full of plants offered some escape, a sense of shelter, but what should be offered in a home was no home to her. These three rooms were the background for each bad memory that her mind had placed in its proper hiding spot.

Stella felt some relief in the fact that Poppie was here with her - relief that he was safe and sound as well as relief in knowing he was there. Mommie was bitter and cruel to Stella when Poppie was near, but the only physical harm that came to her was when they were alone.

Upon entering the house, Poppie began to confront Mommie, demanding to know what had taken place, standing strong, firm, and sober against her. Mommie scoffed at him, disregarding each word as if he weren't speaking.

Stella could not listen. If and when Mommie did speak of the situation it would be to tell Poppie how horrible she was - what a great chore she was to have to raise, what evil, malicious schemes she had devised; it was all lies and manipulation to draw the attention from herself and place blame elsewhere. Poppie knew these statements to be false, but listened each time, clinging to each word and hoping to find a flaw or a reason to accuse her. Mommie was excellent at her craft and could never be cornered within her own lies.

Stella closed herself off from the conversation and walked to the back room, which was the only place she could call her own. She opened the wardrobe and pulled out an older dress, one with which the itchy material had been softened by being beaten and scrubbed upon the rocks of the creek. Peering carefully into the parlor to make sure that Mommie and Poppie were occupied, she carefully removed the sopping wet dress that had wrapped itself around her in the rain. Drying quickly with her weekly linen, she slid the clean dress over her head, swiftly shimmying until she was fully covered. She dried the wet floor with the linen, hung the wet, pink-stained dress to dry, and placed her linen underneath to catch any rain water that may drip to the wooden floor and give reason to flare Mommie's temper.

Examining the room carefully to see that all was clean, tidy, and in order, she walked to the only window that peered through the back wall of the house, overlooking the fields. The window had been left open, but the winds were blowing the opposite direction, allowing the water to stay clear of the floor and walls. She watched the plants dance and the rains fall until dusk settled in, and she no longer heard Mommie's barks at Poppie's pleas.

Her stomach grumbled as she lay down to sleep. There were no kisses goodnight and no one to tuck her in. She had not heard any voices and had assumed Poppie had gone to the back house to drink, away from the house, but sheltered from the rain. Mommie was undoubtedly on the porch having supper for herself.

Stella welcomed the sleep, knowing that even through nightmares, the darkness would ease her pain.

She knew who she was. She hadn't quite figured out the reasoning for her life, but she did know who she was. She was not a "spawn of the devil himself" or "a bastard child" as Mommie so referred to her when she thought Stella's ears weren't wide open.

Stella knew there was so much more to her than that. There was a love in her heart that she could feel, but could not share.

CHAPTER EIGHT

*9*t had become late in the fall when Stella stood at the barn and watched the chickens scratch and peck at the feed she threw to them. Poppie had been around quite often, as had Bessie and Foster, so issues between Mommie and Stella stayed at bay.

As she scattered the feed, her mind was drifting towards other matters. She was turning 7 in January and should have started school already. She had always been excited at the prospect of school and learning and filling her head with as much information as she could possibly hold. She had planned to speak to Bessie about it when she saw her again, but her thoughts were suddenly distracted.

The sound she heard and the dust cloud rising on the road told her there was a vehicle coming down the mountainside. She set down her pail and ran to the dirt road to get a better look; mechanical vehicles were rare in Newport, especially headed down from the hillside. The further up the mountain and into the hollow, the poorer the people. A car coming from this direction had never before been seen in her lifetime. As the puttering sounds of the engine came closer, Mommie came to the side of the house, curious as well.

A dusty, dented, dirt-covered truck was clearly visible as it came around the bend near the top of the mountain. Mommie gasped and held her hands up to her breasts. Stella flicked her head in Mommie's direction, seeing a look in Mommie's eyes she had never seen. She looked happy - and happy she was. Stella stood starstruck and confused, wondering who could cause such a stir in Mommie.

The black truck pulled between the tall tobacco barn and the small white house, puttering for a moment before the engine was cut. Mommie walked cautiously towards the vehicle with Stella close on her heels.

Two people sat inside the truck. A tall, dark-haired man was driving. He was handsome, but unshaven and haggard. The woman beside him was the most beautiful woman Stella thought Newport could have ever seen. She had a small frame, soft face, and almost black shoulder length hair. At the crown of her head, to the left side, was a streak of white. It was a bolt of lightning in a black sky, not only adding to her beauty but lending a mysterious air.

Stella was close at Mommie's side, half hiding behind her leg, as they stood yards away from the truck. Tears welled in Mommie's eyes as Stella's small voice quietly asked, "Who is it, Mommie?"

Silence drifted before her cracked response. "That there's yer daddy."

Stella's world began to swirl into a slow motion that caused her to feel light-headed and faint. She stared unbelievingly as the larger than life man exited the truck and walked to them.

He put his arms around Mommie and hugged her briefly, seemingly without emotion. He seemed to purposely ignore Stella, as if she weren't even there. His attention was drawn to the fields where Poppie was working.

Poppie, suddenly understanding the commotion, dropped the hoe he held in his hands and ran as if he were a boy, rejuvenated and invigorated by the sight of this man. He reached the truck with amazingly fast speed, grabbed his prodigal son, and held him tight. Stella's father returned Poppie's squeeze with a broad smile, lifting Poppie's small body off of the ground. Although he towered over Poppie, Poppie held fast to his son with the strength of 10 men.

"Good ta see ya, Poppie. I sure have missed ya."

"Charles. My boy! Ya look, well...ya look so dern growed up!"

Charles smiled as he looked around the farm, soaking it all in. His gaze finally rested on the small child. There was a sparkle in his eye but no words on his tongue. After staring at her with intent fascination for what seemed an eternity for the both of them, he returned to the truck and opened the passenger door.

The elegant woman stepped softly from the truck, looking out of place in her attire. She wore the most beautiful floral print dress that any of them had ever seen. It was styled very elegantly, dipping slightly in the front and hemmed just above the ankles. The sash around her tiny waist was tied into a magnificent bow. Her glamorous shoes made her look taller than she was as the heels were raised at least two inches off of the ground; this fascinated Stella, and for that matter, it seemed to interest Mommie and Poppie as well. Her makeup was light and natural. Stella thought she was beautiful enough to pose for the cover of a fashion magazine right there under the apple tree.

Stella looked down at her drab dress and bare feet. The woman saw her concern and smiled gently at the child. She was just as curious about the child as the child was of her. Mommie stared suspiciously at the woman, but the woman did not seem to notice. If she did, she did not care. This added to Stella's instant admiration of her.

"Poppie, this is Evelyn. I like ta call her Ev."

Evelyn smiled and held out her dainty hand towards Poppie. "It's very nice to meet you, Mr. Resenger."

He wasn't sure what to say or do. He took her hand and gently shook it, leaving a small cloud of dust as he quickly let go. Poppie looked somewhat embarrassed, but Evelyn did not seem to mind and never let Poppie feel uncomfortable.

"Well, it's, uh, nice ta meet ya, too." He was pleasant, trying to smile, but confused.

Evelyn turned to Charles and motioned towards Mommie. "And this is your mother, Charles?"

In a quieter, less proud voice than he had spoken with Poppie, he introduced the two. Although Evelyn was extremely cordial and polite in any way she knew to be, Mommie barely spoke to her, even letting out a "humph" now and then. After a moment, Evelyn gave up, not willing to waste the energy on a childish game such as what was occurring.

Evelyn's attention immediately turned to Stella. Bending down to meet her eye to eye, Evelyn spoke in a sweet, gentle tone. "And who might this be?"

Mommie instantly threw her head back and roared in an outburst of loud cackling laughter that caused the black crows in the trees to squawk and scatter. Poppie never spoke, nor did he take his eyes off of Stella. Charles cleared his throat and stammered for words that would not form.

Evelyn stood upright and looked from Charles to the child and back again. Tears welled in Stella's eyes, and there was a look of loss on Charles's face. However, what Evelyn noticed most was the resemblance. At that exact moment, through Mommie's laughter, Poppie's silence, Charles's loss, and Stella's tears, Evelyn realized that the man she had married had a child that he had never mentioned.

Stella, as well as everyone involved, understood full well the situation at hand. Her father had come back for the first time in almost seven years. She had never laid eyes on him before. The woman he returned with had never even been told that Stella existed. So many thoughts rushed through her tiny mind that she felt a need to run…and run she did. She darted away from the crowd, tears stinging behind her lids and streaming down her sweat-soaked face.

She ran faster and harder, trying to block out Mommie's laughter, her father's silence, the entire situation. Running until she could no longer run, thoughts still raced through her head so fast it made her dizzy and light-headed. She held her hand against a large tree and rested, trying to catch her breath. She wiped the tears from her eyes and suddenly realized that she had lost her bearings; she was running just to run. When she looked around, she saw that she was yards away from Dunn's Cemetery. She slowly and sadly slid down the side of the tree, sitting on the ground and staring at her forbidden place.

Day was turning to night, but Stella sat staring. She heard the footsteps, but somehow blocked them out, not turning to see who was coming or caring in the least. She was wrapped in her own thoughts and emotions. Even Mommie's switch couldn't harm her at this moment. She stared at the headstones, wondering which was her mother's and wondering why it couldn't have been her that didn't live that fateful day. She also wondered what life would have been like if they had both lived. Time crept through her mind, though it was moving swiftly in her life, more swiftly than she could have imagined.

"How ya been?"

Stella jerked her head around toward the voice that had snapped her back into reality. The gargantuan man that had been called her "daddy" was sitting next to her under the tree, looking at the cemetery as well.

How have I been? Her wandering mind narrowed and focused on that one particular question. How had she been? Did he mean right now at this moment? Or was he referring to the six and a half years she had been alive? The truth was, Charles didn't know what he had meant either, or what response she could possibly come up with to a question such as that.

Stella looked back to the cemetery, and there they both sat silent as the sun lowered behind them. Neither spoke. In the black of night he stood and reached for her hand. She took it, without question, and let him lead the way. A droplet of rain splashed into the center of where their hands had met for the first time. She gazed up at his tall, shadowy figure as he looked upon her smallness. He smiled a broad smile, and without words, they exchanged a moment that neither could describe, but both knew all was well.

They descended the hillside by the trail, the opposite way that Stella had run up, through bushes, trees, and briars. Halfway down the trail, she realized that, as close as she had been for all that time, she still had not seen her mother's grave. But in her hand she held the man she had always dreamed would one day come and sweep her away from all of this.

"It ain't been too good." She said it so quietly that he barely heard her. The rain started down a little harder. He had not heard his daughter. He had heard his beloved, dead wife. She had her voice. She had her look. She was just as Ella had been. And he had loved her so.

He stopped at the end of the trail as the rain sprinkled in their faces. He turned her towards him by holding her shoulders. He knelt down his large frame directly in front of her and studied her intently. Large tears formed in his eyes as he took her and embraced her.

"My child. You are my child. What have I done?" he howled at the darkness.

She took his embrace and returned it tightly, squeezing as hard as her tiny arms would allow. Although she did not understand, she physically felt his pain. She was sensitive to pain. She had felt so much; she was able to feel the pain of others as well.

She forgave him. She didn't even know what or why he was forgiven, but he was. He was forgiven completely.

"I forgive ya, Daddy," she whispered softly into his ear. The words felt strange and sounded even eerier as she had felt she would never be able to utter them.

Charles hugged his child so tightly that she thought she may break, but it was the happiest ache she had ever felt. Charles was rushed with an overflow of memories: of Ella's death, baby Stella's birth, the blood, the grave, the funeral, leaving. He wept uncontrollably as his small child comforted him. It was the first time he had cried in six years.

The rain continued to sprinkle as the night grew darker. Evelyn stood on the front porch of the clapboard house, wrapped in a hand-knitted shawl. She watched as Charles connected with this child he seemed to have forgotten about. Although she did not understand, she allowed what needed to occur. She had taken a vow to God to stand by this man in good times and bad. She would follow those vows. Slipping her small hand under her shawl, she rubbed the spot on her belly where the tiny seed that had been planted was slowly growing.

Charles regained himself and dried his tears. "Reckon it ain't been all that good fer ya, has it, girl." He was silent for a moment as he glanced back up the trail. He continued without moving his eyes. "I ain't got no excuse fer what I done ta ya, Stella." He stammered as he said her name.

Stella did not want to continue the conversation this way as she had already forgiven him.

"I ain't never been up there." She looked up the trail as well. "That there's the closest I been." She was quiet for a moment before she continued with, "Mommie says I ain't allowed."

He gazed at her with a sparkle in his eye and a smile on his lips. "She's a mean one, ain't she?"

"Yep." Stella couldn't help but smile, too. It had just occurred to her that he was raised by the same woman.

"Well, come on then," he said with a smile. "I ain't been there since we laid her in the ground. It's time ya met yer mother." He smiled a broad smile, showing her just how handsome he really was, as he continued, "I tell ya a lil' secret." He bent down close to her ear and whispered, "I ain't afraid of Mommie no more."

They both giggled as they started back up the trail.

Evelyn, still watching, went over the events that she and Charles had discussed when Stella ran from them.

Charles was married once before. They had a child, and his wife died in childbirth. Charles left shortly after. She had known none of these things. As she looked around earlier, she also realized that the "huge" farm that he owned in Newport was not huge by any means. This was the first time she had doubted her beloved husband. Up to this point, he had been the perfect gentleman. He worked alongside her family in the cotton mills in North Carolina, and her entire family loved him. She thought she had made the right choice in marrying him, although she had wondered why he hadn't told his family in Newport. Doubts about him filled her mind because of his lies, but she pushed them away, deep down inside. This child needed Charles and Evelyn more than Evelyn needed anger to dwell.

The rain continued to sprinkle as she watched them walk back up the hill. In the dusk, she had made out the headstones and knew there was a cemetery that they were close to. That was where they were headed, and she knew that they were going to see her grave - his first wife, of whom she did not know.

Evelyn returned to the house and warmed herself by the potbelly stove. The drizzle of rain had given her a chill. Mommie was not in sight. She was more than likely in one of the two small bedrooms that connected to the parlor. Poppie sat on the tattered couch. Evelyn joined him, and they made polite conversation for a small time. She knew that Poppie was a good man and immediately enjoyed his company. She tried to keep her mind on the conversation, but her thoughts kept fleeting back to Charles and Stella, making it hard for her to concentrate. Poppie understood this and, in his fashion, fell silent. It wasn't an awkward silence, but a silence of reflection, which they both needed. Poppie slid his hand on top of hers as they fell into their own thoughts. Evelyn appreciated the comfort.

Charles and Stella had reached the cemetery, although Stella was leery to step closer.

"It's alright," Charles said, assuring her. "I'm right here. Ya can trust me."

Through the darkness they stepped into the cemetery. Stella tried to avoid any ground that she felt may have someone underneath as she didn't want to be disrespectful. This cemetery had been close enough to reach each and every day of her life, yet she had never been. Bessie had told her once that her father had held her as a tiny babe when they laid her mother in the ground, but of course, this she could not remember.

They reached a spot in the small cemetery that did not have a large headstone, but was obviously a gravesite.

Charles fell to his knees and wailed painfully into the night, frightening Stella. Mommie heard his cry. She ached for her son's emotions, but she would not feel his pain. She could not. To feel his pain would be to admit that she had caused much of it.

Evelyn and Poppie heard his cry of pain as well, but they still sat silent and thoughtful. Stella stood solid as a stone statue, absorbing every moment of the mixed emotions mesmerizing her thoughts.

Charles's sobs silenced to sniffles. He removed the fresh flowers that either Foster or Bessie had left for her to reveal a tiny stone set into the ground.

Ella Resenger
1905 – 1924

She was there. For the first time in her life, she was standing directly in front of the place her mother was laid to rest. A feeling came over her that she could not describe. She sat slowly on the wet ground and gazed hazily through the drizzle at the tiny plaque and the pretty, fresh cut flowers, now wet from the sprinkling. She tried to understand the pain of a father she did not know for a mother she had not known, nor would she ever know.

Charles sat beside his child and placed his jacket around her shoulders to stop her shivering. Sitting beside her, he draped his arm around her, warming and comforting her. The tiny plaque, wet from the rain, shone and cast shadows at the same time in the darkness. She touched the ground softly where her mother lay.

"Daddy?" she whispered, again feeling strange with the word.

"Yeah?"

"I've missed you an' my mother both a lot. I'm glad ya came back." She paused before adding, "I wasn't sure ya ever would."

His voice changed. There was a silent seriousness that had not been heard before. "I'm sorry, Stella. I truly am." He meant what he said. He did not understand why he hadn't been there for her earlier. She was a perfect child in every way, and he loved her dearly. He knew that he always had and always would. Somehow leaving that mountain with his heartache behind him included a child he should have loved and cared for.

"It's all gonna be alright, now. It is." These were the only words he had left to offer.

As they descended the trail once more, holding his hand, much tighter and assured this time, Stella's mind began to let go of the pain it held and move to the current situation. She glanced at her handsome father.

"She's pretty. Who is she?"

Charles just smiled.

CHAPTER NINE

Stella woke to the rooster's crow and lay silent on the makeshift bed on the floor in the parlor. She could hear muffled voices, soon recognizing that they were the voices of her father and his new bride. She tried to block out all other noises, house creaks and pops from the stove so that she could make out what they were saying. She distinctly heard Evelyn's voice say that she would not be bullied by that woman. Stella smirked, knowing full well that she had meant Mommie. There was more said: something about the farm, and then she heard her name. She held her breath to hear what would come next.

The door to the rooms opened without warning, and Mommie emerged.

"Git yerself on up, girl. I know ya's awake. Work don't neva' stop."

Stella rose quickly and rubbed her face and any sleep from her eyes. She pulled on her dress over her nightgown for the warmth. She hurriedly put on her boots and tattered coat to gather water and wood. Before she had her hand on the door, her father had emerged and said he would help her.

Mommie smirked. "T'ain't work but for one. If'n yer makin' yerself useful, git it yerself. There's plenty more to be done right 'chere."

Charles winked at Stella, just out of Mommie's sight.

Stella began making preparations for breakfast, setting two extra places for Charles and Evelyn. It crowded the small enough table, and

Mommie grunted under her breath about it, but she didn't make her change it.

Evelyn emerged shortly after Charles, looking just as stunning, but in a dress not quite as nice as the one she had worn when she had first arrived.

"Can I help you with anything, Mrs. Resenger?"

Mommie did not speak; she did not grunt, or growl; she was completely silent.

"How about you, Stella?" Evelyn turned to Stella and leaned to face her. "Would you like some help?"

Stella thought of a million things that had to be done in the house daily, but she stood stunned. She was stunned at the fact that someone would actually be asking her if she needed any help.

"Girl don' need no help. She be fine on her own. If'n ya've made up them beds, then ya've done enough. We've managed this long without no help from ya."

Stella and Evelyn took that as a direct remark towards Charles.

Charles walked through the door, bringing a burst of cold air in with him. In trying to shut the door quickly, he accidentally spilled water from the pail. Stella instantly jumped up and ran for linens to clean up the mess.

Evelyn grabbed her arm gently. "Now, there's something I can do. I can clean up my husband's mess." She said it in such a way that it did not sound smug; her voice sounded so polite and helpful that it could almost be construed as sarcasm. Stella remained to her chore at hand even through the glaring eyes of Mommie. Evelyn cleaned up the mess quickly and efficiently, which only seemed to agitate Mommie more.

Breakfast was quiet - eerily quiet, where you could hear each clink of the fork on the plate. After everyone had finished, Evelyn and Stella began to clear the table. Mommie sat and watched their every move. After breakfast had been cleared away to Mommie's liking, she rose from the table.

"Wait, Mommie," Charles's voice boomed over the silence.

Mommie stood motionless for a moment then sat back down.

"There's something we got ta tell ya."

Mommie's eyes flashed fire. Poppie, who had been silent throughout breakfast looked inquisitive. Stella didn't breathe, excited and frightened at what was to come.

Charles stood up and walked to Evelyn's side. Evelyn smiled, mostly at Poppie and Stella, with a flashing glance at Mommie.

"I know'd it! I know'd you'd come back here! And in another mess! How dare ya bring this inta my house again?"

Stella stood confused. Poppie smiled and a tear streamed his cheek.

"Don'cha start, Mommie! I mean it! Don'cha start! And don't think you gonna be laying a single hand on her when the baby comes!" Charles's voice was strong and demanding. Evelyn looked confused by his statement, but did not waver.

Baby?

Stella understood. Not only did she have a new mother, she was going to have a baby brother or sister! She smiled Poppie's same smile.

"You came back last time, and yer comin' back now. Ya know ya need me." Mommie's voice was quiet, but mean and condescending.

"NO, Mommie! We don't need you. We came back here for Poppie and for sweet Stella. Evelyn and I want to share this experience with them. YOU have nothin' ta do wit it!"

Poppie took Stella and Evelyn onto the porch while Charles and Mommie argued viciously.

"How do you feel about all of this, Stella?" Evelyn asked sweetly.

She loved the way Evelyn talked; her speech was similar to hers in accent, but different, more refined. What surprised Stella most was that she was being asked her opinion. She felt as if, for the first time, someone truly cared about what she had to say.

Before she could answer, the old, beat up International was drudging its way up the mountainside. Bessie jumped out before Foster had come to a complete stop.

"Poppie? It true? He back? Where is he?" She was already out of breath.

"Calm yerself down there, girly. He's in there a talkin' to yer Mommie. Best leave 'em be."

"Stella, darlin'! How are you?" Bessie had Stella in her arms almost smothering her with her bear hug.

"It's alright, Bessie. Everythin's fine. I talked to him last night. And guess what? I finally got ta go. We went up to th' cemetery. I finally saw her restin' place!"

Bessie held her again and rocked her slightly. Evelyn's eyes showed a sign of sorrow.

"Somebody shoulda' done taken ya up there a long time ago," Bessie said as she smoothed her dark hair.

Something in Bessie's eyes shifted, and it seemed as if she was seeing Evelyn for the first time. She stared straight at her as she loosened her grip on Stella.

"This is Evelyn. This is Daddy's new wife! And guess what else? They gonna have a baby!" The excitement of the 6-year-old within her could not be contained.

"Hello, I'm Evelyn." She smiled at Stella's immediate revelation. "It's very nice to meet you."

Bessie was stunned, but very cordial. "You gonna have to excuse the way I'm acting, I suppose. We just ain't heard from Charles since he left. We didn't know…." Her voice trailed off.

Foster and Poppie, as men will sometimes do, sat back and listened to the drama that unfolded before them.

"It's alright. It really is. I've been getting a lot of that." Evelyn's voice was meek, mild, and inviting.

Bessie smiled at Evelyn's response, and soon the two were talking like old friends. The ruckus from inside had subsided, although no one got up to check the situation. Soon Charles had joined the others on the porch.

Time flew by quickly as the day passed. The usual work and chaos of the day was gone. Stella listened to the katydids sing their monotonous song, the crickets chirping their never-ending symphony, and the bullfrogs that lived just below the hill, trying to join in but just slightly off beat.

She had often listened to the same sounds many times before, thinking she was as the bullfrog, just slightly off. Tonight, she was different. She was part of something and it felt good. And warm. And safe.

Stella awoke on her makeshift bed on the floor and tried to focus. She must have fallen asleep on the porch and had been carried in by someone; she imagined her daddy with his big, strong stature. It was the middle of the night, but Stella could see a dim light coming from the porch. She quietly slipped on her boots and coat and stepped outside.

"You neither?" Evelyn asked

"Me neither, what?"

"Couldn't sleep?"

"No, I jus' woke up and saw the light on the porch."

"Hope I didn't disturb you."

"Nah."

They both sat there in the silence of the dead of night for a moment.

"Your daddy did wrong in not telling me about you. And he did wrong in not telling you about me. I'm sure this has all been a bit much for you, God bless your heart."

Stella sat momentarily silent as she formed her response. "He's my daddy. I've thought about him everyday of my life, and now he's here. And he has you." She smiled. "That's good. And you're gonna have a baby! It's all so exciting."

"So, you aren't angry at him at all? Your daddy, I mean."

Stella's eyes trailed away from her gaze. "It was easy to forgive him. Aside from leaving me here, he ain't never hurt me. It's mighty easy to forgive someone that ain't ever hurt ya."

Evelyn smiled. "We best both be getting back to bed 'fore we're caught!"

Stella smiled a warm smile - a smile that felt like no other.

With the dawn came the thick fog. The same fog that had always brought with it misery now seemed majestic. Sunlight glowed through the fog, casting tiny rays of hope into Stella's heart. She rose quickly and began her chores, with no prompting from Mommie. In fact, she had neither seen nor heard from Mommie since the argument she had with Charles the previous morning. When she returned with the water, Charles and Evelyn were in the parlor.

"Ya sure are an early riser," Charles said lovingly. He had already gathered wood while she was at the creek.

"Guess I just fell asleep too early."

"Well, you poor thing. You were just so tuckered out that you feel asleep right out there on the porch. Charles, I mean, your daddy had to carry you in." Evelyn's tender voice sounded like soft raindrops on the leaves. Stella smiled that the thought of her daddy carrying her in had really happened.

"'T'was a lot to soak in, yesterday, huh, chil'?"

"I reckon she's about half starved to death. Fell asleep 'fore we could get any supper into her."

Stella noticed that Evelyn was cooking; she was cooking with Mommie's cookware in Mommie's domain.

"Where's Mommie?" Stella asked timidly.

"Don't quite know. She may still be sleeping. I didn't check, but thought I best start us some breakfast." Evelyn continued her work as if all was right with the world. She was infectious; when she felt joy, the people around her felt joy.

Poppie came from the back rooms, flipping a suspender up and wiping his eye. "Mommie din' come ta bed last night."

"Oh, my!" Evelyn exclaimed, dropping the spatula. "Suppose she's alright?"

The burst of cold air from the front door answered their question.

"Where ya been, Mommie?" Charles asked; concern was in his voice for the first time with Mommie.

"I's fine. Din' want ta be in this house no more with the likes of yuns." She sounded cold and bitter - scorned.

"Oh, come now, Mommie." Poppie placed his arm around her and walked her to the stove. "Nothin's bad as you seem it to be."

Mommie did not fight Poppie. She didn't glare at Evelyn cooking. She didn't send a spiteful message to Charles. She didn't hold the wrath for the child that she had been left to raise. She seemed a woman defeated.

They ate breakfast in silence again, but with an understanding. Charles was back, and he had gained control. His wife would have her child at the farm. Mommie would not be present during the birth.

Stella felt something that seemed like relief, although she had only felt this feeling for brief periods of time while in the presence of Bessie or Foster.

The day went on as it usually would: cooking, canning, cleaning.

Mommie was right in her words that the work never stopped, but, no one felt begrudged. Everyone did what needed to be done without question. The work was easier with Charles and Evelyn there. There wasn't as much to do as the chores had been spread out.

Stella found herself having more time to play and imagine. She would sometimes play games on the porch with Evelyn in the dusk of evening, both ignoring Mommie's scowls. Some days Mommie would stay in her room for hours on end. Stella wondered what kept her so occupied.

Evelyn grew ever so slightly around her tummy. One cold day, she asked Charles to take her to town for some things she needed. When they returned, Stella was sent on a mission to Foster and Bessie's. She was told to tell them that they were invited for dinner. Bessie fiddled with this and that, taking her time in preparing herself. Finally, they all climbed into Foster's old truck and headed up the mountain. When they returned, the house looked dark. Mommie was out near the barn, but other than that, the house was silent.

"Wonder what's goin' on?" Foster said as he turned off the engine. "Best we go and see."

Stella was confused as to why the lanterns weren't lit. Had they left? Did she misunderstand?

Foster swung open the door with Stella facing inward. A kerosene lamp slowly lit, while Poppie, Charles, and Evelyn all yelled, "SURPRISE!!!"

Stella looked at Foster, then at Bessie. She didn't understand what was happening.

Evelyn picked up a small round cake that was frosted with chocolate. Neat, tiny letters spelled out "Happy Birthday". Stella stood stunned; no one had ever celebrated her birthday before. She had always figured that Mommie had forbidden it. She herself didn't even know the exact date. She did know that her father would have known for sure.

Tears welled up in her eyes as they all sang a chorus of "Happy Birthday" to her. Bessie stood beside her and held her shoulders.

"Well, now, there's nothing to cry about, honey. We just wanted to surprise you is all." Evelyn's soft voice broke through the chorus.

"We ain't neva had a birthday for her before," Bessie whispered to Evelyn over Stella's small head.

Anger flashed through Charles's eyes. "No wonder she din't want ta be in here!" He headed for the door, headed for Mommie, but Evelyn's gentle touch stopped him in his tracks.

"Now is not the time." Charles softened with Evelyn's words.

Stella celebrated an evening dedicated to her. They ate their supper and had the fine cake for desert; the focus was all on Stella. After Bessie and Evelyn had cleared the table, Evelyn returned with a large package wrapped in brown paper and tied with a string.

"What's that?" Stella asked, barely above a whisper.

"Well, it wouldn't be a birthday without a present, now would it?" Evelyn and Bessie both beamed.

Stella took the package and delicately untied the string that held it together. She carefully un-wrapped the brown paper and lifted the box. Inside was a dress - a beautiful store bought dress. It had a tag on it from the department store downtown that she had never been allowed to go in. She touched the material, smoothing her hand over it.

Stella's teary eyes looked at Bessie with concern. "But, last time...."

"Was the last time," Charles bellowed. Taking a moment to lower his tone he added, "Bessie tole' me what happened, and it won't never happen again."

Tears filled Stella's eyes again as she lifted the dress from the box and held it to her small frame. Since it was winter and cold, the material was thick, but soft; it was like none she had ever felt before. The sleeves were long enough to reach her hands, with tiny lace surrounding each wrist.

"It's beautiful! It's just beautiful!"

She looked at the faces surrounding her. They were all filled with joy - the same full, uninhibited joy that she felt for the first time in her life.

CHAPTER TEN

The following Sunday, Stella arose to the smell of Evelyn cooking fried bacon. She had a brief flash of Beatrice, but she had to quickly put that out of her mind. She had been told many times and had learned very early that you eat what God has given to you.

"Can I help you wit' anythin'?" Stella asked groggily. She hadn't slept well the night before due to the bitter cold. Even being next to the coal stove was of little comfort as the winds raged through the clapboard house.

"I'll have this done soon, honey. You just go and get ready."

Stella thought for a moment before asking, "Ready for what?"

"Well, it is Sunday, 'chil'! The Lord's Day. We'll be going to Sunday services just after we have some breakfast in our bellies."

"We don't usually go to church on such cold and bitter days. It's too far a walk, and Mommie refuses to ride in Foster's truck."

"Well, we have our own truck. She's welcome to come if she likes. Either way, you, your daddy, and me, we're going to church."

Stella beamed.

"And don't forget to wear your pretty new dress," Evelyn added, not looking up from her cooking.

Charles emerged from the back room, half dressed for church himself.

"Good morning, my beautiful girls!"

Stella's eyes sparkled. Evelyn just smiled, keeping her eyes on the bacon frying.

It was all so sudden that everything seemed to fall into place.

Stella asked to change in their room, where her dress had been guarded as if by a watchdog most of the night. She washed her face and hands in the basin well before touching the beautiful fabric.

She slipped the dress over her shoulders and let it fall to the ground. Looking at herself in the looking glass, she saw someone she had not noticed before. She was looking at someone with a smile and a full heart.

Mommie slung open the adjoining room door and looked at Stella in her new dress.

"At least that 'un covers ya up. Better than that thing Bessie made for ya," Mommie slammed the door behind her and left Stella reeling.

Had that been a compliment? Surely not. Her mind wandered, pondering this question as she buttoned the back of her dress with some struggle. She slipped on her ragged boots and was thankful that the dress almost touched the floor so that the boots would at least be slightly covered. She ran a comb through her long, curly, dark locks and entered the parlor.

"Now, there's a beauty, if I ever saw one!" Charles exclaimed.

Mommie didn't scowl. Her face seemed emotionless as she helped with breakfast. Evelyn beamed at Stella.

"I don't think you could look any prettier if you tried!"

They sat for breakfast, which Poppie did not join. After breakfast Mommie stated that they should head on out. She was going to stay and clean up and look after Poppie. It seemed he had caught a cold.

"We'd love ta have ya with us, Mommie," Charles admitted.

"Would ya, now?" Mommie's tone was harsh, bitter, and dripping with sarcasm.

Mommie began clearing the small table. Evelyn asked if she could help her, but Mommie, in her stubborn way, said she'd be just fine.

Evelyn went to the back room for what seemed no longer than 10 minutes. When she entered the parlor, Stella was revered at her appearance again. She was certainly the most beautiful woman that Stella had ever seen.

"Ready?" She seemed to gleam with her bible clutched in her delicate lace-glove-covered hands.

"All set!" Charles walked out to the vehicle to start it up and help Evelyn and Stella into the truck. It wasn't warm, not by any means, but it offered protection from the cold outside. By the time the Church of God was in sight, the heater began to work.

They stepped from the truck, one by one. Stella was grateful to see Foster and Bessie walking through the icy, dirt park lot.

Bessie, in her perky way, said, "Oh, how much fun! I thought we'd all go in together! We've been watching for ya ta come!"

The family walked to the stone steps surrounded by the white columns that lead to the white double doors to the church. They were greeted by Preacher Rayfield at the door.

"Charles? Is that really you? Oh my, how good it is to see you!" He grabbed Charles's hand and shook it heartily. After his excitement had worn down a bit, introductions were made between the preacher and Evelyn. They kept conversation for a short amount of time about her home in North Carolina. Preacher Rayfield had no words, but a broad smile on his face, as he greeted Stella. She had no trouble returning the smile as her own had been there all morning long.

As soon as they entered the church, leaving Preacher Rayfield to his Sunday morning greetings, evil, malicious whispers could be heard throughout the church.

"Is that Charles Resenger?"

"Who's he wit' now? Who you think that woman is?"

"That Stella with 'em? He thinkin' he just gonna come back after all these years and ever'thin' be alright?"

"How can he come back here like this? After doin' what he did to his mama . . . ."

"And what about that chil'! Growin' up the way she has, and him not nary a word."

The whispers continued, but both Charles and Evelyn held their head's high as they all walked to the front pew. The music began, and the whispering subsided. Stella did her best to pay attention to the sermon and block out the ugly things she had heard walking in. Stella concentrated on Evelyn's voice. Just as she spoke, she sang; she was an angel sent from God.

After services, the bitter women, whilst walking out, became abruptly friendly and phony, asking this and that. Charles gave them only the information they needed and nothing more.

The three piled into the dusty, beat up truck, and Evelyn asked Charles something Stella could not hear. Instead of taking the short, dirt road back to the farm, Charles went straight about a mile, and they came to the county school. He stopped just outside the play area.

Stella looked at Evelyn, then at Charles, confused.

"We'll be enrolling you here tomorrow. It's high time you were in school," Evelyn stated. And with that, they drove back to the farm.

Stella was speechless. So many thoughts raced through her tiny mind that she didn't know what to think, much less say. She spent the day in a daze, not noticing Mommie, the house, the farm, anything. She was going to school, and that was what had consumed her ever curious mind.

She did her chores mindlessly, lost in herself and what seemed to be her new life. At dusk, Evelyn asked Stella to come into the back room. She opened a black, metal chest with a silver lock that had been brought along with them. She pulled out a few small dresses. These dresses had been what Evelyn had been doing in the back room. She had been making these dresses for Stella.

"Can't go to school in the same dress everyday, now can you?"

"But, Evelyn, I can't take these. You worked so hard, and they're beautiful!"

"That's why you'll take them! I made 'em especially for you."

"Are you sure? I mean, you really want me to wear these?"

"I want you to have what you deserve."

That was her response. Nothing more.

After supper was eaten and cleaned up, Stella got herself ready for bed. Mommie had not spoken to her since that Sunday morning, so she had no idea what Mommie thought about Stella going to school. School was forbidden for Stella by Mommie. She had said awful things as to why - things Stella didn't want to remember.

The following morning, Stella rose early, helped with her chores, and dressed in one of the dresses that Evelyn had given her. Mommie scowled when she saw her. The sleeves only covered the elbow and the hem was not as long as Stella, or Mommie, was used to. Although it was obvious Mommie didn't approve, she again remained silent.

Charles appeared and said, "Are ya all ready for school?" His happiness was apparent.

"She certainly looks like it, but, hmmm, I think she's a missing something." Evelyn pulled out a set of writing books and pencils tied together in string to carry. She also produced a sack lunch.

Again, Stella beamed. She had only dreamed of this moment.

Before she knew it, they were at the school; she was enrolled and was sitting in a large classroom full of students of all different ages. The teacher introduced her. She quietly said her name and took her seat. Most of the students were kind, and Mrs. Hill was lovely. Stella enjoyed her day so much that she couldn't wait to return. The end of the day saddened her. She walked home that day, as she would everyday, with pride.

The weeks grew into months as the warm air began to graze cheeks and lips. Evelyn's tummy grew more and more each day. The more she grew, the less she did, but she was still extremely active. Stella would often watch Evelyn while she would rest, sitting in the back yard, studying the tobacco plants from planting to harvest. She seemed to soak in every detail. She worked in the vegetable garden on cooler days until she could no longer lean or squat. She kept herself busy, learning each and every detail of the farm.

Stella was learning every detail taught to her in school. Evelyn and Stella had started a habit of reading or playing a game on the porch as the sun lowered his beams behind the misty mountaintops.

Evelyn was extremely strong. She was often told to rest by one person or another, excluding Mommie, who had stopped communications altogether with much of anyone. Evelyn did not heed the words. She worked as hard as she could each day. It had become her way to take over Mommie's cooking; it had become her way to be the lady of the farm. It was a strange transition. Mommie, some days, merely watched the tragedy that trudged just ahead of her. She waited, worried, knowing, but not knowing, what was to come.

Evelyn and Charles took Stella to church each week, and she was at school each day. The return of her father had broken her free from her prison. She was also allowed to play more often, lightening her load of chores. Her imagination took her to places new and undiscovered. She allowed herself to dream, to love, to care, to read, and to pray.

Late one night, on a dark and humid evening, it began.

Charles caused a ruckus that could have woken the neighbors on the next farm. He was screaming at Mommie to get out with a grievous tone. Stella rose quickly and dressed. Charles opened the door to the back rooms, looked straight at Stella with the eyes of a wild man, and told her to run get Bessie. Before she could get out the door, Mommie had left, silently and sullenly. Stella saw her walking up the northern side of the mountain and not downward toward Bessie's.

Stella ran as fast as she could. She banged on the door and yelled, "IT'S TIME!"

It was a familiar situation that sent shivers down Bessie's spine. In no time at all they were loaded in the International and headed up the mountain. Not one of them muttered a word.

The screams from the house were all too close and familiar to Bessie, Foster, and Charles's hearts. Although men were not allowed in the room during childbirth, Charles refused to leave. Again, Poppie and Foster, as well as Stella, were asked for particular items from time to time while they paced the parlor.

In less than two hours, there was the shrill cry of a baby.

Stella looked at Foster and Poppie with wide, excited, but frightened eyes. Their return gazes were only looks of fear and concern.

A few moments later, Bessie opened the door, wiping her bloodied hands on a rag.

"They's both fine. It's a boy," she said with gushing relief and a smile.

Foster jumped up and let out a howl. Bessie scolded him, and the baby boy began to cry again. This cry was more like a scream.

Poppie smiled a smile that was rare for Poppie and said, "He got some lungs on him, that's for sure! May jus' have ourselves a wild one, here."

Everyone chuckled.

Bessie forced Foster, Stella, and Poppie to wash their hands thoroughly before entering the back room. Stella smiled to herself. This child, her brother, had been born in the same room where she had been born. Her mother had died there as well, of course, but this was no occasion for sadness and remembrances such as these. This was a cause for celebration and joy, and praises to God for this new life He had given them.

Foster, Poppie, and Bessie entered the room as quietly as possible, while Stella tiptoed behind them, peering through their legs to see what she could.

The child had stopped screaming. Evelyn sat up in the bed, holding the baby boy wrapped in clean linens. As the crowd grew closer, the small child stared at each one with extreme intensity. It was intensity so strong that each person looking into his eyes was immediately filled with the same sense.

"He's a strong one, he is, don'cha think, Poppie?"

"He do look awful strong, son." Poppie slapped his hand on Charles's back. "Congratulations, son."

"Thank ya, Poppie."

"He's a fine, handsome man!" Bessie exclaimed, rushing to Evelyn's side.

Charles stood at her side as well and took the baby from her arms, handing him to Bessie.

"Ya done good, Ev. Ya done real good. I'm awful proud of ya." A smile had spread across Charles's face. Stella imagined what this scene must have looked like the day she was born, filled with horror and pain.

Evelyn smiled her beautiful smile, but weakness had faded it some as she also stared at their new creation. "We'll call him John Henry," she said quietly just before drifting off to sleep.

The next few weeks were spent caring for a head-strong demanding baby. Evelyn was exhausted and Bessie came by to help as much as she could. Stella, on the other hand, barely left his side. She was at Evelyn and John Henry's beck and call. Evelyn became stronger very quickly. She would tell Stella to go play or study her lessons, but Stella would remain at their side.

Stella had not heard a word from Mommie since the cold night of her very first birthday party. Mommie had kept her distance, so much so that Stella's small, fragile mind began to think of her as some kind of figment of her imagination. Mommie had just been a bad dream.

But, Mommie lurked. Just a little ways off in the distance; she was there, listening - waiting.

One dark, stormy spring evening, just a few months after John Henry was born, a storm like no other in Stella's memory began. The rage of the storm without was incomparable to the darkness and gloom that ignited inside of Stella that night.

She awoke, not from the thunder storm outside, but from the storm that erupted in the back bedrooms.

"We ARE taking him to North Carolina, and she WILL continue school. And, now, that's just all there is to it!" Evelyn's voice was sharp and angered. Stella had never heard her this way.

"So's yuns just come here and thinkin' ya done saved the day, and now ya're gonna roll on back out." Mommie's voice was forced and harsh.

"It isn't like that, and you know it."

"I don't know no such thing! Don't ya be telling me what I know and what I don't know!"

Charles's voice boomed at her. "She means what she says, Mommie! You hold your tongue!"

Stella lay there silently in the night, concentrating on the conversation, but confused as to what was happening. Sleep had evaded her most of the night, so she rose with the crow of the first rooster, diligently starting her chores. It was Saturday, which meant more work. It seemed hours before anyone else rose. As she threw chicken feed, she heard the door open and close, but did not turn around. She noticed Charles loading a suitcase and a smaller bag into the trailer of the truck. The raindrops, now just large blobs here and there, touched Stella's face. Continuing her work, Charles came and stood beside her.

"We gotta head back to North Carolina now. Ev's family needs to meet the baby."

"I'm guessin' I ain't goin' with ya." Stella's tone was flat and pain stricken.

"Ya still got ya a month or so of school left. We din' wanna take ya out so soon. We'll be back to get ya as soon as we can."

Tears fell down Stella's cheeks as she nodded. Just like everything else in her life, this was something she could not fix; she had no control over it.

She held her head high as she caught a glimpse of Mommie, who smirked in her enjoyment of her granddaughter's pain.

"Now maybe ya mightin' know how I feel," Mommie hissed as she came close and stood in front of Stella.

Stella only moved to the side and kept working. She completed her tasks mindlessly, not caring if they were done well or correctly. Stella spied the back house out of the corner of her eye and shivered.

Evelyn came out of the clapboard house, looking more beautiful than ever and holding her newborn son. She beckoned for Stella to come over.

"Here ya go. It's all yours now." She handed Stella a large, silver key on a dangling chain. "Take good care of it!" She leaned and kissed Stella on the cheek. "We'll be back for you real soon, honey, I promise!"

Stella fingered the key to the large, black trunk that had been left in the back room.

"I don't want ya ta go." Stella's voice was barely a whisper.

"I know you don't, honey. But, like I said, we'll be back soon."

Charles motioned for Evelyn, and he placed her and the baby into the truck. Stella hugged them both gently, unable to control the stream of tears running down her face.

Charles squeezed Stella tightly and said, "We will be back for ya. I'm neva gonna forget ya again."

Stella's tears turned to sobs as the vehicle pulled out of the grassy patch near the barn. The truck headed north, up the mountain. Stella was overcome with emotion and ran after the truck.

"Please don't leave me! Please! Please don't go!" She ran, screaming and crying, until her knees hit the dirt road in the cloud of dust spun up by the truck. She screamed to the heavens and pounded her tiny fists on the soft, moist, dirt road. "NO, NO, NO!"

She felt gentle hands on her shoulders, turning to see Poppie.

"Le's get inside, chil'." As little as Poppie had said, with a touch of his hand she knew that he was now her only ally in this house of pain.

They walked through the door and saw Mommie holding a rolling pin. Neither was sure of what she aimed to do with it, so they both kept a distance.

"So ya thought they was comin' ta save ya or somethin', din' ya?

"They'll be back fer me," Stella stated flatly, without confidence.

Mommie chuckled. "Maybe in another six years or so. Ya ain't neva been nothin' but a burden to ever'one. They don't want ya. Nobody does."

Tears again welled in Stella's eyes. Tears she refused to release. Hope remained in her heart, but she knew that only time would tell.

CHAPTER ELEVEN

$\mathcal{T}$he days passed slowly and painfully for Stella. The joy of going to school to learn was now missing, as Mommie forced her to wake very early in the morning to complete ridiculous tasks and chores before her day at school had even begun. After her return, Mommie would have more chores for Stella to complete. She was tired most of the time and was not the same girl that had entered school in the middle of the year. Mrs. Hill had noticed her sudden decline, but had not spoken. Mrs. Hill knew Stella's family through town talk and was just as frightened of Mommie and her will as many others. By the end of the school year, Stella's grades had dropped dramatically.

Stella waited for letters to come from Evelyn and Charles. Each day she would rush to check the tin mailbox. Not much mail made it to the Resenger farm, if ever, but Stella knew that Evelyn would not break her promise. A letter would surely come soon.

Months had passed since her father, brother, and Evelyn had left, but there was still no word. One hot summer afternoon, Stella stood at the front of the tobacco barn, which faced the dirt road.

"Miss Stella!" A voice from above could be heard through the rustling of the mountain leaves in the wind. She stepped further out of the open air barn to see the postman walking down the dirt road on his long trek. She watched him, not quite sure that she had heard him say her name.

"Miss Stella," he said again as he approached. Stella stood staring at him. Had a letter finally arrived from Charles and Evelyn?

As the postmaster drew closer, he said, "Ya've gotten so many letters from up there in Hickory, NC. I was just wonderin' why ya ain't wrote nothin' back? I can come by and pick up a letter ta send out fer ya. Ya ain't got to go inta town or anythin'."

Stella's mind was sent reeling. Letters? Many letters? So many letters?

"How long they been a comin'?" she asked him timidly.

"Gracious, girl. I don't know. Been a long time, that's fer sure." He paused and studied Stella's face. "Ya been gettin' 'em ain't ya?"

Stella didn't answer. She looked back to the field where she saw Mommie tending to the hill of green plants, bending to pull tobacco bugs as she spotted them. Leaving the postman, Stella turned toward the house and, feeling her actions were not her own, entered the small white structure. She stood in the parlor a moment, not noticing the heat that filled the room as well as her cheeks. She turned and walked through the door leading to the back rooms and stood by Mommie and Poppie's bed. Bending down, she lifted the bedspread to peek underneath. Nothing had been placed there. She stood and gathered in her surroundings. She slowly walked to the end of the bed and opened the armoire. She pushed clothing aside and revealed a small wooden box with a lock. Carefully removing the box as not to disturb anything, she sat at the foot of the bed and placed the box on her lap. Examining the lock, she discovered that it had not been latched the entire way; the box had been put away hastily. She pulled the lock gently, and it released easily. Slowly, carefully, she opened the lid. Her eyes grew wide at the sight of a stack of letters, all opened and read.

There was a darkness that settled all around her as she gently pulled the letters from their hiding spot. More than a dozen letters resided in the tiny box, all of them addressed to Stella at the Resenger farm with a return address from Hickory, NC. The letters had been placed from newest to old. Each time a new letter came it was placed on the top of the stack. Stella flipped to the letter on the bottom of the stack. It had been sent only two weeks after they had left.

The bright flash of lightening that lit the room and the loud crash of thunder that followed did not faze Stella. Rain pounded the tin roof, a deafening sound in the sudden strong summer storm. Unaware of her surroundings, she carefully pulled the letter from the envelope and began to read.

Clean, beautifully written cursive letters filled the page.

> *Dear Stella,*
>
> *I hope this letter finds you well. We made it back to Hickory, which was a very long ride due to your tiny brother being so demanding! It was wonderful to meet you and get to know you.*
>
> *You were a big help during our time there and I don't know how I would have managed without you. I am so proud to have a stepdaughter like you. You are a very special girl, Stella, and we both love you very much.*
>
> *All my love, Evelyn*

Stella folded the letter and placed it back into the envelope. She put the envelope back into place and examined the envelope of the next. Another bright crack of lightening filled the room, this time revealing a shadow on the wall in front of her. She turned her head toward the door to see Mommie's eyes blazing with fury. Stella placed the box beside her on the bed and stood to meet Mommie's gaze.

Mommie swooped in like an eagle and in seconds had Stella's hair in her rough hand, pulling her into the parlor. Stella winced at the pain, but she refused to cry out.

"HOW DARE YOU!" Mommie bellowed.

Stella sat where Mommie had dropped her. She stared at Mommie with eyes deep and dark, stained with anger and betrayal. Mommie huffed and puffed as if a fire breathing dragon were about to char Stella.

"How dare me?" Stella spoke without wavering - not with bewilderment, but with crazed questioning. "How dare ME?" Stella stood as tall as her small frame would allow and stood close to Mommie. Mommie's look of shock amused Stella and fueled her strength.

"How dare you keep them letters from me," she hissed through clenched teeth, the grammar she had been taught in school gone. "Ya wanted me ta think they din't want me. Ya wanted me ta think that they thought the same of me as you do. Well, they don't; and they won't ever!"

The storm cracked again and thunder shook the tiny house, sending a shudder into Mommie's spine.

"Ya ain't never meant nothin' ta me and ya neva' will! Ya're just mean and nasty and ain't nobody EVA gonna love ya!" Stella's cheeks were bright red and tears of anger stung her eyes. She seemed to grow taller and stronger with each word.

Mommie stood staring blindly at the girl turned woman before her eyes.

"Ya know it, don't ya?" Stella spoke quietly now with a quirky smile Mommie had never seen. "Ya know what I say is true, and ya hate it, don't ya?" Stella laughed out loud, a cackling cry of her own joy. "Ya done it to yerself!" Her voice grew stronger now. "All of it!"

Stella stormed past Mommie, pushing her body out of the way with great force, and walked into Mommie's bedroom where the box of letters still lay, envelopes now scattered across the floor. She gathered the letters and placed them all neatly inside the box, making sure not to clasp the lock. With her head held high, Stella walked back to the parlor where Mommie still stood, stunned by the set of events that had just occurred. She walked past Mommie and towards the door.

"Where ya think ya're goin'?" Mommie asked with the last bit of dignity that remained with her.

Stella never spoke as the screen door slammed, drowning out Mommie's words. She walked into the large, heavy raindrops aimlessly, holding the sturdy wooden box close to her chest. She walked through the rain, allowing the water to flood her mind, washing away the evil that had possessed her with Mommie. The rain started to let up, and Stella realized her surroundings, noticing that she was close to Foster and Bessie's house. She walked the last half mile or so and steadily climbed the steps of the rock porch. Without announcing her arrival, she sat on the porch, leaned against the house and began reading the precious letters that had been kept from her knowledge.

After what seemed hours, Bessie emerged from the house. The rain had subsided and birds were chirping in the glow of the new sunlight that glistened on the wet leaves.

"Whatcha doin' here, chil'?" Bessie was concerned when she saw her niece drenched to the bone and surrounded by envelopes.

Stella looked up at Bessie, noticing her for the first time. "She kept 'em from me," she said in a whisper. "She kept 'em all."

"What are ya talkin' about, girl?" Bessie walked to Stella and picked up an envelope, then another, and another. "Mommie? Mommie kept ya from seein' all these?" Bessie asked, but she knew the answer. Stella just looked at Bessie. She still held a letter.

Bessie slid her body to the floor of the porch beside Stella, taking the letter from her hand.

> *Dear Stella,*
> *We've been so worried about you since you haven't written back. We have been waiting for your reply. We have decided to come back to Newport to see you. John Henry and my sister, Mabel, will be coming with us. Please tell all of the family we are coming soon for a visit.*
> *All my love, Evelyn*

"Is this the last one?" Bessie asked. Stella nodded. Bessie looked at the date on the letter and said, "Well, this was just sent two weeks ago. They could be here anytime! We have to go tell Mommie and Poppie."

"I can't." Stella stopped Bessie.

"Whatcha mean, ya can't?"

Stella looked at the rock floor and told Bessie each word that she had said to Mommie after finding the letters. When she looked up at Bessie, Bessie's color seemed to have faded, and now she sat silently staring.

"Aunt Bessie?"

Bessie looked at Stella, her face changed expression, and she threw her head back and laughed like Stella had never heard her laugh before. It was infectious, because soon after, Stella began to laugh as well. Both of them laughed until their sides hurt and tears ran down their cheeks.

When they had caught their breath, Bessie said, "Well, I guess that threw her for a loop!"

Stella smiled and replied, "Yep."

Bessie convinced Stella to return to the farm, but they found the house quiet - eerily quiet. Bessie opened the door and stepped into the parlor. Stella followed, walked past Bessie, and stepped quietly into the back rooms, where she saw full well what silences surrounded them.

Mommie sat on her bed, yards of burlap material surrounding her. The silver metal lock on the large black chest that Evelyn had given to Stella had been pried open, damaged beyond repair. The beautiful dresses that Evelyn had made for Stella had burlap pieces sloppily sewn onto the arms and hemlines, making them much longer than intended, as well as extremely ugly.

"MOMMIE, NO!" Stella's shrill scream spilled out as she rummaged through the black chest. There wasn't a dress untouched. She picked one up and examined it, realizing that the way they were sewn in would prevent the patch work from being removed without ripping the dress material.

Bessie entered the room and stood in amazement. She saw the shattered child sitting on the floor, ruined dresses scattered across her lap and the chest. Mommie sat sewing, absorbed in her work, with a slight smile across her wrinkled face.

"What have ya done?" Bessie's question was directed at Mommie, and her voice was more malicious than Stella had heard in the past.

"I made 'em presentable. She ain't goin' out in that trash no more."

Mommie dropped the last dress and left the room. Stella sat holding her once beautiful dresses, crying silently. Bessie put her arm around Stella for a moment, but she had no words.

Stella examined each dress. Tears were rolling down her cheeks.

The next morning was a Sunday. Mommie had Stella up before the rooster's crow. Normally, Mommie would not allow any work that was not a necessity to be done on the Lord's Day, but this morning Mommie worked Stella like a mule. She was then forced to clean herself up, don one of her newly altered dresses, and walk with Mommie to church. Many of the women and men looked at Stella with surprise and wondering; others knew that this was surely some evil that Mommie had created as punishment for Stella. Children, on the other hand, were not so kind, and Stella was laughed at and made fun of by the majority of them.

That evening, Stella sat quietly in her room thinking of writing a letter back to Evelyn and her father, but decided that she would wait for their arrival. Her hopes began to fade when after three days they still had not arrived. One evening, soon after, she heard an automobile coming down the mountainside. She had been drawing water from the creek, and the buckets splashed and spilled over as she ran up the hillside towards the road. Mommie stood in the yard scowling at her, but she said nothing. Stella didn't notice anything except for the car pulling in next to the barn and its passengers.

Stella was amazed at how much John Henry had grown. He was wobbling around on his own and had a sweet tuft of black hair on his head. Charles and Evelyn hugged and kissed Stella and introduced her to Mabel, whom Stella took to instantly. Mabel was Evelyn's sister and was very beautiful, just as Evelyn. She had a larger build than Evelyn, but they had similar striking features. Although Mabel didn't have the same dramatic streak of white hair that Evelyn had, touches of her hair had turned white at a very young age. Each of them spoke at the same time, gushing about this and that. JH, as Charles called him, a nickname which seemed to suit him, ran all around the yard.

"Mommie?" Charles called. "You just gonna stand over there in the yard and not say hello?" As he walked towards her, Evelyn approached Stella, eyeing the condition of the dress she wore.

"Well, honey, it don't make no nevermind. They were getting too small for you anyway. You're growing so big!" Evelyn's look of disapproval washed over Mommie, although she ignored the flood.

There was nothing more said about the dresses. Stella had not even noticed that the dresses were becoming too small for her. The next day, Evelyn, Mabel, and Stella drove to town for material to make new dresses. Evelyn did her best to make Stella's situation seem lighter, but she knew the darkness that dwelled within her.

Their stay was short. Mommie made herself invisible most of the time, but Poppie enjoyed the lively company and sat on the porch in the brisk evenings to talk with his son and watch his grandson play. Evelyn and Mabel worked feverishly to complete a new set of dresses for Stella that were suitable for the upcoming winter months and that would be more appropriate for Mommie's tastes. Stella had told Evelyn and Charles of Mommie's plot to keep the letters they had sent from her. While no discussions were made in front of Stella, she did hear muffled whispers now and then between Evelyn and Mommie.

Almost as soon as they had come, they were gone.

CHAPTER TWELVE

$\mathcal{S}$tella remained a child broken, and days continued this way. Mommie was crueler now than ever. Stella wrote letters to Evelyn as often as she could and made sure the postman gave her letters directly to her. The summer months came and went, and Mommie worked Stella relentlessly. She tried to read when she could, but Mommie kept her so busy that activities such as these and play were unattainable.

When school began again, Stella was only allowed to go on certain days - the days Mommie would allow. She worked hard at her studies, but she was only afforded the time allotted at school to keep up.

Birthdays and Christmases came and went without celebration. The only joy gained from these occasions came in the care packages sent by Evelyn and Charles. Mommie had even stopped allowing Foster and Bessie to buy Stella gifts. Stella hid the packages she received from Evelyn and her father, even though Mommie had all but stopped trying to destroy the items that came from them.

Letters arrived around twice a month, all of them written and signed by Evelyn. The letters back and forth were all that kept Stella going some days. Poppie, on his bad days, could scarcely be found, and Mommie was always there, always watching, waiting for a mistake to allow her to pounce on Stella and lock her away or worse. Stella knew not to anger Mommie. She knew the fury that lay just underneath the surface.

Visits from Charles and Evelyn were very few and far between. Each time they would come, they would stay for a short amount of time, and then they were off again to their beloved home and family in North Carolina, leaving Stella once again in her own silent hell.

She grew this way. She became a woman this way. She became strong this way.

"Miss Stella!" The postman called to her as he always did. Mommie was standing close by, gathering tools to head for the fields. "I have 'nother letter fer ya," he paused. "Also gots one fer ya, Mrs. Resenger."

Mommie walked closer, seizing the letter he held for her. Stella spied that it was from the same address and in the same script as her own letter.

"Thank you, Raymond." Stella smiled politely.

"Ya've just grown up to be such a fine young lady, ya have," said the postman as he smiled and continued his stroll down the mountain.

Mommie grunted as she read the letter she had already ripped open.

"Looks like they's a comin' fer ya. 'Bout time." Her words fell flat as she walked away.

Stella carefully pulled back the envelope and retrieved the letter.

> *Dear Stella,*
>   *I am writing to tell you that your father is coming to Newport to bring you here for a visit. It is high time that my family gets to meet you. JH misses you so much, as do Charles, Mabel, and I. He'll be there for you as soon as your studies are over for the year. I have written to Mommie as well to let her know.*
>   *All my love, Mama*

Mama. Even though Evelyn had insisted that Stella call her this many years ago, the word always stayed on her tongue and in her mind. Evelyn *was* a mother to her - a mother she so desperately needed.

Stella held the letter to her chest and glanced at Mommie, who had already started working the fields. She was sure that Mommie would have been happy to be rid of her forever, but the letter said only for a visit. Oh, how she wished she could stay.

The next few weeks passed slowly for Stella. She continued her studies as best she could, kept up with her chores, and tried to stay out of Mommie's way. Poppie had been excited for Stella and her upcoming visit, but he seemed somewhat saddened that she wouldn't be at the farm to keep him company. Closer to the end of school, Mommie became more and more distant, and Stella began packing. She had no idea how long she would be staying, so she packed all that she had. She also didn't want to run the risk of Mommie damaging her items while she was away. Knowing that all of her belongings would fit into one trunk was unsettling to Stella, but her mind was focused on greater things.

One fine spring day, as Stella worked in the vegetable garden, she heard the sound she had been waiting for. Looking up, she saw the dirt cloud that rose behind her father's vehicle as it made the slow descent. Soon, he was pulled beside the barn, and a dirt covered Stella was running towards his embrace.

There were very few pleasantries as Mommie and Poppie said their goodbyes. Charles informed them that Stella would be staying for the entire summer. Stella's heart leapt. Charles half expected Mommie to protest, having to be left without Stella's help, but no protest came. Charles and Stella felt most sorry for Poppie. He hugged his granddaughter tight and wished her well. He wiped a tear from his eye before anyone was able to catch a glimpse of it.

Soon, they were in Charles's new Dodge sedan and were headed upward. She was excited about seeing her family in North Carolina, but more so for the journey over countryside she had never before seen. For hours they traveled in silence, through switchback turns, through the mountains, and along the French Broad River. If Charles was driving too quickly, Stella would hold in a gasp as she thought the new sedan would plummet from the high cliffs.

Charles's fatigue began to show, and soon they were stopping in Hot Springs, North Carolina. Charles pulled into a gravel lot where a hotel stood. Stella's eyes grew wide in amazement. Charles began to tell Stella of a grand hotel that had stood here not 20 years ago and had burned, but Stella could not imagine anything grander than what lay before her. Acres of flowers and trees surrounded the large building, and a few people bustled all around. Charles walked with Stella into the front foyer of the hotel and asked for a room. He was given a key, and they followed a young man that took their luggage. Stella had never witnessed anything like this other than in books, and she soon became aware that the things that she read weren't always just made up in someone else's imagination. These things actually existed outside of her simple existence on a mountain farm.

Upon entering the room, Stella let out a gasp. Crisp linens covered two beds donning plush, flowered bedcovers. Windows covered in lace overlooked the grounds, covered in short grass and neatly trimmed hedges. A door in the room led to a balcony where Stella stood astounded. She realized that she had lived her life from the side of a mountain, but this view was from the top. Mountain peaks lay below them as far as she could see. Wispy clouds circled the tops of these mountains, giving her a new perspective of the beauty that had always been around her, but out of her reach.

After washing up, Charles and Stella left their lovely room and entered a new part of the hotel. There were many tables in the large room, all covered with fine white linens. Upon each table sat a lit candle, although they were not needed due to the light from the many windows. Stella stood behind Charles, very unsure of herself and what she should do. A man in a white coat with a black bowtie came and spoke with Charles momentarily before ushering them to a nearby table. Charles had to tell Stella to sit when the waiter pulled out a chair for her. She did, and the waiter picked up a fine linen from the table, folded into an odd shape, and shook the material. The fold fell loose, and he placed what was her napkin into her lap, startling Stella. Charles chuckled.

"I guess I forget I was just like you once. It's a li'l unsettling at first. I had never been to a place like this either until I met Evelyn. I mean, now don't get me wrong her family ain't highfalutin or nothin', but she sure did know a lot more about all this here stuff than me." Charles continued to talk about his early encounters after leaving Newport, but Stella was awestruck at the sights and sounds. A couple sat at a corner table, sampling treasures off of one another's plates. Many men wandered about, attending to this and that, all dressed identical to the man that had seated them. One walked from table to table, pushing a cart of some of the most delectable looking foods she had ever seen. Charles explained that it was a dessert cart, and after they had eaten their supper, they would sample some and order a dessert of their own.

"Pullin' out all the stops fer ya on this here trip, I sure am. All fer you, my sweet Stella."

Stella blushed thinking that all of this was for her benefit. As she smiled and looked down, Charles couldn't help but think that she was so much like Ella. She had grown into a beautiful young woman, and she had every feature of her mother's.

A man came to the table to take their order, but Stella had no idea what to say, even after suggestions from the waiter. Charles finally ordered for her as well as for himself. They dined on fruit cocktail, buttered peas, and the finest rabbit Stella had ever tasted. Stella savored every bite as if it were her last. When they were finished, the man with the dessert cart came to their table, much to Stella's glee. She had eaten so much already that she didn't know if she could fit in another bite, but the smells of the peach cobblers and apple pies opened a tiny part of her small stomach to let more flavor in. She ached a pain that she had never felt - a feeling of being too full.

They returned to their room and settled in for the night. Stella looked through the small amount of things she had brought in with her and found a nightgown. She walked down the hall to a shared washroom. The sink basin was attached to the wall with a silver handle.

Stella's curiosity set in. She pulled the handle and squealed with delight when water came rushing forth. She also recognized what was a flushing toilet and felt compelled to use it.

Upon returning to the room, she noticed that the sun had set. Charles began to talk, out loud but more to himself, of days gone by, stories from his childhood, and of Ella. As much as Stella wanted to listen and learn, she could not remain awake. Sleep gushed over her with a wave as she lay with her head upon the finest pillow.

When morning came, Stella knew that Charles no longer felt the urge to talk of things past. She was saddened by her inability to listen, but she had gained an experience that would last her whole life. For that, she was grateful.

They gathered their things and returned to the sedan, leaving the fine hotel behind them. Stella was bit saddened that they were leaving, but looking forward to new things to come soon overpowered her sadness.

The continuing drive was slow and long. Due in part to the overwhelming trip and sights never before seen, Stella kept dozing off, but she tried desperately to stay awake in order to see more of the countryside she had never known. Conversation was short and brief between Stella and Charles. Although Stella tried to bring up the talk from the night before, Charles became sullen and quiet. He had been back in her life many years now, but he still carried much guilt. Talking about Stella's wretched life with Mommie only created more guilt for him to suffer. If words were spoken at all, it was of Evelyn's family and home.

Hours and hours they drove. The first part of their second day was spent climbing higher into the mountain ranges. They drove through farm after farm and small town after small town. The sun lowered, and Stella could no longer keep her eyes open. She fell into a deep sleep where dreams of better days and a better life lay ahead of her.

"Stella?" Charles's soft voice and gentle touch woke Stella. "Stella, honey, we're here."

Stella sat up in the seat where she had been curled up and wiped her eyes. They were nearing a small valley amidst beautiful small, rolling hills. A small lake could be seen in the background through heavy trees wearing an early morning haze. Stella's eyes widened as she soaked in her surroundings. Charles turned onto a dirt road that was surrounded by white fencing. What lay at the end of the drive caused Stella to gasp. The double story white house stood bold and sturdy. Large white columns towered through both stories. The upper level contained a covered terrace, and on the bottom level sat two white rocking chairs with fine, full ferns in each corner.

"What'd ya think?"

"It's beautiful!" Her astonishment was all too real.

Within seconds, Evelyn was outside with JH and Mabel. JH's excitement couldn't be contained.

Stella jumped from the car and ran to grab him and swing him around. "You just get bigger and bigger every time I see you!"

"I know," he said with excitement, "I'm gettin' HUGE!"

All of them laughed, and Stella hugged and kissed everyone. By that time, more people were coming out of the house. Grandma and Grandpa Lenfield and all of Evelyn's sisters came to the porch. Stella became surrounded. Evelyn could see that Stella was overwhelmed and brought her inside where everyone followed. Everyone found a seat in the large, beautiful parlor and began talking. JH stayed right at Stella's side while she was introduced to all of her step-aunts.

Mabeline was the oldest of the clan. Next was Judith, who everyone called Jude. Belle was just a bit older than Evelyn. Lyle would have been the next in age, but he had died tragically a few years prior during a tonsillectomy in his early 20s. Sadness filled all of their voices as they spoke of him. Mabel came next and then there was Marlene.

"I think it's funny that I'm your aunt, but you're older than me!" Marlene was filled with excitement, just as JH. Marlene was 13, three years younger than Stella.

"That is funny, isn't it?" Stella laughed at all of the attention and commotion. She was delighted with this new family she was so willingly accepted into.

The hound dogs outside howled, causing Stella to startle. A few seconds later, the door opened and closed with a bang. Around the corner walked a young man who was close to Stella's age. He was tall, handsome and beautiful in the way that Stella had decided all Lenfield's were. His painfully blue eyes met hers for a moment, and a flutter was felt in Stella's heart.

"Well, if it isn't our Henry!" Grandpa Lenfield beamed.

"Stella, this is my youngest brother, Henry. You and he are just about the same age." Evelyn smiled at the both of them.

Stella stood to shake his hand and said, "It's very good to meet you, Henry."

Henry looked amused and smiled a crooked smile. "So this is the Stella everyone's been talkin' about. Sure is good to finally meet you after all they been sayin' about ya." He winked his eye at her in a way where no one else could see, and it made her turn away and blush.

The commotion continued, and after a few moments, Grandma Lenfield spoke up and told Charles to get Stella's things to her room and help her get settled in. He knew Stella was in need of rest and freshening up. Charles and Henry climbed the stairs with Stella's trunk and entered a room that was bright and airy. The windows had been opened, and pretty pink curtains fluttered in the breeze. The bed was large and comfortable looking with a beautiful pink bedcover that had been woven and embroidered by hand. There were picture hangings of floral arrangements all around the room.

"Oh, Daddy! It's too much! Look at how pretty it all is!" Henry beamed at her gleeful reaction.

Charles gave her a strange smile with a dark look in his eyes before kissing her on the forehead. "I hope ya like it, Stella."

"I love it, Daddy. Thank you."

The strange darkness returned to his eyes before he closed the door after he and Henry had exited, leaving Stella alone in her room.

A light rapping on the bedroom door woke Stella. The door squeaked open as Stella rubbed her eyes. She hadn't remembered falling asleep. Dusk had replaced the streams of sunshine pouring in the window, and the beautiful breeze now brought with it a slight chill.

"Ya been up here a while. Ya that sleepy?"

It was Henry speaking to her. She could make out his figure in the hazy light.

"I guess I was. Must be the excitement and all," she stated.

Henry strolled into the room and sat at the foot of the plush bed, facing Stella. She sat silently, studying his lovely face and dark, tousled hair. They each stayed that way, examining each other eternally, if just for a moment.

"I din' wanna wake ya up, but it's fixin' ta get dark, and I was wanting ta show ya around a bit."

"Oh, that sounds fun. I'd like that. I'll take a few minutes to clean up and I'll be right down."

Henry smiled and smacked the bed. "Sounds great! See ya in a few!"

Stella rose, changed her clothes, and washed up in the basin that had been left by her bed. As she came down the staircase, she glanced at the luxurious bathroom; it was so different from Aunt Bessie's powder room.

"Never been in one?" Henry stood at the bottom of the stairs watching her.

Stella lowered her head, not wanting him to see her blush.

"I was in one at a hotel in Hot Springs on the trip. It was real nice."

"Ev tole' me ya was pretty poor on that farm. I mean, we ain't got much, but I guess I take for granted what we do have." His voice was soft and sincere, understanding. "I wish we had that 'lectricty. It be a while before we get that, though, I guess."

Henry escorted Stella inside the room and showed her how to turn on the water and flush the toilet properly. While she was grateful for his instruction, she felt awkward in the bathroom alone with him, even with the door open. When he was around her, her heart felt flutters she had never known. Even though it made her nervous and feel sick to her stomach, she enjoyed the strange feeling she felt when she was around him. Henry felt the same feelings, but he thought it best to keep them at bay. Her father was married to his sister. They could be nothing more than friends.

The evening was spent with the two of them walking around the lake and woods that surrounded the large house. Every so often, he would stop and point out an unusual tree or animal and tell a funny story about this or that. He wanted to know all about Newport and her life there. She said as little as she could to describe the way she lived. She did not want him to understand the monster she called Mommie. She spoke about school and Poppie, as well as Aunt Bessie and Uncle Foster. Henry rambled on about his family there, funny stories, and fun times past. He became melancholy when he spoke of Lyle and laughed when he said Marlene was a pain in his side. They were captivated by each other's company.

Soon the sun settled full into its house of darkness and Stella became quite frightened of her surroundings. Henry grabbed her by the hand and led her back to the house where lamps lit up the large front porch. His hand felt warm and right in her own. She couldn't remember a time when she had been happier.

The days passed all too quickly. Stella would take part in the chores with her step-aunts, and she learned to become very good at sewing and cooking, among other things. She washed clothes and hung them on the line, beat dust from rugs, and scrubbed floors, all the while enjoying the constant company and chattering of the many sisters. Mabel and Stella became even closer, and Marlene was never far behind. Whenever possible, Stella would spend time with Henry.

She enjoyed every minute of being in North Carolina, but the summer was soon to come to an end.

"What's wrong wit' ya?" Henry asked one night as they both rocked on the porch, listening to the katydids and crickets sing their songs.

"Just sad, I guess. I have to leave soon."

"Doncha miss your family?"

"I guess so."

"I know I'm sure gonna miss you."

These were the last words that were spoken between them before her departure. Henry had been called up to fill in at the cotton mill after one of the workers had been badly hurt. She would not see him again until she came back for another visit.

As her things were loaded into Charles's car for the long journey home, each person came to say their goodbyes. She looked around one last time for Henry, hugged everyone, and climbed into the car. She looked out the side window to see Marlene and JH running after the car and waving. It wasn't until then that Stella realized her face was streaming with tears. Tears for a home she wanted to be her own; tears for a fear of the life that lay over the mountains - unexplainable tears fell. They fell until the heavens opened up before them, and tiny drops began to splash the windshield. She knew them as God's tiny tears that again coincided with her own.

CHAPTER THIRTEEN

$\mathcal{T}$he journey back to the farm had been much less exciting than the trip to Hickory. Stella's mind replayed every incident that took place that summer. The long and strenuous drive between Stella and Charles was silenced, almost secretive.

Hours and hours passed before they were on the down slope of the mountain to the farm. They had not stopped at the hotel, and Charles looked tired and haggard. Stella had been in and out of sleep many times during the trip, but still felt the same exhaustion. Charles pulled into the space beside the farm house and stopped the engine. Stella went to open the door when he touched her arm, stopping her and causing her to face him.

"Don't ya go forgettin' who ya are, girl. Ya're my daughter. Remember that."

"I do, Daddy." Stella responded, even though the statement had confused her immensely.

"Ya better."

He stepped out of the sedan, unloaded her trunk, said hello and goodbye to Poppie, and was off again.

Stella was hurt and unsettled by her father's behavior and began to silently cry again as he drove away. She imagined the little girl she had been, beating her tiny fists into the dirt. Knowing she was much too old for fits such as this and not wanting Mommie to see her anguish, she dried her eyes before returning to the house to help with any chores needed.

Stella lived her existence by cooking, cleaning, harvesting, sewing, school when she could, and writing to her family in North Carolina. It had become her way to take over most of the duties in the house as Mommie spent more and more time in the fields. Poppie's condition continued to deteriorate due to sicknesses brought on by his drinking.

One day Bessie had visited the farm and was talking with Stella as they worked at feeding the chickens. Suddenly, without warning, ominous clouds filled the sky. A strange, eerie feeling surrounded the land. Stella looked up from her duties with the animals and saw a commotion in the fields. Bessie sat down her bucket and began to look in the same direction. Mommie was doing a sort of dance as Poppie ran to her full strength. They glanced at each other in wonder and stared at the odd sight. Soon, Mommie made a turn in her strange dance, and they could both see the snake dangling and swinging in her hand.

"Oh, God, Stella! Run get Foster! Quick!"

Stella threw down her bucket of feed and bolted down the mountainside. She reached her aunt and uncle's home in record time, but Foster was nowhere to be found. She stood in the yard, frantically trying to catch her breath and thinking of where he could be. She remembered that he had been at a new job site and ran to the location. She found him quickly as he was giving orders to the other workers. She breathlessly spat out the words, and soon Foster and Stella were in his beat up work truck headed to the farm.

Upon entering the house, Poppie's haggard look startled them. He sat on the couch in the parlor, eyes lifeless and empty.

"Poppie?" Foster said his name three times before he raised his head to look at them.

"She's bad off. Real bad off."

Bessie heard the voices and stepped from the back rooms. Knowing Poppie could not bear to hear the events again, she took Stella and

Foster outside, towards the back house. The same back house that still caused Stella to shudder after all these years.

"Bessie, we got ta get her to a doctor!" Foster's agitation was showing.

"I know it, Foster, but she's refusing. She won't go and it's real bad."

"Tell me what happened. All I know is that Stella saw a snake in her hands."

Stella stood listening, soaking in every word.

"She was out a workin' the fields. Poppie was clear on the other side, but saw the whole thing. He said she bent to pick up a 'bacco bug when she stepped on a big ol' timber rattler, and it got her. Bit her right on the neck. Deep, too. She got it offa her, but it was hangin' on fer a while. Poppie killed it once he got ta her, but the damage is done. I just don't know what to do. Even if we bring the doc here, she won't see him. I been just tryin' to make her as comfortable as I can."

Tears streamed Bessie's face as she replayed the events.

Stella stood stunned. The woman she despised her entire life lay dying in the clapboard house she hated so badly. A mixture of emotions sprang through her. Feelings of joy made her wish to vomit, yet she could find no sadness, no fitting emotions. Foster looked down and kicked the ground.

"Guessin' I best go in and see her," Foster said solemnly. He knew that a bite in the neck from a rattler wouldn't take long.

"Ya alright?" Bessie asked Stella.

"I don't know what I am, Bessie. I just don't know."

Bessie's eyes became distant. "She wasn't always like she was with you, ya know. She used to be a kind woman. I was proud ta call her Mommie."

"I never saw that, Bessie. Not ever."

"I know. She was awful to ya. She blamed you for what not shoulda been blamed on ya."

"What happened with her and my mother, Bessie? I've overheard things, but no one has ever told me."

"It's best we leave that be, Stella, honey. 'Specially now." She turned and walked slowly, sadly, to the house.

Stella looked out over the tobacco fields that were yellow for harvesting. She wondered who would harvest, hang, and sell them. Poppie was in no shape. Thoughts of working her fingers to the bone to get it done alone filled her head. She thought of the animals, the vegetable garden, and all the work to be done. Who would do it now?

Shame overcame her as she thought of the woman that lay dying inside and being unable to find any emotion for her. She somberly walked to the house to do what she must.

Stella came in and sat next to Poppie, placing her hand on his knee. It took him a moment to realize she was there.

"She's awful bad, Stella, darling. Awful bad."

"I know she is, Poppie. I'm awfully sorry. I wish I could do something."

His frail hand patted hers. "Yer here, honey. Yer here."

Stella went to the table and picked up a piece of paper and a pencil. She scribbled a note, folded it, sealed it in an envelope, and addressed it to Charles and Evelyn. She ran to the road, placed it in the small box and raised the flag, knowing the postman would be coming soon.

Hours passed into days while Stella comforted Poppie, and Foster and Bessie did the best they could to make Mommie comfortable. Stella had refused to go in and see Mommie and would only walk Poppie to the door of the adjoining rooms. Stella would pass from one room to the next, but could not find it in herself to look Mommie's direction. Moans of agony coming from her room left Stella with no emotions, no feelings at all.

One day, as Stella stood in the parlor making supper from what little they had, Foster exited the back rooms looking pale.

"Ya best go in and see her, Stella. Won't be long now I reckon."

Stella stood solemn, knowing that this was something she must do. Her hand quivered as she turned the doorknob and stepped into the tiny room. She did not recognize the woman she saw before her. Open sores oozed blood and puss from the huge, swollen bite marks that were visible on her neck. Her neck and face were so swollen that her skin could burst open at any minute. Sweat beads covered her body as she shivered from chills. Her eyes would roll into the back of her head as she would moan in agony.

The room smelled of vomit, urine, and blood, which churned Stella's stomach, but she could not turn away. She stared at her intently, as if trying to find the answers in the soul of her monster.

"Ya happy?" Mommie asked through staggered breaths.

"Happy? Mommie, no. I wouldn't wish this on anyone. I'm so sorry." Stella knew the words that should be spoken.

"Ya're a better woman than I is, Stella." It was the first time Mommie had ever spoken her name. "Now leave me be," she spat through suffering breaths.

Stella left the room feeling victorious. A lifetime of misery had been boiled down to a deathbed sentence that would stay with her forever. Even though she knew those words to be more than true, to have her say them was the greatest gift Mommie could have given her.

Surprising to everyone, for the next three days Mommie continued to moan and cry out in agony. Oozing boils festered and started to rot. Though she could eat no food, vomit and bile continued to spew forth. Stella helped Bessie, and they would tend to her as needed, the smells so horrid that one or the other would suddenly have to leave the room.

Poppie became a shell of himself. The only woman he had ever loved, good or bad, was dying. He was losing her, and there was nothing he could do to comfort her in her time of need. Foster busied himself with what needed to be done to handle the farm.

Late in the night, a shrill scream came from the back rooms. Stella bolted up from her makeshift bed on the parlor floor. Before she could enter the room, Poppie exited - a tear streaming his face.

"She's gone."

Although Stella had never had to make arrangements for one of her own, she had been to many mountain funerals and knew what had to be done. With Foster's help, they began their preparations. Bessie mostly consoled Poppie. Neither of them could bear what had happened.

Mommie's face was so distorted that she had to be covered for the entire three-day viewing. Many people came from miles and miles around, as Mommie had touched so many lives at one point in time during her life in the Smokies. Stella was fascinated with stories that people told of the good she had done. She wondered why Mommie had never allowed her to see this awe-inspiring woman so many spoke of. Many people gave Stella their condolences, but they looked at her with a knowing eye - a look that told Stella they knew of the hell she had suffered at this woman's hands.

On the third day, the day Mommie was to be laid in the ground, the numerous mountain people began their walk towards Dunn Cemetery, singing their hymns and carrying their dead. Stella stirred with confusion and mixed emotions, feeling dizzy and faint. She stayed behind in the house, finally stepping onto the porch to get some air where she fell directly into Charles's arms.

"Oh, Daddy! I'm glad you're here."

"How ya feelin', Stella, darlin'?"

"I'm not feeling very well at all, actually."

"Are ya sick?"

"No, I just don't...I just don't know."

He hugged her tight.

"They just started the walk up. I was heading that way. I'm sure Bessie will be happy you're here."

"I'm just gonna wait here until she gets back, if'n that's ok with ya."

"Sure, Daddy, I understand." And she did.

She began walking the trail slowly and somberly.

"We commit you to the ground, o Child of God. Ashes to ashes…."

She heard the words, but did not listen. Her eyes were on the casket. She had watched them lay her there, she watched the nails go in, she watched as they slowly lowered her to the dirt, but she couldn't shake the feeling that she would be severely punished for walking the trail to Dunn Cemetery.

The procession back to the house was quiet and solemn. The mountain people slowly said their goodbyes and left the Resenger family to be with their own.

Bessie's face told of her thankfulness to see Charles, but she knew why he had come.

"Get your things, Stella. All of 'em," Bessie told her sadly.

"What do you mean?"

"Ya're daddy has come for ya."

"What do you mean he's come for me? What about Poppie? What about the farm?"

"No sense in arguing, girl. Poppie's too sick ta live on his own, much less take care of the farm. Foster and me will do what we can with the farm, but it's just gonna be ta shut it down. T'aint much else we can do. Land's paid for. We just got ta sell off them animals and such. Ya can't do it yerself. It's the only right thing left ta do. Besides, ya're coming up on 18 soon. It's high time ya find ya're way out of here."

Stella walked as if in a dream to the room she had always called hers. In an instant, the life she knew was no more. Tears filled her eyes as she packed her things in the trunk she cherished. She glanced around her tiny room, soaking in every detail - the frayed bed linens, the tattered curtains hiding the warped glass facing the fields, the hand made wooden armoire that had been handed down through the generations.

She wandered into the room where Mommie and Poppie had always laid their heads - the room which still held the stench of death. She walked to the dressing table at the end of the bed and opened a drawer. Inside were two photographs. One showed an image of Mommie and the other an image of Mommie and Poppie together. She held up the tiny photograph of Mommie and placed it gently in her dress pocket as a lone tear escaped her eye. It was the first and only tear she would ever shed for her.

Stella's things were loaded into the sedan as she said her goodbyes. The tears she shed now were for those she loved and for those that loved her. She had no idea when, or if, she would see any of them again. As often as she had longed to escape from her tormentor, she could not grasp that it would mean leaving so much else she had come to know behind.

Stella's heart slipped away from her as her father pulled out onto the dirt road. Pieces of her soul dripped, spotting the road behind them. She turned slowly to wave goodbye one last time to the family she had known.

CHAPTER FOURTEEN

" *S*tella? Stella!"

Stella opened her eyes to see JH's face inches away from her own. She sat up from her twisted position to realize she was still in the sedan.

"Daddy said ya slept the whole way! Boy! Ya must'a been tired sumthin' awful!"

"JH! You leave her be! Mind your manners, young man!" Evelyn was fussing at him gently.

"You just keep growing," Stella said sleepily as JH stepped back, giving her room to exit.

Evelyn walked to Stella and held her tight.

"I have no idea how you must feel right now, but I'm here for you if you want to talk or anything. Just know I love you."

"I do, Mama. Thank you."

"Well, let's get you inside and get you settled."

Charles jumped into action, causing a whirlwind of commotion around Stella as different family members clamored for her attention, offering condolences and gushing over her permanent move.

It was early morning when they arrived, so Stella busied herself wherever she could to keep her mind off of the series of events that were taking place. She put her things away neatly and settled herself in, jumping right into chores that needed to be done.

"They's already puttin' ya to work, huh?" A deep voice that sounded familiar spoke above Stella as she scrubbed the floor of the kitchen. She looked up to see an older, more handsome version of Henry, which she did not expect.

"Henry?" She stared stunned for a moment as he smiled his unmistakable crooked smile. "Oh, my goodness, how you've grown!"

He wasn't exactly tall, standing at only 5'11", but he carried himself stately. He had very strong features, a chiseled jaw line, and high cheekbones. His dark hair was tousled on top, but high on his neck and above his ears. He held his posture firm, and his blue eyes dazzled her. Stella stood from the floor and met his gaze. In one swift movement he picked her up and twirled her around, causing her to giggle loudly.

"I've missed ya so much. I think about ya all the time," he whispered softly in her ear. Her face and neck felt hot from the redness that filled them. He set her down slowly and gazed into her eyes.

"I, um, I've missed you, too, Henry. It's good to see you." Stella stammered for her words.

"You're more beautiful than I remember." He seemed to be lost in thought, as if talking to himself rather than to her.

Trying to change the subject, she asked, "How have you been?"

Henry stepped back from her, suddenly aware of how close he was.

"I've been good, I guess. Real good. Working a lot. I, um, I got married." He felt sick as he uttered the words. "Her name is Justine. We're gonna have a baby."

"Oh, Henry! That's wonderful!" She tried desperately to hide her disappointment and disheartenment. "Why didn't you write to tell me?"

"Ya know I ain't much fer writing. Ev's the smart one in the family."

Henry changed the subject quickly, feeling uncomfortable discussing Justine with Stella. Stella had always taken a special place in his heart, but she was so far away, and any relationship they would have had would be forbidden simply because of who they were.

They talked about Rhodhiss Mills and how business was growing so quickly that everyone in town seemed to be working there. He helped her to finish the floors while they made small talk, then they wandered outside, carrying their conversation with them.

"How've ya been? Really?" Henry asked once they were nearing the lake.

"I don't know how I've been. It's funny how I keep saying that. Everything has kind of turned upside down on me."

"It's gotta be hard, leaving behind everything ya know and all." Henry gazed at her deeply before he added, "Ya never really talked about yer Mommie much. What was she like?"

"She was a hard, bitter woman that hated me." Stella was stunned that the words had fallen from her tounge as easily as they had.

"Why'nt ya ever say that?"

"I don't like to talk about it, I guess." After a long pause she continued, "I love Poppie, and Foster and Bessie, too. I don't know when I'll see them again, and I'm going to miss them terribly." She began to cry.

Henry put his arms around her, consoling her. At that moment, all of her troubles washed away. She felt as if she belonged there, safe in his arms. Henry felt the wonderful warmth of her embrace and savored the moment.

"Please don't cry, Stella, darlin'. It breaks my heart to see ya cry."

She stood back and wiped her tears dry. "It's good to have you to talk to."

"Whenever ya need me, no matter what, I'll be there."

"But, what about Justine?"

Sadness filled his eyes as he said, "I'll be there for ya, Stella. Always."

She found comfort in his words. His words lulled her to sleep that night as they would for many nights to come. Thoughts of him filled her mind. She knew that it was wrong to think of him this way, but no matter how hard she tried, she couldn't change how she felt. She dreamed of him every night. She longed to be near him every second. Her heart seemed to ache when he was away.

At the mill, Henry would have to force thoughts of Stella out of his mind to concentrate. He found himself sitting alone at lunch breaks, imagining her soft brown hair glistening in the afternoon sunlight, the way she threw her head back when she laughed, the softness of her touch. Every movement she made fascinated him. He would make up excuses to his wife to rush to the Lendfield home each day at the sound of the whistle to see the tender, broken beauty that he wanted to claim for his own. He cursed the fact that Charles and Evelyn had married; he cursed the fact that he had not waited to marry Justine; at the same time, he thanked the Lord above that he knew Stella, no matter what the circumstances.

Soon Labor Day was upon them, and everyone was preparing for a big celebration held by the Mills. Mabel and Stella busied themselves making banners for the big day while Henry kept walking by, asking some silly question or other.

"Why don't ya get outta here! You're getting on my nerves!" Mabel screamed when she had had enough. Stella and Henry giggled, but he left them alone.

"I don't know what he's been up to lately. Acting a fool, he is!" Mabel ranted as she worked. "It's like he's giddy in lo…" She set her paint brush down abruptly and looked at Stella, studying her intently.

Reading her thoughts, she said, "No, Mabel. You're wrong. We're just good friends is all." Stella pleaded to Mabel with her eyes.

Mabel's voice became quiet and still. "I've seen your daddy lookin' at y'uns. Justine, too. Best be careful with whatever it is ya've got goin' on."

Stella couldn't enjoy the celebrations. She replayed Mabel's revelation over and over. Had her father been watching her and Henry? She had noticed a change in Charles lately, but she thought that it had to do with the adjustment of her moving to Hickory. She hadn't even considered what other people would say of her actions with Henry, especially not Justine. For some reason, Justine never entered her mind. After all, they had done no wrong. They spoke of things she could not mention to others. She was comfortable with him. She enjoyed his company. But she knew she was lying to herself. She was in love with him and she knew what horrors that would cause for poor Justine and the rest of the family. She had to bury those emotions deep within.

At the festivities, Henry tried to invite Stella for some watermelon, but she busied herself with JH and Marlene, making excuses. Later in the evening, he tried inviting her on a hayride, but she stayed close to Evelyn and Charles, making it awkward for him to do so. Charles and Evelyn saw his advance, and Stella knew then that there was a darkness in Charles - a darkness that dulled to black when he saw Henry near his only daughter.

Things continued this way over the next few weeks as Stella did all she could to avoid Henry. She sat upon the backyard swing one day, lost in thought, when he caught her off guard.

"Why ain't ya talkin' to me?"

Stella jumped. "I, I, it's just that people are saying stuff. And my daddy's not happy about us being so close. And Justine…."

"Did he say that to ya? And who's sayin' what? I'll teach them a thing or two. We ain't done nuthin' wrong!"

"I know! Please, Henry! Please keep your voice down!"

He ran to her side and fell to his knees.

"I can't help it, Stella! I can't stand not bein' with ya! Please talk to me! I don't care what yer daddy says! I don't care what anybody says!"

Stella ran her fingers through his hair and smiled. He grabbed her hand, held it to his face, and kissed her palm gently.

"I'm in love with ya, Stella. I don't care who thinks it's wrong, I love you."

Stella heard a rustling in the trees and jumped from the swing, pulling her hand away from Henry's embrace. She spied a movement through the corner of her eye. Saying she had to go, she disappeared in a flash.

She tossed and turned that night, dreaming wonderful dreams of love and Henry, then waking in a sweat from a nightmare of Mommie and one of her many horrible punishments. In the earliest morning hours, she awoke and made her way down the stairs and out to the porch. The cold air was moving in swiftly as the months pressed on. She grabbed a sweater and sat in a rocker, looking at the stars through the brisk, fall air.

Stella saw a movement in the yard that startled her. A voice she knew well spoke.

"It's just me." Henry came closer where he could be visible in the pale moonlight. "I din't plan it. I couldn't sleep neither."

"It's all right, Henry," she whispered. "I love you, too."

She walked into the yard and fell into his embrace.

"My daddy can never know. No one can ever know."

"I know," he whispered. "I know."

They departed quickly, for fear they may be caught, but they made plans to meet again the following day when Henry was done at the mill. They met each day as soon as they could, strolling hand in hand, talking about their hopes and dreams. They made sure to stay out of sight at all times, always making excuses for where they were going and where they had been. Stella spent most of her day with the family so as not to raise any suspicion. Most of the other family members thought that Henry was out with friends or home with his wife after work and never questioned his whereabouts.

Mabel spoke with Stella a time or two; Stella assured her that everything was fine, but she also knew that the black darkness that filled her father did not go away and became slowly worse with time. No matter how well they hid their relationship, Charles seemed to know their secret.

Just after Thanksgiving, the family threw a party for Stella's 18th birthday. It was weeks early, but preparations for Christmas would not allow it at any other time. It was a wonderful celebration with cake and presents. Many people gathered for the occasion, and Stella was flattered. Nearing the end of the party when many had left, Stella excused herself for some fresh air. While walking through the tree line, she heard Henry calling her.

"Where did you come from?"

"I followed ya out here. Snuck out the front and came around. Wanna go for a walk?"

"I'd love to."

Stella made a last glace at the house then stepped into the shadows of the trees with Henry. Hand in hand they strolled in silence, listening to the symphony that nature created for them. They reached a clearing in the woods, and Henry laid down his jacket to make Stella a seat. Sitting beside her, he produced a tiny box from his pocket.

"It's for your birthday."

"Henry, you didn't have to do that."

She took the box and gently untied the small blue bow. Inside was a thin neck chain with a tiny heart locket attached.

"I didn't put a picture in it," he said. "Maybe someday we can, but for now, you just have to know who's in your heart"

"I do, Henry. I truly do."

He kissed her.

It was a kiss like none that either of them had ever known. It was at that exact moment that they both knew they were where they belonged. He held her tight and kissed her again, caressing her back and neck. Soon they were captivated in each other's embrace.

"Oh, Stella," he sighed. "I've loved ya since the day I first laid eyes on you."

Stella let herself surrender to the emotion and was lost in his sweet, loving touch. She allowed herself to be carried away, swept into a time and space where it was only the two of them, together forever, without judging eyes and hateful glares. It was there, under the assurance of trust in the bright and shining stars, that Stella knew her first love.

Time passed all too quickly. They never heard the calls. They never saw the lanterns.

"What...have...you...done?" a voice hissed hatefully.

Stella jumped at the sight of Grandpa Lenfield.

"We've been out looking for her. Charles got his shotgun out. He's gonna kill you fer sure if'n he finds ya this way." His voice was low, almost growling. He directed his words at Henry and wouldn't look at Stella. "Ya're wife's half sick with grief and worry." Looking disgusted, he said, "Get that one up, and get her outta here." He turned away from the both of them before adding, "I knew that girl was gonna be trouble."

In an instant, Stella had again become "that one" or "that girl" - someone unworthy of a name.

Stella dressed quickly, not sure if her shivers were from the cold or from her distress. Henry tried to hurry her along, neither of them speaking. She grabbed her coat from the ground, turned to look at him one last time, her eyes glassy, and ran for home.

"Oh, dear, chil'! We've been worried sick about you!" Evelyn was on the porch waiting when she returned. "All of the family's out lookin' for you. Are you all right?"

"I'm fine, Mama. I, um, I got lost is all."

"Goodness! You're half frozen through! Let's get you in and get you warmed up."

Evelyn doted on Stella, giving her attention that she did not want, did not feel she deserved. But she couldn't turn away. She had to bear her shame in front of those she loved. She knew what had happened was wrong; she knew it from the first day she had feelings for Henry. But she had somehow felt she couldn't deny her heart.

"Well, what th' hell is wrong with her then?" Charles's booming voice brought her back to reality. Mabel stood in the parlor speaking to him while Evelyn poured Stella's warm milk.

"Don't fret none. He's just been worried about you. We all were." Evelyn's soft tone gave little comfort to Stella.

Stella stared at the man she knew as her father and studied the changes in him. He seemed heavier, his shoulders slouched. His usually kept hair was messy and graying. Wrinkles had formed across his forehead - wrinkles she had not noticed before. The most frightening thing was the shotgun. He grasped the handle firm with the barrel over his shoulder, ready to aim at a moment's notice.

"Why'nt ya put down the shotgun? She's fine!" Mabel was pleading with what looked like a madman.

He snickered. "Why don't I just hang onto it for a while. If it's all the same to you." His look was sinister.

Evelyn left Stella alone in the kitchen and went to Charles. She soothed him, consoled him. Although he would not give up his gun, he softened just a bit. She led him to the staircase, but he took one last glance at Stella before he left; it was a glance that left her feeling cold as ice.

Mabel went to the kitchen and sat next to Stella, watching her intently.

"What happened?" she asked softly.

"I just got lost. That's all." Stella would not meet her gaze.

"You're lyin' to me. I thought we were closer than that."

"What am I supposed to say, Mabel? I made a terrible, terrible mistake!" She sobbed silently as Mabel stood to hug her.

"It's all right, honey. It's gonna be fine. Ain't nothing you can mess up that we can't fix together. Don't worry. It's all gonna be fine."

Stella sobbed, catching her breath. "Is it?"

CHAPTER FIFTEEN

I *knowed it! I knowed all along what ya was! Ya're a filthy harlot! A*
Jezebel! Just like yer mama was!

Stella startled from sleep and shook her head violently, trying to will
images of Mommie out of her mind. She sat up in her bed and gazed
out the window.

Soon, voices and commotion could be heard through the floor, and
Stella went to investigate. From the top of the stairs she could hear
Charles and Grandpa Lenfield in a heated argument.

"Where's he gone, then? He sure ain't with his wife!"

"I told him ta stay away! That girl of yours ain't nothin' but
trouble!"

"Don'tcha be talking 'bout my daughter like that! Who ya think ya
are, anyhow?"

"I think I know a tramp when I see one!"

Both men were screaming now.

"A TRAMP? How dare ya say that!"

Scuffling could be heard, as well as the women in the house
screaming. Stella stood at the stairs feeling faint and sick. She felt all
color drain from her face. At that moment, Mabel ran up the staircase
to face Stella.

"Get yer things. We gotta get. Quick!"

Panic set in as Stella asked what she should get.

"Everything. All ya got."

"Mabel, what's happening?"

It had been two weeks since Grandpa Lenfield had seen Henry and Stella in the woods. It had also been the last time she had seen Henry. She waited daily to see if he would come, but made a conscious effort not to seem anxious. She had cried herself to sleep every night. She was crushed that Henry had broken his word. He was not there for her when she needed him. He was just another in a long line of people to disappoint her.

Grandpa Lenfield had told Henry to stay away from Stella, and while it broke his heart to do so, he knew that his father would take precautions. He would lose his entire family if he did not obey his father's order. Mr. Lenfield was a powerful man in the community and in his family life. One way or another, he would get what he wanted and what he wanted was for Stella and Henry to be far apart. Henry had defiled the family name, his wife, and his unborn child by being with Stella, his step-niece, and he knew the shame that had been brought with his actions.

Charles had spent each night looking for Henry. At dusk, he would climb into his sedan with his shotgun by his side. While he did not know the extent of the events, he did not like what he knew Henry's intentions to be. He planned to stop any further actions. If it took his gun to do so, then that was how it would be.

Evelyn came into Stella's room. "How are you doing? Mabel said she told you to get your things."

"She did. I'm almost done. What's going on, Mama?"

"I'm not quite sure myself, Stella, honey, but with Daddy and Charles fighting like this, we're going to have to get our own place. Charles has already found us one. I guess they just needed one last blow out, and, boy, was it a doozie!" She smiled her tender smile that seemed to make all troubles disappear.

"Is it my fault?" Stella asked, knowing in her heart that it was.

"No, honey, of course not! I don't know what's got into them, but we've been here too long, anyway. It's high time we found a place to call our own. Mabel is going to come with us. It's already been decided." She smiled her tender smile. "Now don't you worry and just get your things as quick as you can."

Charles came into her room a while later and picked up her trunk. He glanced at Stella momentarily with wild eyes that pierced her soul. Without a word, he left the room carrying her things.

In the sedan, Stella sat silent as JH cried hysterically.

"What's happenin'? Why do we have ta leave? I don't wanna go!"

"You'll do what I say and hush up your mouth!" Charles screamed as he went to smack JH. Evelyn's tiny hand caught his hand with surprising strength.

"Watch yourself, Charles. Calm down."

He hunkered down in the driver's seat and gripped the steering wheel until his knuckles were white. JH snuggled next to Stella as she placed her unsure arm around him. Mabel sat staring out the window, slightly detached from the situation.

After a short trip, they pulled into the drive of a small, but roomy, white house near the edge of town. The yard was neatly trimmed and surrounded with yellow buttercups. Each window was covered with a green awning. The only porch was a tiny concrete slab that led to the front door.

"Oh, Charles! It's lovely!" Evelyn's airy tone cheered everyone.

"I thought ya'd like it." Charles beamed through his darkness. "There's a room for us, one for JH, and then a room for Mabel ta share with Stella. And JH has a shorter walk ta school. What do ya think, little man?"

JH's troubles seemed to disappear as he excitedly climbed over Stella to investigate his new home.

"Can we get a dog, Daddy? Can we?"

"Well, I guess that settles that."

Days passed slowly. Stella found new chores to keep her busy and considered taking a job at the mill with Mabel, but Charles had made her new home a prison, keeping an ever watchful eye on her, refusing to let her leave.

On Christmas Day, JH, Mabel, and Evelyn went to the Lenfield home for morning festivities, but Charles and Stella stayed behind. Each made an excuse, but Stella knew she wasn't welcome.

That evening, Mabel, Evelyn, and Stella created a feast for their own household while JH ran amuck, playing with his new toys. Evelyn had brought a chicken fresh from the Lenfield home and had already wrung its neck. She plucked out feathers by the handful as she spoke to Stella and Mabel. Stella's head began to swim, and her mouth began to water.

As quickly as it came on, she spewed forth vomit that could not be contained.

Evelyn jumped to comfort her. "What's got into you, Stella?" Stella continued to gag and cough. "What's wrong with her, Mabel? Do you think she's getting sick? She's never been squeamish before!"

Mabel looked at Stella in disbelief. Whispering, she told Evelyn, "She's with child."

Stella and Evelyn gasped at her revelation - a revelation that caused Stella to vomit even more.

"But, how?" Evelyn couldn't find her words.

"Henry," Mabel whispered.

"What?" Evelyn faced Stella, white faced, shocked. "Is this true?"

Tears streamed from her eyes as she became aware. Stella slowly nodded her head up and down.

"Oh, Lord, have mercy!" Evelyn wrung her hands as she paced the tiny kitchen. "Oh, what shall we do? What about poor Justine? Oh, what a mess this is!"

Stella silently cried as she bent to help Mabel clean up the mess. She was heartbroken to cause Evelyn so much anguish. Within seconds, she heard a tiny cry come from Evelyn and saw the flash of fear in Mabel's eyes. Before she could react, there was a whoosh; it was the sound of a belt coming loose from its loops. The strap came down hard on Stella's back, tearing her dress and causing her to jolt.

"They was RIGHT! And ta think I wouldn't believe 'em!"

Again and again the blows came as she tried to crawl away.

"Ya've sure done it now, ain't ya?" *Slash*.

"Mommie was right about ya!" *Slash*.

"Ya ain't good for nothing!" *Slash*.

Suddenly something cold and hard hit her as well, along with the strap. She felt the blood ooze from open sores until she fell flat to the floor. She turned to see that he had loosened his grip on the strap and was now hitting her with the thick buckle as well. Mabel jumped onto his back to try and stop him, but his fury drove his madness. Evelyn screamed and tried to cover JH's tearful eyes as he looked on in horror at the sight. Blow after blow came and landed on Stella's frail skin.

Finally, sweet blackness surrounded her, taking her into a dream state where nothing could harm her.

When she woke, it was nighttime. She noted her surroundings to be the back seat of Charles's sedan, and she bolted straight up in spite of the pain.

"It's all right. You're safe now."

Mabel was driving with Evelyn by her side.

"We didn't have time to get you cleaned up, honey. We had to get you out of there. He was planning to kill you." Evelyn spoke with a quivering voice.

"We're taking you some place safe, Stella," Mabel said while looking in the rear view mirror.

Stella leaned and tried to feel her back, but the tightness made it impossible. From her movements and pain, she knew her dress was stuck to open, bloody sores. Soon, they were pulling in front of a quaint, brick building far off the main road to town.

A short, plump, kind looking woman exited the building and headed for the car.

"Why, Eveyln! Mabel! It's so late! Are y'all alright?"

Evelyn looked at the woman with the pain of a thousand lost souls. "We need your help."

The woman's smile faded when she gazed into the back seat.

"Oh, dear God. Who did this ta her?"

"My husband. Her father. She's with child."

"Let's get her in quick. I've got a room ready for her."

It took all three women to remove Stella's damaged body from the back seat. Upon standing, she knew her injuries stretched to the back of her thighs and legs. A thumping sensation crept into the back of her head, and she placed her hand over a large, swollen bump.

"He sure did do a number on her. Don't nobody deserve such as this!"

Soon they were inside the brick building and headed for a staircase. Mabel's strength bore most of Stella's weight as she helped her into a tiny room off the hallway. She slowy sat Stella on the small bed while Evelyn and the woman spoke quietly outside her room.

"What is this place, Mabel?"

"Her name is Miss Mabry. No one knows where she came from; she won't talk about it. But she was in awful shape when she came to Hickory. Someone had hurt her badly. Now she helps women like her. Right here in this house. She's gonna take good care of you."

"You're going to leave me here?"

"We ain't got a choice, Stella. We got ta do what has ta be done. He's gonna be looking for you. We have ta be real careful."

Evelyn came in to introduce Miss Mabry and say her goodbyes. Stella went in and out of conciousness, and when she awoke, Evelyn and Mabel were gone. Miss Mabry stood by her side, cleaning her wounds and comforting her.

"Ya's gonna be fine, Stella. Just fine."

"Are they ever coming back?"

Miss Mabry chuckled softly. "Of course they are, dear. They's just tryin' to keep you safe is all."

Charles became more restless and wild eyed as the weeks passed. He was never seen without carrying his shotgun. Evelyn, Mabel, and JH had all but stopped speaking to him for fear of repercussions. Each day he would drive aimlessly, looking for Stella.

Mabel and Evelyn visited her when they could, but they had to be extremely cautious of their actions so as not to be seen or followed. In early spring, after a short visit with Stella, they returned home to find Charles on the couch, shotgun in hand.

"Where is she?" he asked angrily.

"I've already said that I'm not telling you where she is, Charles." Evelyn stood firm in her actions.

"Mabel, what'd ya do with her?"

"I ain't tellin' ya nothin', Charles."

He stood, groggily, unsteadily.

"Have you been drinking, Charles? You know I don't approve of...."

"I don't care what ya approve!" Charles screamed, cutting her off. "Ya're gonna tell me where she is, or I'm going to...." He raised his shotgun higher.

"What are you going to do, Charles? Are you going to shoot me? Well, you best get busy because I am not telling you where she is!" Evelyn stood tall in his line of sight.

"TELL ME!"

"No."

The blast was loud, echoing in their ears. The room lit up from the explosion of the barrel. Evelyn stood staring at the smoke coming from the end of the gun, wondering what had really just happened.

"Ya shot her! Oh, God! Ya shot her!" Mabel was screaming hysterically as Charles gave a sinister smile.

Eveyln looked down and instantly felt the pain. The bullet had grazed her shoulder. Blood was seeping through her dress sleeve. Mabel was running towards her with linens to apply pressure to the wound. Both of them ignored Charles and the fear that he brought with him as he laughed.

"We gotta get ya to the doctor, Ev!"

"Well, then, y'all do that, and I'm gonna go find Henry." He threw the shotgun over his shoulder and exited the small house of horror, taking his terror with him. He jumped into the sedan, kicking up dirt and gravels as he left.

Mabel and Evelyn dressed the wound and started walking towards Doc Howard's house. A couple of miles down the road, Mr. Lenfield pulled up to them in his truck with JH.

"What's goin' on now?"

"He shot her!" Mabel screamed.

Mr. Lenfield hit the brakes hard and threw the truck into park.

"What? Who shot her?" He was helping Mabel place Evelyn in the truck as they shouted their conversation.

"Who ya think? Charles! He's gone plum crazy! He's out there lookin' for Henry now!"

Fire burned in Mr. Lenfield's eyes as he dropped Evelyn and Mabel at the doctor's house, leaving JH with them.

"I'm headed out ta find him. I'll be back soon."

Before anyone could protest, he was gone.

Charles, knowing the places he had been, started looking elsewhere for Henry. Upon entering Granite Falls, he slowed the sedan to a crawl. He pulled up to a local tavern and stopped the car, waiting for someone to exit.

Hours passed before he spied Henry, but he had found him. Henry had been spending all of his nights in one tavern or other, trying desperately to drink his sorrow away. He had not even been to see Justine for fear of Charles finding him.

Charles jumped out of the sedan with his shotgun slung over his shoulder, as was becoming his way.

"I'm going to KILL you!" Charles stated through clenched teeth when he had caught up to Henry.

Henry cowered for a moment from the barrel of the shotgun being pointed directly at him. He held up his hand and stood firm.

"I guess you have ta do what ya have ta," he proclaimed, unafraid.

Charles thought for a moment before he motioned to the sedan.

"Shootin' is too easy fer ya and what ya've done ta me and Stella. Can't even call her my daughter no more. Get in the car." He shoved Henry in the back with the gun as he slowly walked to the vehicle.

"I'm not sorry, Charles. I love her."

"Ya love her? Ya love her, do ya? SHE'S PREGNANT! AND IT'S YOURS! And I don't see ya doin' a damn thing about it!"

Henry stopped in his tracks. His father had come to see him earlier that same day, but he had not told him.

"How long have ya known?" Henry asked timidly.

"Long enough! Long enough ta know that ya ain't around! Done run off from your responsibility! Done run off from Justine, too, from what I can tell!"

"Charles, I didn't know."

"YOU KNOWED YA TOUCHED HER DIN'T YA? Ya defiled my girl. Ain't my girl no more."

"She never was your girl, Charles! Ya left her alone in that pitiful excuse for a home and didn't even tell Ev about her until it was too late!"

"Shut your mouth and get in the car!"

Henry sat in the passenger seat while Charles revved the engine, holding his shotgun fast in Henry's direction. Charles drove to the outskirts of town and kept driving. Further and further he drove until Henry's heart began to pound. When Charles stopped the car, Henry looked around, noticing nothing but railroad tracks. Charles stepped out and went to the trunk of the car. When he returned, he held a thick rope in his hand.

"Get out," he stated flatly.

"What are we doing here, Charles?"

"I said to get out of the car."

Henry did as he was told, exiting the car to once again face the shotgun.

"Turn around."

Charles began to drape the half-knotted rope around Henry's body, fastening his hands tight. Before he reached his legs, he poked the shotgun into Henry's back, escorting him towards the railroad tracks.

"What are ya doin', Charles?"

"Keep yer mouth shut and keep moving."

When they reached the tracks, Charles kicked Henry in the back of the legs, forcing him down. Once he was on his knees, Charles hit him in the back with the butt of the gun, causing him to fall to a laying position. Charles continued to tie the rope, lashing Henry to the tracks.

"Charles! Charles! Please! Don't do this!"

He worked diligently until he was sure that the knots were secure. He stood back, admired his work, and walked to his sedan.

"Charles! Please!"

Charles started the engine and put the car in gear.

"Charles!"

He smiled once again, satisfied with his accomplishment, and drove away.

CHAPTER SIXTEEN

Stella continued to heal as her tummy grew. Scars were forming on her back that she was sure would be there forever; constant reminders of the trauma she felt she would always know. The new life that formed inside her turned and moved, bringing with it something that seemed like hope, but hope was always just that, - hope.

One peaceful night Stella sat in the front parlor, watching the lightning bugs through the window frame and listening to the sweet lull of the crickets. A slow, faint knocking sound came from the back of the house.

"Now, who could that be?" Miss Mabry questioned. "It's late! And that's someone at the back door! We gotta get you out of sight, Stella!"

Stella's heart pounded from fear as she ran for her room, holding her ever growing tummy. Miss Mabry cautiously walked to the back of the house.

"Who's there?" she asked through the closed door.

There was no answer, only another tiny knocking. She opened the door just slightly, adjusting her foot behind it. There in the darkness she saw Henry. He was worn, haggard, and tired looking. He had neither shaved nor showered.

"Whatcha doin' here so late, boy?"

"Is she here? I have to see her."

"Is who here?" Miss Mabry was ever courageous, she knew never to give away someone she was set to protect.

Stella heard Henry's voice and crept slowly down the staircase.

"Henry?"

He rushed passed Miss Mabry as if she weren't there and held Stella gently, swaying back and forth.

"I'm so glad you're OK."

"What's happened to you, Henry? You look awful." She could only imagine what things had occurred in his life. It had been months now since they had seen or spoken to one another.

"Yer daddy tried ta kill me. Searched until he found me then tied me to the tracks out past Granite Falls."

Stella gasped. "Oh, no, Henry! I'm so sorry! Are you all right?"

"Oh, Stella, please don't be sorry. I deserve everythin' I get. I'm fine. Some friends of mine just happened to be passing by and saw me. They helped me and got me off the track before the train could come." He paused, gazing at Stella with pain in his eyes. "As soon as they got me undone, they told me Justine was havin' the baby. I hadn't been to see her, neither. I done ya both wrong, Stella." He hung his head.

"Is she, the baby?" Stella stammered for words.

"They's fine. Both of 'em. Got a healthy baby boy. She named him Thomas." He looked down at Stella's protruding stomach. "I sure have made a mess of things."

"It's all right, Henry. I'm safe now. Everything is fine." She assured him, but she was still so unsure herself.

"Charles has gone crazy." He gazed towards the front of the house, ever watchful of him. "When he found out I wasn't dead, he done something awful." He looked out the window and swallowed hard. "He's filed a complaint with the sheriff and says I, well, I raped ya."

"He did what?" Stella was stunned at his announcement.

"It's turned into a mess, it has. It's gonna go to court. Some kind of hearing they said. Dad ain't letting him do it without a fight. Justine won't see me and won't let me see the baby. It's all just such a mess." He choked back a tear.

Stella felt dizzy and confused. She reached for words that would not come.

"I don't know what ta do, Stella. I've made a mess of everythin'." He buried his head in her bosom, and she stroked his hair.

Wisdom and her comprehension of the situation told her that this would be the last time she would ever be close enough to touch Henry. She soaked in his smell, his touch, his face; she remembered every detail of that moment.

"Just remember I love ya, Stella. I've loved ya since the day I laid eyes on ya. I shoulda waited fer ya. I've made of mess of it all. Just a mess."

In a flash, he was gone. Silently sullen, sulking through the thick night air, he made his way.

Stella found herself alone again, surrounded by nothing but her feelings and fears. She felt she should be accustomed to this uncertainty, the feeling of being abandoned, but there was no comfort in past grievances. She was alone now in a way that she had never been alone before.

She slept the sleep of the restless, fitful dreams abounding. She tossed and turned, waking many times during the night. She rose at the first signs of daylight, no longer able to confine herself to the nightmares. In the early morning hours, Mabel burst through the door.

"We got a problem, Stella. It's a big one." She was breathing heavy.

"I talked to Henry last night. He told me."

"You what? How did you talk to Henry? Did he come here?"

"Yes. He came by late last night. He told me Daddy tried to kill him and that he's accused Henry of raping me."

"That's what I'm here for. They's gonna be a court hearing, and they say you have to be there. It's gonna be bad, Stella. I'm real worried."

"I don't see how they can hurt me any more than I've already been hurt, Mabel. Of course I'll say that what Henry and I did was wrong, and that it wasn't his fault. He needs to be with Justine and the new baby. I'm going to be fine."

"You've always been a strong one. I admire that about you the most. We'll get through this together."

The following week, there was a clamoring at the courthouse. People were coming from miles around to be at the hearing. The Lenfield family was very prominent in Hickory, and it seemed gossip had made it across much of the mountain.

Stella felt sick as she walked through the crowd towards the courthouse with Mabel and Evelyn. She tried desperately to tune out the words of the cold and bitter that spat at her as she entered. Her knees buckled when she saw Charles, freezing in fear.

"They's too many people around for him to hurt ya. Don't worry. He won't do nothing here." Mabel spoke softly in her ear, assuring her as she draped her arm through Stella's. Evelyn stood firm and held her head high, making sure not to turn in Charles's direction.

They took a seat in the front of the courtroom; Stella nestled between her protectors.

Grandpa Lenfield entered the courtroom, followed by Henry and five other men. They took their seats on the opposite side of the room, sitting near a man in a suit. Although Grandpa Lenfield looked pained, he would not make eye contact with Stella, Evelyn, or Mabel. Henry only looked at the floor and fiddled with his fingers.

"All rise!"

A judge entered the room and took his seat at the bench. Stella followed the actions of the others in the courtroom.

"We're here today for a preliminary hearing in the case of Resenger vs. Lenfield. I see there are many people here today. I just want to warn you all now that if there are any outbursts, I will clear this courtroom." He shuffled some papers laid in front of him then added, "Well, let's get on with this. Prosecutor?"

A man in a suit that sat next to Charles stood to address the judge.

"We are here today on the testimony of one witness, Mr. Charles Resenger. He has stated that his daughter, Stella Resenger has been raped by Mr. Henry Lenfield. She is now with child due to this horrible incident."

"And what evidence does Mr. Resenger have?"

"Mr. Resenger's testimony is that he overheard a conversation between his daughter, Stella, and one of his sisters-in-law where Stella stated that Mr. Lenfield had raped her. He states that she is too afraid to come forward to place these accusations against Mr. Lenfield. He is here to speak on her behalf."

"You don't have much of a case, here," the Judge stated. He shuffled some more papers before asking the defense to stand.

The man in a suit that sat next to Grandpa Lenfield stood.

"Your honor, we have been brought here today as a waste of time to this court. We have sworn affidavits from Henry Lenfield stating that the sexual relations between himself and Stella Resenger were, in fact, consensual. We also have sworn statements from Alexander Johnson, John Thurman, Jake Surmond, George Miller, and Andrew Gorman, all present here today, that they have also had consensual sexual relations with Miss Resenger. It is obvious that these are false allegations that have been brought forth by Mr. Resenger and that Miss Resenger is nothing more than a slovenly woman with an angry father."

There was a small gasp from what seemed everyone in the courtroom. Stella felt all color drain from her face and was sure she was about to vomit. She looked in Henry's direction, but he continued to look at the floor. She glanced at the other men sitting with Grandpa Lenfield, wondering why in the world they would say such things. She had never seen these men before. One of the men looked at her, then he quickly shifted his eyes the other direction. Mabel squeezed her hand tight.

The events that followed swirled through Stella's head as each man's sworn statement was read in front of the court. Stella felt lightheaded and faint. She could not focus on the words that were being spoken.

Suddenly, without warning, Charles jumped to his feet and lunged at Henry.

"I'm gonna KILL ya!"

The courtroom erupted.

Bang. Bang. Bang.

"Order!"

Three guards jumped on Charles and wrestled him to the ground.

Bang. Bang. Bang.

"Order! I will have order in this courtroom! Guards, get that man out of here!"

The guards contained Charles and brought him to a standing position with his hands cuffed behind his back.

"Know this, Mr. Resenger. I am throwing this case out for lack of evidence. I had better not ever see you in front of my bench again."

Bang.

The judge grabbed his paperwork and left the courtroom, clearly perturbed with the situation. Charles was taken through another door, escorted by the guards that had contained him.

Stella turned to Evelyn, who had silent tears streaming her face.

"It's a lie, Mama. All of that was a lie."

"I know that, honey. Don't you worry what these people have to say."

Evelyn stood and walked boldly to her father. "How could you? How could you do such a thing?"

"What's going on, Mabel? Please tell me what's happening!"

Mabel stood and pulled Stella's arm until she stood as well. "Hold your head high," she stated. They walked through the crowd of judgmental onlookers. Stella made eye contact with several people and could clearly see their contempt for her and her situation.

Outside, people gathered to utter hateful words and pour out nasty accusations. Mabel and Stella walked steadily through the crowd, making their way slowly. Evelyn soon caught up with them as they turned a corner into an alley where Miss Mabry waited for them in her car. No words were spoken as the women returned to the safety of Miss Mabry's home.

Stella spent the next few months in agony, locked away from society, away from hateful glares and evil words. She found herself replaying the events over and over again in her head until she thought she would go mad.

"Ya got ta stop actin' this a way," Miss Mabry stated one hot summer day. "Sure, ya made a mistake, but any fool would know that what's been said about ya ain't true."

"How would they know that, Miss Mabry?"

Miss Mabry didn't have an answer.

Stella continued to grow in her pregnancy and would feel the baby do flip flops through the summer heat; she began to grow more and more tired and weak. Soon, Miss Mabry catered to her every need while trying to keep her as cool as possible through the blistering sun.

"Something's happening!" Stella screamed through tears. "Miss Mabry, help me! Something's wrong!"

Miss Mabry ran to the kitchen where Stella stood in a puddle of water.

Stella screamed and doubled over in pain.

"It's time," Miss Mabry stated. "Let's get you to the doctor."

It's time. It's time. The words echoed in Stella's head. She remembered the screams, the pain, and the blood of when her brother had been born. She became suddenly frightened - daunted and dismayed at the demoralization approaching.

Miss Mabry loaded Stella into the backseat of her car and headed into town. She drove through the streets of Hickory and out towards Granite Falls.

"Where are we going, Miss Mabry?" Stella uttered through staggered breaths.

"Can't take ya to the hospital in Hickory. He'd find ya fer sure."

She continued to drive past Granite Falls and into Marion. Stella tried to contain her screams on the drive. They soon pulled in front of a large red brick building that read 'McDowell Hospital' on the side. Once at the doors, they were met by a kind looking woman in a white outfit.

"Why, Miss Mabry! How are you? I haven't seen you in...."

"No time, Sandy," Miss Mabry cut her off. "I got a girl that's in labor here. We need some help."

"Oh, my!" Sandy rushed through the doors, returning with two men dressed in white with a wheelchair. Stella screamed in agony as they removed her from the car and took her inside. Miss Mabry followed, stopping just before they took her into a large room separated by curtains.

"Now, I ain't leavin' ya, chil'. I got ta go find Evelyn and Mabel. We'll be back as soon as I find 'em. Ya ain't gonna be alone for this."

Stella doubled over again with a scream. Before she knew it, Miss Mabry was gone. The words she had said replayed in Stella's mind. *I'm not alone. They'll be back.* But, they were gone. She was alone. All alone.

"Isn't that the girl from that dirtiness that happened over in Hickory?" Stella heard a male voice say through a nearby curtain.

"Hush, up, Carl. That ain't none of your business," a woman's voice replied.

Stella's agony continued as two other nurses helped her change into a flimsy gown.

"She's pretty far along," one of them stated. "We best go get the doctor."

"Wait!" Stella cried out. "My mama isn't here yet."

"Sweetheart, we may not have that much time."

Stella screamed out again in agony. The pain was so severe, she was sure something was wrong. She took deep breaths as the nurse had told her, but it didn't help the pain; nothing helped the pain.

A dark haired man dressed in blue walked into the room and looked under Stella's gown. She tried to move or protest, to stop him somehow, but the shearing sting left her defenseless.

"We need to get her sedated."

She was soon surrounded by nurses, one of them placing a clear mask over her face. The pain subsided, as did she. She dreamt wonderful dreams of a beautiful life where her children ran happy and carefree. They never felt pain; they never felt anger; they only felt love.

"Mr. Resenger, you have to put that shotgun away. You can't have that in here!"

Stella woke from her grogginess, not sure if she had heard it or if it had been a part of her dream.

"Where is she? I know ya got her in here someplace. I know it! Now, where is she?"

She sat straight up, ignoring the pain, and looked around.

"Mr. Resenger, please, you have to calm down."

Fear struck her heart like lightening. He had found her. He was there to kill her.

"DON'T TELL ME TA CALM DOWN! WHERE IS SHE!?"

She scampered around the room, gathering the clothing she had came in. She stripped off her hospital gown as quickly as possible, thankful for the comfortable largeness of the dress that had been made to cover her bulging stomach. As quietly as possible, she walked passed other patients covered by hanging curtains, and walked to the open window. Painfully, she slid one leg over the ledge, lifted the other leg with her arms, and slowly lowered herself to the ground.

Following the tree lines on the streets, she walked in agony through throbbing tenderness. She walked until she saw the bus station. Stepping inside, she spied the service window. Pulling out the money she had tucked away that Miss Mabry had given her, she carefully counted the bills.

"One ticket to Knoxville, Tennessee, please," she spoke softly.

"Round trip or one-way?"

Quietly, shifting her eyes to the floor, she stated, "One-way, please."

The bus loaded and was off. She was riding away from the heartache, away from the pain, away from the fear, and away from a child that was her own. As the bus crossed the mountain, across the state line, the Tennessee rain began to fall. Stella didn't wipe her face as she allowed her tears to flow with it.

GENERATION THREE
ELISA MAE

CHAPTER SEVENTEEN

*E*lisa Mae held firmly to Evelyn's hand outside the courthouse in Newport.

"Mama, why is Mama Stella crying?"

"Well, that's because she wants you to go home with her."

"I'll go with her if she won't cry."

Evelyn smiled gently at the small child.

"She would like that very much, but I don't think your daddy will allow that."

Stella held on to Burke as they spoke at their car, away from Evelyn and Elisa Mae.

Evelyn thought back to the day she had brought her home. She was surprised at the strength and power she possessed when she looked straight at an angered Charles and a terrified JH, holding a brand new bundle of baby, and said, "Her name is Elisa Mae, and we're keeping her."

Even though JH was 13, and pure boy, he was thrilled with his new baby sister.

Charles came nearer and, for a moment, just a glimpse in time when he laid eyes on her, a tiny, shimmering light replaced the darkness he now carried eternally. The bitter loss of his first love, the disgust with himself over leaving his daughter with Mommie, the way his daughter had been raised, and what he felt she had become, the things he had done after she had conceived in sin - it was all too much for his mind to cope with. He had slowly and surely lost control, just as he had seen his mother do. While he remained angry, bitter, and ornery, he vowed to protect this child at any cost.

Charles, Evelyn, JH, and Elisa Mae moved back to the farm in Tennessee after Elisa Mae was born; they moved away from hateful glares and spiteful words in Hickory. Words and gestures such as these were still prevalent in Newport, but often people respected Evelyn too much to mutter them aloud. In Elisa Mae's young life, she had heard the word "bastard" many times, knowing that it referred to her, but she had no idea what it meant.

Charles and Evelyn had accepted Mommie and Poppie's previous roles and duties in their tobacco farm lifestyle. The farm had been so run down that it took them many years to make it yield the green and yellow stalks it once proudly carried.

Stella had gotten on that bus, but she had always looked back. For more than five years she looked back.

As soon as Mabel had learned that Stella had disappeared, she followed her to Knoxville where they had both received jobs at Brookside Mills. Mabel was quickly hired on due to the knowledge of her work in the North Carolina cotton mills, and she soon got Stella hired on as well. They lived together in a boarding house and would visit Evelyn and Elisa Mae as much as possible, forever trying to avoid Charles and his bitter hatefulness. It would break Stella's heart in two each and every time she would have to leave Elisa Mae with Charles.

Mrs. Crane owned the boarding house where Mabel and Stella resided. Mrs. Crane had a son named Burke who had just come home from the war. Mrs. Crane, forever the matchmaker for her son, introduced the two upon his return, and he and Stella felt instant love in their hearts. They had a proper courtship, fell in love, and were married. Burke always knew about Elisa Mae and both he and Stella wanted to have her in their lives, but Charles wouldn't allow it. He had maintained strict control over Elisa Mae since the day she was brought home from the hospital. Stella had tried many times to take Elisa Mae to be with her, but she had failed in her efforts. Although there was never any real closeness between Charles and Stella, their relationship had now turned to cold, hard ice.

Elisa Mae was too young to understand what was happening in this place and time. She knew many things for sure. She knew that Evelyn was her mama. She knew that JH was her older brother. She knew that Charles was her daddy. She also knew that Stella was her real mother. Evelyn's infinite wisdom of God's words and her own had made it understandable for Elisa Mae.

Stella and Burke walked from the car towards Evelyn and Elisa Mae. Stella tried to wipe her tears, but they continued to stream.

"I'll come visit you as often as I can. Just always know deep in your heart that I love you and always will."

"I love you, too, Mama Stella. Don't be sad." The child's small voice was soft and sincere. Stella hugged her tight and walked away, sobbing.

Burke knelt in front of Elisa Mae, held her gaze for a long moment, and then squeezed her with all his might. Although he was crushing her tiny frame, she was joyful for his bear hug.

"We love you. We'll visit you real soon, I promise."

Elisa Mae had mixed emotions, unsure of what was happening. Before she could question, they were gone. All the while, Evelyn stood at her side, guiding her assurance that all would be fine.

Charles had waited purposefully for Stella and Burke to leave before descending the courthouse stairs towards Evelyn and Elisa Mae, holding the official paperwork in his hands.

"Daddy, why was Mama Stella crying so hard?"

"We ain't a worryin' 'bout that no more. She just didn't get her way. And from now on, I want ya ta stop calling her Mama Stella." He motioned towards Evelyn. "That there's your mama. Plain and simple."

"But," she dared to question him.

"No buts about it. That's it."

Elisa Mae became silent. She knew not to challenge Daddy. Ever.

"See this?" Charles held up a crisp ten-dollar bill. "We're gonna take this over to the bank and get you a savin's account. Your first legal transaction as a Resenger. A true Resenger."

"Charles, shouldn't we go over and file the papers first like they said?" Evelyn questioned.

"They'll be time for that later."

They all climbed into Charles's dusty truck, Elisa Mae in the center beside Evelyn, and Charles's shotgun between her and Charles. His shotgun was common place now. Wherever he went, the shotgun went with him.

They drove away from the courthouse and had their celebration - a celebration that Elisa Mae did not understand.

The drive up the dirt road on the way home to the farm house was always Elisa Mae's favorite. She would turn full around to look out the back window, watching the dust make its large, brownish-red cloud as they drove across it. The farm had changed from what Evelyn and Charles remembered, mostly due to their hard work. A new fence now surrounded the yard part of the property. Two dogs ran back and forth, excited to see their owners returning. The tobacco fields flourished. Evelyn had kept the hydrangeas that sat at the porch column bases. Mommie had planted them so long ago that they had become a part of the house. The barn had been mended time and again, but it remained sturdy and firm. The apple tree was no longer a large sapling, but a huge tree, bearing fruit for all to share. Evelyn had also planted a grape vine between the barn and the house, which was doing quite well. The most extreme difference was the addition they had made to the once square clapboard house.

The house now had another bedroom and a large kitchen, with windows lining the entire front side. Charles had worked endlessly at Evelyn's request to have a proper kitchen. Now, instead of one small parlor, there was an entrance on the right that led to a tiny hallway. To the left was a bedroom with a door that led to the back yard and to the right was the entranceway into the kitchen. A well had been dug, and a door from the kitchen was only steps away from the red pump.

Charles pulled into the drive between the barn and house, and Elisa Mae climbed over Evelyn to exit the truck.

"Elisa Mae, don't you get that pretty dress all dirty. If you're going to play, you need to go put on one of your old dresses."

"Yes, Ma'am."

She scampered into the house and went to her room; it was the same room where Stella had endured years of hardship. While Elisa Mae was always cautious of Charles, she did not fear him. She knew that others feared him, and she had seen many instances that would cause their fear, but while he didn't speak much, he was never angry or bitter with her.

JH came from the back room and looked at Elisa Mae when she exited, wearing an older dress of softened burlap.

"How'd it go?" he asked.

"What do you mean?"

"Oh, well, you're here, so never mind." Changing the subject, he added, "You excited about starting school?"

"Oh, yes! I am! I get to ride the school bus and everything!"

"Yes you do! And guess what? I'm going to save you a seat!"

"We'll ride the same bus to school?"

"Well, we go to the same school, silly. This year, anyway. This will be my last year in school."

"But, why?"

"I graduate after this year. That means you don't go to school anymore."

"What will you do then?"

"I'm not too sure, yet, squirt. I'll figure something out. Maybe the army."

"What's this about the army?" Evelyn questioned as she entered the parlor.

"Nothin', Mama. Just talking to Elisa Mae."

"About the army?"

JH shifted his eyes away and he made an excuse to leave. Elisa Mae followed him outside and began to play in the yard, chasing the dogs. Worry ran across Evelyn's face, but she knew in her heart that she couldn't keep her son forever.

In the following weeks, Evelyn kept herself busy making new dresses for Elisa Mae for her first year of school. She allowed her to wear one to church one Sunday morning. JH had driven them because Charles had refused to go. While leaving the church, Preacher Baker commented on how pretty Elisa Mae's dress was.

"My mama made it for me!" She beamed as she twirled around.

"Not any mama that bastard child will ever know," a voice muttered behind them.

They all heard the comment, but tried to ignore it - all but JH. He swung full around and faced the woman that had said it.

In a deep, harsh tone he flatly stated, "That IS her mama. Legal and all. And you ever call that child a bastard again, I'll personally...."

"JH!" Evelyn stopped him. "It's best we leave now."

JH turned around, and you could see the red anger rising up his chest, neck, and face.

Evelyn turned back to the preacher and asked if he could come for dinner on Thursday night. Preacher Baker, being a widower, never turned down a home cooked meal, and plans were set. Evelyn took once last graceful glance at the woman that had made the comment and turned to leave, grasping Elisa Mae's hand.

The three drove home in silence. When they arrived, Bessie and Foster were at the house.

Elisa Mae jumped out of the truck excitedly.

"Where's Little Grandpa?"

When no one answered her, she became worried. She knew that he often drank too much moonshine and would wander off. The adults gathered around, talking quietly.

"I'll find him." JH said suddenly. "I think I know where he might be." He hopped in the farm truck and was gone.

"I swear, Ev, I jus' don' know what to do with Poppie no more. It's jus' gettin' worse 'n worse. It's like he's this a way even if he ain't drinkin'.'"

"It'll be fine, Bessie." Evelyn comforted her. "I'll help you out more. It's going to be just fine."

Charles seemed indifferent, but he seemed indifferent to everything. To everyone else, wait and worry was always the reaction.

Hours later, JH returned with Poppie. JH helped him out of the truck, leaning him against the side while he closed the door.

"Little Grandpa!" Elisa Mae shouted and ran to him.

Before JH had even seen her, she had thrown her arms around Poppie, causing him to fall on top of her. She cried out in pain as JH lifted him off of her swiftly.

"ENOUGH!" Bessie screamed from the porch. "I've had it! Ya can have him. I'm DONE!"

She stomped her way to Foster's truck, and he followed. Without another word, they drove away.

"JH, get him into the parlor and lay him on the couch. Elisa Mae, stand up, honey. Let me see you."

Elisa Mae stood, bearing a large scrape from her knee to her thigh and an already bruising elbow.

"Let's get you inside and clean you up."

After settling Poppie on the couch, JH started cooking supper. Evelyn cleaned and bandaged Elisa Mae then came to the kitchen to help. After Elisa Mae had set the table, she called Charles to come eat.

They all sat at the table, thanked the Lord for their meal, and began eating.

"I've found a real good job outside of Knoxville," Charles stated. "Was gonna tell ya earlier, but with Poppie and all. Anyway, it's in this place they's callin' Oak Ridge. It's a security guard position. Thing is, though, I cain't tell ya no more than that."

"What do you mean you can't tell us anything more than that?" Evelyn questioned.

"That's the thing, Ev. It's a government job. They's been a working on somethin' real top secret out there, and I don't even know what. It's top pay, Ev. Real top pay. I've got ta be gone for a while, though. A long while."

"How long?"

"Could be months. I just ain't sure. JH can help ya with the crops, and it would help us out. Ya know it would."

"Well, I've never been able to stop you from anything before. I don't guess I'm going to start now."

The rest of supper was eaten in silence. Evelyn's mind raced. Thoughts of caring for Poppie, Elisa Mae starting school, JH thinking of joining the army, taking care of the farm, and Charles not being around for help made her head swim. She was unable to sleep that night and was up at the earliest light.

Elisa Mae jumped from the bed as soon as she heard the rooster's crow. She threw open her wardrobe and went from dress to dress, deciding which she should wear on such an important day. She finally chose a blue floral dress that felt like silk on her skin. Picking up her brush, she walked to the looking glass and brushed her long, dark curls. She washed her face in the basin and looked back in the glass.

"This is it," she said aloud, "my first day of school."

She laced up her brand new boots and stepped out of her room and into Charles and Evelyn's room on her way to the parlor. Charles stood at the end of their bed, packing a large suitcase.

"Well, don't you look handsome!" he proclaimed.

"I'm a girl, Daddy. I'm pretty."

"Yes, ya are."

A searing pain flashed through him as he said the words - words that cut his frail mind so deep that he wasn't sure if he had said them to Ella, Stella, or Elisa Mae. He hugged this child, a child that he was unsure of. He knew her. He knew that he did, yet he could not place her. He loved her. He knew that as well.

"Daddy? Are you all right, Daddy?"

Charles snapped back just slightly and loosened his embrace.

"I love ya, girl."

"I love you, too, Daddy."

Elisa Mae made her way through the parlor and into the kitchen.

"Sit yourself down there, Miss Elisa Mae. We have to get some breakfast in you for your first day of school!"

She was so excited she was about to burst. When she sat at the table, she saw a small stack of books tied with a string and a lunch sack.

"Are those for me?" she asked, astonished.

"They sure are! I can't send you off to school without the proper materials!" Evelyn beamed at Elisa Mae's excitement and wonder.

She ate her breakfast so quickly that Evelyn had to tell her several times to slow down. Elisa Mae couldn't stand still as Evelyn cleared the table and cleaned up the breakfast dishes. Once the kitchen was cleaned, Elisa Mae proudly held her books and items and headed for the door. Evelyn gave her a big hug and many well wishes.

"Wait. Where's JH?"

"I'm not sure, honey. He left a little earlier."

Elisa Mae couldn't hide her disappointment.

"Well, what's wrong, honey?"

"He promised to save me a seat on the bus."

"Maybe he just forgot. I'm sure there'll be a seat for you, and you'll make lots of new friends."

"Do you think so?"

"I know so."

Evelyn hugged her again and Elisa Mae set out. She walked to the end of the dusty dirt road and stood at the corner of the main road, waiting with all the other children. The longer she waited, the more her stomach churned. Butterflies ran rampant.

Finally, the bus arrived. She followed the other children, one by one, onto the giant yellow school bus. She turned her head from side to side, looking for a seat.

"Elisa Mae!"

She looked to the back of the bus and saw JH in a seat by himself. She walked his direction.

"You saved me a seat." She smiled.

"I made ya a promise, didn't I?"

CHAPTER EIGHTEEN

$\mathcal{T}$hursday came, and the next day Charles would be leaving for his new job in Oak Ridge. That evening, the preacher came and knocked on the door. Charles opened the door angrily with his gun slung over his shoulder.

"Oh, uh, hello, Charles." Preacher Baker stammered for words.

"Charles! Put that thing away! I've invited the preacher for supper!" Evelyn tried to hide her embarrassment of the situation while trying desperately to not let Charles get out of control. With all that had been happening, she had completely forgotten about having a guest.

Soon things were calmed, and everyone sat at the table. Grace was given, and everyone began to eat - everyone but Charles. Charles stared wildly at the preacher. Conversation was made by Preacher Baker, Evelyn, Elisa Mae, JH, and even Poppie, but Charles never uttered a word. Soon, nearing the end of their meal, Charles let out a large, guttural growl and flipped the table on its side. Dishes smashed to the floor, and everyone jumped up from their chairs.

"You ain't nothin' but a damn freeloader! Ya come here ta eat my food, ya gonna take my wife while I'm gone, too?"

Everyone was bewildered, and no one knew quite what to do or say. Evelyn was immediately on the floor, clearing the mess. JH and Elisa Mae stood frozen in position, waiting for the worst.

"Get the hell outta my house!" Charles bellowed.

Preacher Baker practically ran out of the kitchen door, across the front of the house, and jumped into his car. The tires only spun in the dirt when he hit the gas. On his third try, he was almost out of the driveway when Charles came out with his shotgun aimed at the car. Two rounds went off as Preacher Baker's car swerved down the dirt road.

Charles flung his gun over his shoulder, walked to the back room, and got his suitcase.

"Ain't a waitin' 'til mornin'. I'll be goin' now. Can't trust none of yuns."

"Charles, wait!" Evelyn tried to get him to stay and talk, but there was no use. He was in his car and gone.

"Why'd he do that, Mama?" Elisa Mae's soft hand clung to Evelyn's.

"I don't know why he does much of anything anymore, chil'." She looked distant, but there was a slight change in her. She slowly let out a sigh of relief. Her largest worry had just driven away.

Elisa Mae was a wonderful student, and going to school made her happy. She learned of things that existed outside of her small mountain range, and she soon wanted to explore the world. She understood why JH would want to join the army, but she also knew that she loved those mountains - the misty morning haze rising likes smoke circles in the earliest rays of the sun, the lull of the crickets and katydids at dusk, singing in perfect harmony with the tiny rays of lightning bugs - and she knew she would be homesick for them if she were elsewhere.

JH and Elisa Mae would rush home each day after school to help Evelyn with chores and with caring for Poppie. Since the day Bessie had left him in their care, she had barely spoken to them. Poppie would wander through the woods near the creek, getting his moonshine from a stiller further up the mountain. JH had tried to intervene, but to no avail. These were men that you did not reckon with. If Poppie was going to them to get his moonshine, he would have it. Most days, if Evelyn wasn't already searching for him, JH and Elisa Mae would set out to do so upon their return. Poppie would start drinking before he would come home and lose his way, forgetting which creek lead towards the farm or if he had come up or down the mountainside. JH was always cautious to keep Elisa Mae near him and would never let her get too close to the stills.

Weeks passed into months, and the postman frequently delivered letters from Charles with no return address. They were always short and addressed to Evelyn. He never mentioned work, only that he was doing well and would send money. Evelyn was hurt at his lack of communication, but she seemed to be thrilled each time a letter would arrive. She had trusted the Lord with this man and had made an oath to be his wife. She would forever be just that.

Aside from having more work to do on the farm, Elisa Mae was happy with Charles's absence. The tension that was always present when he was near had faded, and she felt happy and carefree.

From the beginning of school, Elisa Mae had become fast friends with Lorene. As soon as chores were done, she was off to run wild through the hills with her new friend. If they weren't at the swimming hole in the creek, they were exploring some unknown set of woods. There was always excitement and fun all around. Elisa Mae and Lorene would catch Junebugs, tie strings around them, and keep them for the day as pets. They always made sure to loosen the string and let them free at dusk. They caught lightning bugs in mason jars with holes poked in the lids, which lit their way when they played in the dark. Many times she had climbed the hill to the cemetery and saw the gravesite of Ella Resenger, knowing that she had been Stella's mother. She would sit in fascination, wondering who she was, what she looked like, what she enjoyed.

Elisa Mae grew this way. She was able to be a child. She had worries; she was sick often in the winter months, Little Grandpa was constantly on her mind, and she fretted over the thought of her big brother leaving, but she was a child.

Charles came home from his work in early August. He was there for Elisa Mae's 7th birthday and to see his only son off to the army. School had ended, and JH was following through with his plans. Charles entered the parlor like a whirlwind, bearing gifts for everyone and being unusually jolly. He picked up Evelyn and twirled her around. He hugged Elisa Mae tightly and shook JH's hand vigorously. He sat and spoke to everyone for quite a while, happy to be near his family again.

An hour or so passed, and everyone was in great spirits. Charles entered the bedroom to put his suitcase away, and everyone heard a loud crash of glass breaking.

Terror struck through Evelyn as she muttered, "The photograph."

Elisa Mae knew which photograph she referred to. She had placed it in their room a couple of weeks after Charles had left. Elisa Mae had stared at the handsome man in the glass frame. Something had seemed so familiar about him, but she hadn't inquired as to who he was.

"I thought I made it clear that I don' want ta see that man ever again! Even in a photograph!" Charles had re-entered the parlor and was screaming viciously at Evelyn.

"Marlene sent it to me. I haven't seen him in so long, I just…."

"I don' care whatcha have ta say. Ain't gonna be nothing in this house to remind me of that man ever again!" He stomped away, outside into the rain that had began to pour. He shoved his hands into his pockets and walked aimlessly.

"Want me to go get him, Mama?" JH questioned.

"Leave him be. Just let him cool off some. It's my fault. I should've known better."

Evelyn walked to the small bedroom to clean up yet another mess left for her by Charles.

"Who is it, JH?" Elisa Mae's voice was soft.

JH looked distant, as if his mind had been sent into the past. "Just someone we used to know." He walked away, leaving Elisa Mae with her questions unanswered.

Charles came home later that night, calmer, but sullen and quiet.

The following day, Stella and Burke came to town, as did Mabel. Although Stella couldn't stand the thought of facing Charles, she knew she had to see her younger brother off, and she had never missed a birthday for Elisa Mae.

During their stay, Stella and Burke announced that they were going to have a baby.

"Oh, how wonderful! A baby!" proclaimed Evelyn.

Charles stood up and walked out the front door, out into the drizzling darkness of the night. Stella tried to ignore his hateful gesture, but she couldn't hide her hurt. Mabel and Evelyn gushed on about a new baby, and JH hugged Stella and congratulated her. Elisa Mae wasn't sure of how this would affect her.

After the adults had settled down in their conversation, Evelyn asked Elisa Mae what she thought of all this.

"Well, I'm not quite sure. Does that mean I'm going to have a baby brother or sister?"

"Well, yes! That's what it means! The baby will live with them in Knoxville, of course, but they'll visit just as they always do."

"Sure we will!" Stella beamed. "Are you excited about a new baby?"

"I'd love one!"

Everyone giggled, and celebrations began. There was so much to celebrate. There was a wonderful new baby on the way, Elisa Mae was turning 7, and JH was doing something noble and meaningful with his life. The war had ended three years prior, and although there was still turmoil, Evelyn felt comfortable and proud about sending him off.

The weekend was full of cakes, gifts, and feasts. Charles was present for the celebrations, but did not partake with the rest of his family. He stayed angry and bitter throughout their stay. On Monday morning, they all went to the bus station to see JH off on his new career as a military man. Elisa Mae's emotions couldn't be contained as she said her goodbyes to JH.

"I'm going to miss you so much," she said through teary eyes.

JH leaned down to face her. "I'm going to write you all the time - letters especially for you. It will be just like I'm here with you." He hated to leave her alone, but he felt certain she would be safe from Charles and his scornful ways. His concerns lied mostly with Evelyn and all the worries he was leaving her with.

"I'm so proud of you, son."

"I'm gonna miss you, Mama," JH said through the lump forming in his throat.

"Well, I'm going to miss you, too, son, but think of all the adventures ahead of you!"

JH was silent as he hugged his mother tightly. "Are you gonna be alright?"

"Of course I will, JH. Don't you worry about a thing. Remember to keep God in your heart and always know that you are in mine."

He boarded the large, silvery-grey bus and looked back one last time. Stella, Burke, Mabel, Elisa Mae, Poppie, and Evelyn all stood waving their goodbyes. Charles looked at the ground, but before the bus could close its doors, he stepped up onto the small platform.

"Don'cha forget about us, son." JH turned to look at him, and for the first time since he was a small child, they embraced.

"I won't, Daddy. I love you."

"I love ya, too. I hope ya know that."

"I do, Daddy. I do."

Charles stepped down and the doors closed.

Soon, Stella, Burke, and Mabel were saying their goodbyes as well, and they headed back to their home in Knoxville. Elisa Mae felt lonely on the silent trip back to the farm. She did not even turn to watch the dust cloud form as they drove up the mountainside. She entered their small home and went to her room. Soon, the *tink, tink, tink* of raindrops on the tin roof lulled her into a deep sleep. She dreamed of boarding a big silvery-grey bus to a destination unknown.

Although Charles had planned on returning to Knoxville for work, the hardest months of the tobacco farm were upon them. The large, green plants had to be cut, stalked, graded, and hung to dry by the end of August. Although many small farmers throughout the mountainside would ask for Evelyn's help with grading their own tobacco, she was never able due to the tremendous amount of work that their own small farm would require. From August through November, Elisa Mae would cry at the sight of Evelyn's bleeding, blistered hands. Evelyn would always comfort her in saying that all hard work yielded pain in one form or another.

Elisa Mae would help as much as she could, but she seemed to be in the way during those months. Although there was much work for her to do, she was kept busy during that time watching out for Poppie; Charles and Evelyn were unable due to their tremendous workload now that they no longer had JH to help.

In late November, Charles was extremely satisfied with the crops. It had been a very good year. He decided to take Elisa Mae with him to the auction house with their load of stalks. Elisa Mae was fascinated by the men in suits who had come from far away to bid on the local farmer's crops. Evelyn was so skilled with grading the tobacco that for several years they had received very high bids at auction. This year was no exception. Their stalks received the highest bids, and Elisa Mae finally understood the meaning of "fruits of their labor." Although she was confused at the actions and speech of the auctions, she knew they had done well in that she had never seen so much money at one time.

Charles went directly to the bank after auction and stopped at the local department store to buy a new dress for his wife. He knew that he would not be able to produce such accomplishments without her and her skills. He wanted to thank her, and the gift of a dress for Evelyn thrilled Elisa Mae.

Upon their return home, Charles carried the packaged dress under his arm and held Elisa Mae's hand as she skipped to the house. Charles was in rare, but wonderful, spirits.

Their celebration came to a startling halt when they entered the parlor and saw Evelyn's face as she sat on the couch, holding a letter in her trembling hand.

Charles dropped the package to the floor and rushed to her side.

"What is it, Ev? What's happened?"

Tears filled her eyes as she said, "I have to go back to Hickory. He's being charged with murder."

"What? Who are ya…" his voice trailed off as he looked at the floor. "Him," he stated flatly.

"I know how you feel about him, Charles, but he's my brother. I have to be there for him."

"Ya're right. Ya have ta go. I'll stay here at the farm with Elisa Mae. Has anyone told Mabel?"

"Marlene sent a letter to the both of us. I expect she'll be here shortly."

"Better git yer thin's packed then."

He left the room without another word.

Elisa Mae followed her distraught mother into the bedroom.

"What's happened, Mama?"

"My brother in Hickory is going to have to go through a trail. He killed a man. Mabel and I will be traveling to Hickory to be there for him. I'm going to need you to be the big girl that you are and help your Daddy and Little Grandpa with anything they need while I'm gone."

"Can't I go with you?"

"I'm sorry, honey, but a trial such as this is no place for a child." She broke into tears that would not stop. Elisa Mae became increasingly concerned for to cry was not Evelyn's way.

Evelyn stepped away from her suitcase, knelt beside her bed, and folded her hands to pray. Elisa Mae left her alone for her time with God and wandered to the yard where Charles stood angry and dour, staring at nothing in particular. She knew never to approach him in this state, and she longed for JH and his comfort.

Early the next day, Mabel arrived, and Evelyn's suitcase was loaded into the sedan she shared with Stella and Burke. Saying their goodbyes quickly, they were gone, leaving so much unanswered. Elisa Mae sucked back her tears as she watched them drive up the mountainside. Thunderous clouds rolled above, but she did not move. She watched the sedan until it disappeared over the mountainside. Looking at the empty fields, she shivered as the bitter cold rain began to fall.

CHAPTER NINETEEN

*E*lisa Mae's time on the farm alone with Charles and Little Grandpa was difficult. She took refuge in her schoolwork, taking care of the farm animals and playing with Lorene when she could. Charles, while not cruel, was indifferent to Elisa Mae, only speaking if he was giving an order for a chore she should complete. Little Grandpa was the only person she could talk to at home, but on some days, couldn't understand what he was saying when he did speak to her.

She gained great delight in letters that came to the home from Evelyn. Although the nature of the letters were grim, she wrote as often as she could. It was apparent that the events taking place in Hickory were taking an extreme toll on her and Mabel. When a letter would arrive, Charles would wait for Elisa Mae's return from school to read it aloud to her.

He knew deep in his mind that Elisa Mae did not know that the man spoken of in the letters was her true father, but that someday she would. It was his own way of placing a black mark in the child's heart for the man that Charles hated most in the world.

Many letters came describing the events of the trial and what had taken place. It seemed that Evelyn's brother had been driving home from work in the cotton mill one rainy night. He spotted a fellow co-worker that was walking from work. She was soaked to the bone and had no umbrella. He asked if she would like a ride. She had hesitated, but he had insisted. He drove her directly home where he was greeted by the woman's husband. Because Evelyn's brother had a reputation as a "ladies man," a term Elisa Mae did not understand or question, the husband of his co-worker assumed that there was a relationship going on between the two and vowed right then and there to kill Evylen's brother.

Rumors had quickly spread throughout the town and many were concerned for his safety, including himself. The man had vowed over and over again to kill him. He had purchased a small hand pistol to keep with him at all times in case a situation arose. A few weeks after the incident began the man came to the cotton mill nearing the end of Evylen's brother's shift. He was drunk and belligerent, screaming for Henry and that he was there to kill him. He had on an overcoat and kept his right hand tucked inside the coat, between the buttons. Henry told him to not come any closer, but the man persisted, coming nearer and nearer. Before he could react, Henry, in fear for his life, removed his pocket pistol and shot the man. After the police arrived, it was discovered that the man did not even have a weapon, and Evelyn's brother was taken into custody.

Elisa Mae had played out the events in her head the way she would if she were reading a book. She could imagine the fear that Evelyn's brother must have had in that situation. She understood why he would shoot the man, but taking another person's life was not something she could fathom. She carried no ill feelings towards Evelyn's brother for the state of events; she felt disheartened, concerned for this man that would have to live with his actions eternally.

The winter months were hard for Elisa Mae. It was a harsh, bitter cold winter, and she became ill as she did most winters. She longed for Evelyn's soft embrace, her warm words and caring touch. She received none of these things from Charles and was sent to her bed, where she would cringe at the howling winds that blew through the clapboard walls. She became desperately lonely and would delight in the letters that would come specifically addressed to her from either Evelyn or JH.

Nearing Christmas, she received a package from JH with a return address from his new station in Japan. Poppie had received the package for her and had come to her room to deliver it. She was barely able to sit up in her weakened condition, so Poppie sat on the feather bed with her and began to unwrap the package for her, pointing out the lettering from the postal services in Japan and speaking of how far the package had traveled. Elisa Mae marveled in the moment, happy that Little Grandpa was lucid enough to share this time with her and exuberant with his company.

"Well, will ya look at that?"

"What is it, Little Grandpa?"

"It seems ta be a puzzle box o' some sorts. Gonna take ya a mighty long time to figure this 'un out."

He handed the box to her and she turned it over and over in her hands. There was no obvious opening or closing, only small, almost invisible lines that made her understand that it was no ordinary block of wood. It was a light, wooden box with vibrant decorations of landscapes she had never before seen. One side pictured a woman with piles of dark hair atop her head, wearing a long, strange looking red dress. She was walking a trail made of stone. The other side was a beautiful garden with strangely shaped hedges and tiny, trimmed trees.

"Can you read the letter to me, Little Grandpa?" She was so tired that her eyes were closing, but she wanted to remember this moment with him.

"I ain't much fer readin', chil'. Never really learnt how."

"It's all right, Little Grandpa. I'll teach you someday."

He chuckled as he patted her leg, "I'd like that, Elisa Mae. I sure would like that a lot."

She laid her head back on the pillow and closed her eyes, clutching tight to the beautiful box.

She awoke to the howling winds and the sight of Charles pulling wet, almost frozen linens from the cracks in the walls and replacing them with fresh, dry linens. The window appeared white from the snow that came down hard and blew sideways in the malicious winds.

"Daddy?" Elisa Mae gasped for air.

Charles rushed to her side.

"Daddy? I can't catch my breath."

Charles lifted her from the bed and she coughed and stammered with the movement.

"Elisa Mae!" Evelyn's voice startled Charles, but to Elisa Mae, it was as if she were in the presence of an angel.

"Mama?" Elisa Mae's staggered breathing and high fever caused her to wonder if she were seeing a vision.

"Why, Charles? Why didn't you tell me she was this sick?"

"I din't realize it were that bad 'til just now."

They carried their conversation to the parlor, but the thin walls revealed her anger with him.

"Has she seen the doctor?"

"Ev, I really din't know she was this bad off. I'll run and fetch him now."

"It's no use, Charles. The roads are all covered. It's taken Mabel and me three days to get here. We just barely made it ourselves. Let me tend to her."

Evelyn's comforting hand was quickly laid upon Elisa Mae. Mabel was already setting water on the stove to warm and was rushing to and fro, fetching cool linens to place on Elisa Mae's blistering hot skin.

Elisa Mae heard Evelyn tell Mabel that she had pneumonia again. She was quite familiar with this illness as she had had it many times in the past. She drifted in and out of consciousness, no longer afraid, assured that her mama was there and all would now be fine.

Elisa Mae awoke to the blinding light of the sun shining straight into the sparkling snow. She lifted her hand over her eye, which hurt from the blazing glow; she was amazed at how much snow had fallen. The highest drifts reached well past the window sills. She arose from her bed, aware of the silence that surrounded her. She heard no voices, no roosters crowing or horses neighing, no more howling winds. She stepped barefoot to the ice cold, hard floor and jumped back onto the soft bed, searching for her woolen socks.

Walking in wild wonder to the window, she gazed at the sights before her. The sky was the bluest of blue with wispy, thin clouds streaked throughout. The mountainside, with all its trees and land, was fresh and clean, a large blanket of sparkling snow covering everything in sight. Things she knew to be there were buried - the grapevine Evelyn had planted, the laundry line, the dog houses - only the roof of the chicken coop could be seen.

Shivering from standing too close to the window, she quietly opened her wardrobe, not wanting to disturb the silence of nature, and took down a heavy robe. Wrapping it around her and tying a knot in the front, she walked through her cracked door and into the parlor. Charles, Evelyn and Mabel all sat silent in the small room filled with the warmth of the potbelly stove.

Evelyn's face lit up and tears came to her eyes when Elisa Mae entered the room.

"Praise Jesus! She's all right!" She jumped up and ran to her, holding her tightly in her thin, but strong arms.

"I'm all right, Mama. I feel fine now."

Charles had a glimmer of a tear in his eye when he came to her. He gazed at her for a moment and hugged her close.

"Don'cha ever scare me like that again, ya hear me?"

"I'm sorry, Daddy." Elisa Mae was somewhat frightened, but she also understood that this was somehow his way of saying that he was glad she was better.

He smiled gently and hugged her tight once again.

Mabel knelt down to her and looked directly into her eyes. "Ya had us scared, Miss Elisa Mae. I'm so happy you're better." Mabel never showed much emotion, but her feeling of relief was apparent.

"You sit yourself down there in front of the stove while I go clean up your room and linens."

Evelyn hugged Elisa Mae tightly once more before she was off to her duties. Mabel followed.

A few moments later, Mabel returned with the wooden box that JH had sent.

"This yours? Ya been sleepin' with it?"

"Oh, yes! JH sent it to me. Poppie brought it to me when I first got sick. I never read the letter. Could you find it for me?"

"Let me go look for it."

Elisa Mae studied the box carefully again, once more turning it over and over in her hands. A few moments later, Mabel returned with the letter that Elisa Mae had requested.

> *Dear Elisa Mae,*
> *I hope you get this before Christmas. I found it while I was out and thought about you. I miss you very much and can't wait to see you again. I'm very excited to tell you about all the things I've seen and done!*
> *Love always, JH*

Elisa Mae set the letter down beside her and studied the box more intently.

"Ya plum missed Christmas all together, young 'un." Charles said unexpectedly. "We left the little tree and all yer presents there fer ya."

Elisa Mae turned to see the tiny tree that had been decorated for Christmas sitting in the corner of the parlor. Underneath it were presents - some large, some small.

"What day is it, Daddy?"

"It's purt' near New Year. When the sun goes down and comes up again, we'll have another year under our belts."

"It's New Year's Eve?"

"It sure is!" Evelyn sang as she walked into the parlor from the back room.

"How long did I sleep, Mama?"

"Well, now, that's nothing for you to worry about. You're all better now and look at all those presents you have to open!"

Elisa Mae smiled, aside from her realization at how sick she had actually been.

Evelyn and Mabel worked in the kitchen, preparing the best meal they could and Elisa Mae delighted when she saw the food, surprised at how famished she actually was.

During their meal, Charles said, "I'm goin' to talk ta some people about gettin' us some 'lectricity in the house. Gonna have some insulation put in, too."

"Charles, that's wonderful, but won't that be expensive?" Evelyn questioned.

"Well, ya know we did real well at auction this year, and I was paid real good money for that guard's job and all. I jus' can't have them winds blowin' through the house like they do in winters like this no more. And it'd be nice fer Elisa Mae to have a light to read them books she likes so much." He smiled gently at her beaming face. "I was also plannin' on goin' back to Knoxville with Mabel and workin' at Brookside for a while, after this damn snow clears, that is."

"Well, it seems like you've got it all worked out! It would be nice to have some lights around here." Evelyn smiled sweetly as she finished her meal and began clearing dishes with Mabel and Elisa Mae.

Returning to the parlor, Elisa Mae was handed her bright, festive packages one by one. She opened a nice winter sweater, hand knitted by Marlene, two beautiful dresses made for her by Evelyn, a wonderful book of paper dolls from Mabel and a book called *Charlotte's Web* by E.B. White from Charles.

"Oh, Daddy! I've heard of this book, and I can't wait to read it!"

He was enthralled as she reveled in the book, turning each page carefully and examining the pictures. Evelyn cleaned up the mess of papers and wrappings while Mabel and Elisa Mae started delicately cutting out the paper dolls and their clothing from their paper linings. She played for hours, feeling tired, but without pain. Soon, dusk fell and Evelyn was sending Elisa Mae back to bed, feeling too much excitement and not enough rest could make her fall back into her illness.

Elisa Mae sat in her freshly cleaned bed holding the puzzle box that JH had sent her. She studied the lines intently by the candlelight. On one small side of the rectangular box was a piece about an inch wide that had veiled lines on each side. She pushed on the piece ever so slightly, and to her amazement, it moved. She pushed a little harder, but it would only move a small amount. She had seen the lines on the top of the box, the side with the woman in the red dress, and she pushed lightly on that piece, again delighted that it moved as well. Flipping the box back and forth with two pieces out of place, she could only see one more set of lines, belonging to the other side of the small end, but the top being moved just slightly caused that side to be inaccessible. She went back to the first piece and pushed again, this time realizing that it moved even further. Following her pattern, she returned to the top piece and it moved again as well. Back and forth she went with those two pieces until the lid slid completely off of the box.

"Elisa Mae, what are you doing in here? You've just about burned up that candle. You need to get to sleep!" Evelyn fussed at her gently.

"But, Mama, please! I almost have it figured out!"

Evelyn smiled at her and her diligent work with the puzzle box.

"Just a few more minutes and then it is bed for you."

"Yes, Ma'am."

Elisa Mae turned back to the box and looked inside. It was empty, but judging by its depth, she knew there was more to uncover. She turned her attention back to the opposite small end of the rectangle and pushed down on the piece. It didn't move. When she pushed upward, however, it moved up completely, revealing a tiny, round wooden handle. She pulled on it gently, and an entire piece came out of hiding from under the box. It made a chime - a chime more beautiful and exotic than any she had ever heard. Noticing there were also veiled lines on this piece, she pushed slightly and gasped when it opened up, uncovering a hidden compartment. Inside was a tiny piece of paper, written in JH's script.

Discover the secrets of this box and you can discover the secrets of yourself.

She read it over and over again, folded it, and placed it carefully inside the compartment. Then, meticulously, one by one, she replaced the parts of the box exactly as she had taken them apart.

CHAPTER TWENTY

*T*he years passed quickly for Elisa Mae.

She soon had two sisters: a young girl named Rose, and a toddler, Catherine, that had also been born to Stella and Burke. Oddly, to Elisa Mae, they didn't seem like sisters to her as she was rarely able to see either of them.

JH had returned from his station in Japan and had decided not to return to Newport, but rather to live in Knoxville where he worked at a large grocery store called Cas Walker's. So, while Elisa Mae missed him, he was still close enough that she felt the comfort of his presence.

Charles would work in Knoxville at Brookside Mill with Mabel and Stella during the off season, and during harvest times he would return to the farm and help with the crops.

Most of Elisa Mae's time was spent either with Lorene or alone on the farm with Evelyn and Poppie. There were many chores to be completed each day and the work was hard, but Elisa Mae didn't mind. She threw herself into school and her studies. She was an excellent student and volunteered for many after school activities.

Lorene had become interested in boys quite early, but Elisa Mae shied away from them, leaning more on her interest in knowledge than on boys. She knew that something about her existence was different. She had heard the hateful names her whole life and knew that she was associated with something dirty and wrong. She did not want to ever give the impression that she herself was either of those things.

On cold, dreary nights - nights that Elisa Mae was not able to wander and discover all that nature and the mountains had to offer - Evelyn and Elisa Mae would cut their own paper dolls from an old copy of a Sears catalogue. Elisa Mae would always envision her father figure in her paper doll family to be strong, handsome, and kind. He would be happy and carefree; she would have had the assurance that everything would be fine just because he was there.

"Mama, who is my real daddy?" Elisa Mae blurted out on just such a night while she flipped through the pages searching for a daddy for her paper doll family. She had grown to an age where she understood what a bastard was. She knew that Charles and Evelyn had adopted her and that Stella was her real mother, but the question of who her real father was ate at her from the inside out.

Evelyn didn't answer. She had tears in her eyes, but she remained silent. She slowly stood up from the parlor floor and politely asked Elisa Mae to clean up the mess from the paper dolls when she was finished playing. Elisa Mae knew that she had hurt her mama in some way and vowed never to ask about her real father again. Evelyn was everything to Elisa Mae and to hurt her was too much to bear.

Evelyn walked to the kitchen to begin preparing supper. Electricity had become common place in a short amount of time, as had a telephone. Food was kept fresh in the Frigidaire, and the small radio in the kitchen usually belted out the sounds of gospel music, but this evening, Evelyn needed silence for her thoughts and could not be distracted by the sound. Elisa Mae thought it strange the way Evelyn cooked supper, as if she were going through automatic motions.

After a while, Evelyn emerged from the kitchen and entered the parlor, leaving supper to simmer on the new, large white stove.

"It's time we had a talk. Come with me."

A flash of fear ran from Elisa Mae's heart into her cheeks, causing her to flush. A rage of lightning bolted through the sky, followed by a thunderous boom that shook the house's foundation. Elisa Mae wasn't sure what was to come, but she knew from the sinking feeling in her stomach that she would not like it.

Evelyn walked to the back rooms, and Elisa Mae followed. Evelyn knelt at her bed and asked Elisa Mae to kneel with her. They both folded their hands as Evelyn said her prayer. "Dear Lord, give me the strength and the courage and the wisdom to answer this child's questions that she may understand and not grow spiteful. Help me to guide her in her way and in her understanding. Stand with her always, Dear Jesus, that she may always know that she is stronger than anything that threatens to destroy her. In Your Heavenly name I pray, Amen."

Elisa Mae was even more frightened once the prayer had been said, but she somehow knew that this was one of the most important things to happen in her life. Evelyn sat on the bed and Elisa Mae followed her actions.

"You've always known that I'm not your real mama, right?"

Elisa Mae nodded.

"And you know I'm not really Stella's mama, right?"

"Yes. Daddy had another wife named Ella who was Stella's mama, but she died. I've seen her grave before."

"Yes, of course you have. Well, when I was very young I met Charles and we came to this very farm where I first met Stella."

"She didn't live with you?"

"No. She lived here on the farm with Poppie and Charles's mother, Mommie. Charles and I lived with my family in North Carolina. Stella came to visit us a few times, but it wasn't until Mommie died that she came to North Carolina to live with us."

"She must have been really sad."

"Well, Mommie wasn't a very nice person. Stella was very hurt and confused when she came to live with us."

"Was Mommie mean to Stella, Mama?"

"She was, child, she was." Her voice quivered as she spoke. "But, that's a conversation for another day."

Elisa Mae remained silent with her questions.

Evelyn sighed and looked out the window at the downpour of rain that began to beat on the sill. She distanced herself somewhat, not wanting to explain the rest of the story to this growing child she held so dear. Minutes trickled as the rain fell and splattered. Turning back, she placed her arms around Elisa Mae's shoulders.

Finally, she took a deep breath and continued, "Stella fell in love with my brother, Henry. He is your birth father." She paused and took another deep breath. "He was a handsome fella, he sure was. Still is, too. All the ladies would swoon over him." She smiled slightly, and Elisa Mae noticed how her eyes lit up when she spoke of him. "He loved Stella, too. He did. But, he was already married, and his wife was expecting a baby." Pausing momentarily she stated, "You have a brother that is just about the same age as you. After you and he were born, Henry's wife had another baby that died in its sleep. She was a girl. Henry came home to find her rocking the dead baby in her arms. She'd been that way for hours. It was just awful." Evelyn shook her head of the thought, not wanting to bring back the memory.

Elisa Mae's head began to swim, and her chest felt heavy.

"Charles became very, very angry and did a lot of nasty things during that time," Evelyn continued. "He hated Henry and still does. That's why we don't visit North Carolina much and why he doesn't like for me to go." She took another deep breath and let out a long sigh before going on. "When Stella had you, she felt that she didn't have a choice but to leave you with me. She didn't want to break up Henry's marriage to Justine, and she knew she couldn't raise you alone. She has always loved you, I want you to know that." She paused for another moment, adding, "You must never tell your daddy I told you these things. I promise you that someday you will meet your birth father, but you must never, ever mention him to your daddy."

"Yes, Ma'am."

Evelyn hugged her tight and retuned to her duties in the kitchen. Elisa Mae sat stunned, unmoving. She somehow knew that Evelyn had made a great sacrifice for her, and she wondered how she would ever be able to repay her. Thoughts raced through her mind. She imagined that if she were able to find him, to meet him, things would be better. She wouldn't feel any anger, she wouldn't feel any pain. Most of all, he would make her feel pretty. Having been called a bastard her entire life, pretty was a word that Elisa Mae felt did not describe her.

Her thoughts were sent reeling with the thought of having a brother her same age. She wanted to talk to JH. She could not imagine any other brother. She stood from the bed and walked to the black telephone that sat on the small table in the parlor. Flipping through the small, black address book she found the number she was searching for and began to tediously circle the 0 through the rotary telephone. When the operator answered, she told her that she was making a long distance call and gave her the numbers needed. Soon, there was the sound of a connect and ringing.

"Hello, Cas Walker's. Where our melons are thumpin' good. Can I help you?"

"Could I speak with JH Resenger, please?"

"Well, certainly, little lady! This must be Miss Elisa Mae! We've all heard lots about you! Let me run fetch him for ya."

"Thank you." Elisa Mae sat patiently on the other end of the receiver while she heard all sorts of bustle and commotion through the line. Finally, JH answered.

"Elisa Mae? You OK? Everything alright?"

"Yes, I'm fine. I guess. I just wanted to talk to you is all."

"Sounds like something's wrong."

"Well, I don't know. I just. Um, …Mama talked to me and told me a lot of stuff."

"What kind of stuff?"

Elisa Mae sucked in her breath. "She, um…." Her voice cracked. "She told me about my real daddy and said I had a brother my age and a baby sister that died." Tears streamed her cheeks and she wiped them swiftly.

"I worked the morning shift today. I'll be off work in an hour and I'll head that way. Hold tight. I'll be there as soon as I can."

"Alright," Her voice quivered as she slowly replaced the receiver.

She aimlessly walked to the kitchen to help Evelyn continue preparing supper. Elisa Mae used automatic motions now, too; both were lost in their own thoughts.

It was just past dusk when Elisa Mae spotted JH's Ford truck rolling up the road with its dust cloud following.

"Well, who could this be?" Evelyn said out loud, but more to herself.

"It's JH!" Elisa Mae almost squealed with delight.

Elisa Mae, Evelyn, and Poppie came to the front porch and waited as he pulled in. Elisa Mae ran to the truck as he came to a stop.

"Thank you for coming," she whispered as she hugged him.

"I told ya I'd always be here for ya."

"JH! It's so good to see you!" Evelyn was walking his way, wiping her hands on her apron. "What are you doing here?"

"Well, I was just missing y'all. I wanted to take Elisa Mae for an ice cream, too."

"It's getting pretty late, JH. She has school tomorrow."

"I know. We won't be long." He was already opening the truck door for Elisa Mae to enter. "I'll visit with you some more when we get back."

Evelyn just shook her head and smiled.

"Love you, Mama!" JH shouted as he jumped in the truck and backed out.

Elisa Mae loved to be in JH's truck. It was louder and faster than any other vehicle she had ever ridden in. He drove into town and pulled up to Stokely's Drug Store. They went in and walked across the black and white tile floors to the counter where they sat and JH ordered a milkshake. Neither he nor Elisa Mae had spoken a word since they had left the farm. Elisa Mae watched the young man with the white cap spin the milkshake in the tin cup. He came back and placed the shake in front of them with two straws. Elisa Mae picked up her straw and sucked, delighting in the flavor of the cold chocolate. People passing were giving their hellos to JH.

"You gonna drink it all?" he asked.

Elisa Mae almost shot shake through her nose when she laughed.

They both laughed for a moment before JH asked, "So, Mama told ya everything I guess."

Elisa Mae set the straw back in the tin cup and nodded her head.

"She told me never to tell Daddy she told me."

"That'd be best," he stated. "Daddy's mean and ornery enough as it is. You mention Henry to him, he goes insane."

"Do you know him?"

"Well, sure I do. I know him well. I haven't seen him in a long time, but yeah, I know him."

"Is it the same man that went to prison?"

JH nodded his head slowly. "It is. I want you to know he feels real bad about that. I don't know if he could feel any worse."

"I'm not mad at him or anything," she stated. "I really felt sorry for him when it happened."

"He's out of prison now. Did she tell you that?"

"No."

"He got out early for good behavior. He lives in Virginia now. He had to get special permission to leave the state, but it was easy for him because they need so many people up in Norfolk to work on them ships. Abe, Marlene's husband, works up there with him."

Elisa Mae's thoughts took on shapes of their own as they drank their milkshake in silence.

"Did she tell you she'd take you to meet him?" JH asked after a long while.

"She said I'd meet him someday."

"Then I'll be with you when someday comes."

"You mean it?"

"Of course I do. I'm making a promise to you right now that I will never let anything hurt you. Ever. If you're afraid to meet him or you're nervous, or whatever, I want to be there for you."

"Thank you, JH. I love you." She stood from her stool and hugged him tight.

"I love you, too, squirt. Remember, whenever you need me," he said as he winked at her.

As they were leaving, he stopped in the parking lot to talk to June. He had had his eye on her for a while now. She was a pretty girl with hair as black as the midnight sky. They spoke for a while before he entered the truck.

"You like her," Elisa Mae teased.

"Shut up." He smiled as he said it.

"You're going to marry her."

"Shut up."

"JH and June, sittin' in a tree," she sang.

He smiled broadly as he allowed her to continue.

CHAPTER TWENTY-ONE

*O*n the summer that Elisa Mae was to turn 15, Evelyn made good on her promise. She was taking her to see her family in North Carolina and to meet Henry, her real father, for the first time.

JH had returned to Newport and had married June, just as Elisa Mae had predicted. A couple of acres on the land further up the mountain that had housed fields of tobacco had been cleared, and JH and June's home now sat there, along with a barn, chicken coop, and other necessary items needed to maintain a home in the mountains. The tobacco fields were the shared responsibility of JH as well as Charles, Evelyn, and Mabel. Mabel had returned to the farm, and she took over the room that had been built for JH. The room became forever known as *Mabel's Room*.

JH and June drove to North Carolina ahead of Mabel, Evelyn, and Elisa Mae. Charles had been called to work in Knoxville, and while he knew they were going for a visit, he had no idea that Henry would be there.

Elisa Mae marveled at the trip up the mountainside. She soaked in every inch of green leaves and swaying trees, the rushing mountain river, deer and squirrel running to and fro. She appreciated the harmony and the nature that surrounded her, and she reveled in it. She had daydreams of better days ahead – glamorous days, exciting days.

The long drive passed quickly, and Elisa Mae was soon gushed over by aunts she knew that had visited Newport and cousins galore that overwhelmed her. JH rushed out and swooped in, taking her inside, away from the madness that surrounded her. June laughed as she saw Elisa Mae's stunned face.

"Everyone's been talkin' 'bout ya fer days. Excitement and all. They'll calm down in a bit."

Elisa Mae relaxed just slightly as the aunts and cousins and Grandma and Grandpa Lenfield entered the house.

"Slow down," JH ordered. "Y'all are scarin' her half to death!"

Grandma and Grandpa Lenfield approached and gave Elisa Mae big hugs and kisses. It had been years since they had seen her. Their conversation was based around how much she'd grown.

"Give us a chance to see her!" Marlene pushed her way into the crowd to hug Elisa Mae. "My how we've missed you!"

All the aunts agreed. The conversation became loud again as everyone spoke over each other.

"I've missed you all, too. So much," Elisa Mae said loudly over all their voices. "I'm so happy to see you all. I guess I just need a minute to catch my breath!" She smiled sweetly at all of them, and they could all see the love in her heart.

Soon, she calmed down as one by one, cousin by cousin, everyone was introduced.

The rest of the evening was a whirlwind of activity and commotion. Elisa Mae fell into her bed that night and into a deep sleep, dreaming of a family she'd never known and the love, care, and devotion they would offer.

She rose early, with the rooster's crow as was her way. She walked down the staircase quietly, not wanting to disturb anyone who was not yet awake. She entered the kitchen where Marlene and Evelyn stood whispering over coffee at the table.

"Well, good morning!" Evelyn sang in her lovely voice.

"Good morning. What's going on?"

Evelyn and Marlene exchanged glances and were silent for a moment.

"Well, Elisa Mae, your father is here in town, with his boy, Tommy. He's wanting to meet you."

Elisa Mae froze in place. She knew that this was her reasoning for coming here, but the thought of actually meeting him face to face had not occurred to her until that very moment. She sat silent, thinking, pondering. Soon, without a word, she stood up and walked to the bedroom that had been set for her visit.

What seemed like hours later, there was a light rapping on the door.

"Come in," Elisa Mae managed to squeak out.

JH entered and sat next to her on the bed. "How ya doin', squirt?"

Elisa Mae couldn't contain her tears as they rushed forth. "What am I going to do, JH? What am I going to say to him? I'm so scared right now. I really am!"

"I know ya are. Who wouldn't be? Tell ya what. Ya go in there and wash up your face and take you a good long nap. It'll do ya good. When ya get up, me, you, and June will go to a drive-in movie. Any movie you want to see. It'll help get your mind off of things."

"Thanks, JH. I love you." She hugged his neck tight before following his instructions.

She decided to take a bath in the luxurious bathtub that she had yet to see. The suds around her body relaxed and calmed her. After she bathed, she chose a light sundress for her evening out. She tried to nap as JH had told her to, but sleep evaded her. She tossed and turned, wondering what was to become of her and her life now. In the blink of an eye, all had changed.

Nearing dusk, JH lightly rapped on the door once more. "You about ready?"

"Yes. I'm almost done."

"That dress sure does look pretty on ya, Elisa Mae."

She blushed at the thought and was instantly grateful for the love and support of Mama and JH.

Elisa Mae had so much going through her mind that she couldn't even concentrate on the movie at the drive-in. She couldn't tell you the name or the actors, and truth be told, she really didn't care. Thoughts of a new father and brother consumed her.

"Tell me about him," Elisa Mae whispered.

JH thought for a moment. "He's a good man. A fine man. He tries real hard, but he just can't ever get it straight. That's his downfall, I guess. He likes to drink too much, and he loves women. All women. He's a true ladies man, and everyone knows it. Gets him into trouble a lot."

June poked JH in the ribs.

"Like with my mama, Stella, and all," Elisa Mae pondered aloud.

"Yeah, like that." He turned around in the backseat to face Elisa Mae. "You've heard bad stuff said about you your whole life. I'm sure you know what those things mean by now. I want you to know that you are NOT a bastard. You are a loved, cared for young woman that just about anybody would lay their life down for." He paused momentarily. "Look, if you don't want to meet him, don't meet him. No one, and I mean no one, is going to make you do anything you don't want to do. Don't you dare make him think you aren't good enough or that you're inferior to him. You've been called a bastard your whole life and it ain't true. It just ain't true. None of anything that happened was your fault. None of it."

He had tears forming in his eyes, and June touched him lightly on the arm, letting him know she was there and understood.

That night, while Elisa Mae fell into sleep, she had made up her mind that she did not want to meet Henry. She slept in a bit later than usual and when she did wake, she found Evelyn and Marlene canning apples in the kitchen with the back door wide open, letting in the fresh air. Elisa Mae hadn't even had the chance to say good-morning when Marlene screamed, "Oh dear God, I've cut my finger."

Blood rushed forth from Marlene's sliced finger while Evelyn and Elisa Mae ran to bring fresh linens to seal the wound.

"I didn't know I'd cause *that* much commotion," a deep, handsome voice spoke behind them. "Are you alright, Marlene?"

"Yes, I think its fine. No need for stitches or anything. You startled me bad when I saw ya at the back door."

Elisa Mae stood stiff with fear. She could feel his presence, feeling, knowing he was a part of her. She turned slowly to face him. She saw that he was wearing a grey suit with a red tie. His dark, wavy hair was combed back, and his blue eyes sparkled, just as Evelyn had described him. He was extraordinarily handsome in every way.

Evelyn stayed utterly silent, as if all words had escaped her. She tended to Marlene's wound to keep herself occupied.

"Are you Elisa Mae?" He directed the question to her, but she could not look into his eyes.

"I am."

"Well, I guess that makes me your daddy."

"That's what I've been told."

Their conversation was distant, almost bitter. Henry tried to lighten the load by offering to take her shopping and buy her a new dress – whatever she wanted.

"Only if Mama can come," was Elisa Mae's shy response.

Henry looked around cautiously, his eyes darting back and forth. "Your mama? She here?"

"She means me, Henry. I'm her mama," Evelyn broke her silence.

"Of course you are!" He looked at Evelyn as if he were just seeing her, picked her up and swung her tiny frame through the air until she begged him to stop. "You wouldn't believe how much I've missed ya."

"Oh, yes I would, because I've missed you just the same!" Evelyn had a light that shone bright in her eyes when she was near him. Charles's forced distance between them had made their relationship even closer. When they were able to communicate, it was obvious that each held a very deep love for the other.

Elisa Mae moved slowly, almost cautiously, as she dressed. She chose the finest dress she had brought, a light-colored, cool green dress that came off the shoulders just slightly. She painstakingly combed through her dark curls, twisting them with her fingers as she went.

Evelyn entered her room. "Are you nervous?"

Elisa Mae, who had been pinching her cheeks and biting her lips for color, stopped and stared at Evelyn in the mirror. "Yes, Mama. I am. Would you look at me? I feel like I'm getting ready for a date or something!"

"Well, you are in a way."

"It's just so strange, Mama. I don't know what to say."

"Say what's in your heart, girl. That's all you have to do." Evelyn patted her shoulder. "You ready?"

"Ready as I'll ever be, I guess."

Henry took Evelyn and Elisa Mae to the finest department store that Elisa Mae had ever seen. There were sales clerks everywhere, women spraying you with a new line of perfume, racks and racks of clothing and shoes - Elisa's Mae's eyes lit up in wonder and amazement.

They laughed and talked like old friends, all of them shopping, each lost in their enjoyment of the situation. Elisa Mae was smitten with Henry. She was proud he was her father. She knew of his faults; she had decided early on that all men had faults, but she could overlook his, because to her, he could easily become her world.

After hours of shopping, they left the fashionable department store with a beautiful new dress, a new bathing suit, and a stunning new necklace. Elisa Mae was thrilled in a way she had never known before.

She dreamed again that night of better days to come.

Early the next day, Elisa Mae got dressed and went to the kitchen to begin her day helping with the various chores and tasks to be done. Evelyn shooed her out of the kitchen and told her to go play, that there was plenty of help.

Elisa Mae walked outside and around the house to the swing that sat in the yard. She sat in the swing, swaying back and forth slowly, replaying the perfect events that had happened the day prior. Something smacked her on the arm, and it stung a bit. She dismissed it, thinking a bug had flown into her, but it happened again and then a third time. She began to look around and finally spied the boys on the balcony, throwing spit wads at her.

They were perched upon the wrap around porch on the second tier of the home. She knew that Larry and Marlon were cousins, but she didn't know the third boy. Their eyes met, and for the first time, her heart skipped a beat for a boy. She was enjoying their attention and giggling when the third boy started to run down the side staircase towards her. Larry yelled something at him and tried to stop him, but he was gone in a flash and at Elisa Mae's side in an instant. Their eyes met, and they both smiled a smile that warmed their hearts.

"Elisa Mae! We have to talk!" Larry called from the upper balcony.

She looked up at him to say OK, but the boy gently pulled her face to his and looked into her eyes.

"I think you're really cute, and I'd like to take you to the drive-in tonight."

Elisa Mae blushed as she had never actually been asked out by a boy before. Up to this point, she had tried to ignore their advances.

"I know you're my cousin and Aunt Ev is your mama, but Marlon said you're adopted, so that means we ain't really kin."

"You sure do know a lot about me."

"I think you are the prettiest girl I've ever laid eyes on. You're my kissin' cousin, and I'm gonna kiss you tonight." He smiled a crooked smile, a familiar smile. "I'm guessin' that's rude. My name is Tommy Lenfield. Henry is my dad. He's Ev's brother."

Elisa Mae couldn't find her breath. Her chest felt heavy and painful.

"Ya alright?" Tommy was worried with her reaction.

Larry ran up to them just in time to see Elisa Mae stand from the swing and run into the house crying. She ran straight to Evelyn and flung her arms around her.

"What is it, honey? What's happened?

"I want to go home! I want to go home now!" Elisa Mae screamed through her tears. Her words flowed fast and free as she told her the events that had taken place.

"He doesn't know about me, Mama! No one's ever told him! He's going to hate me!"

"Now, now, it'll be alright." Evelyn stroked Elisa Mae's hair, but concern covered her face.

The commotion brought JH, June, Mabel, and Marlene into the kitchen, which caused more commotion. JH was cussing and screaming, Mabel was trying to calm Elisa Mae who was still crying hysterically, and Marlene was calling Henry telling him he needed to get to the house now.

Elisa Mae ran to her room, crying uncontrollably. Understanding that she could not be consoled, the others left her to be alone with her thoughts and her pains. She closed the door and locked the lock, not wanting to speak with anyone.

She soon heard a vehicle pulling into the drive and saw Henry taking Tommy with him. Tommy had stood looking at the house, obviously wondering what was occurring, but he now seemed concerned with his father's presence. Elisa Mae backed away from the window, threw herself to the bed, and cried until there were no more tears to cry.

She wondered if anyone had ever felt this betrayal she felt – the betrayal of the denial of her existence. She felt certain that Tommy would hate her and would never want to see her again. Henry would certainly understand that Elisa Mae was a burden to his family and would want nothing more to do with her.

She stood from the bed and removed the necklace her father had given her. She placed it neatly on the vanity and walked away. Dressing for bed, she dreamed fretful dreams filled with horror and dread.

Evelyn was knocking loudly at the locked door sometime in the late morning hours. Elisa Mae had finally fallen into a deep sleep around 2 AM, causing her to be groggy and hard to wake. She rose from the bed and unlocked the door, letting her mama inside.

"How are you feeling?"

"Not so good, Mama. I didn't sleep well at all last night. I know we have a family outing planned today, but I really don't feel like being around anybody. Is that alright?"

"That's perfectly fine, sweetheart. You've been through a lot. You get some rest, and you'll feel better this evening." Evelyn patted her on the knee and kissed her forehead. "You're a strong girl. You're going to make it through this."

Elisa Mae was slow in getting up and dressing. She didn't care much what she looked like and barely ran a comb through her hair. In the late morning, when everyone had gone, she ventured outside to the swing. She swung slowly back and forth, trying to collect her thoughts.

"Ya know what my daddy told me last night?"

The voice from behind her made Elisa Mae jump and goose bumps broke out all over her body.

She turned to face him. "Yes."

"It true?"

"That's what I've been told."

He came around to the swing and sat beside her. Tears formed in the corners of his eyes as he looked at the ground. "I can't believe they never told me I had another sister. They told me I had a baby sister that died. I go see her grave. But they never told me about you. Why would they never tell me about you?"

"I'm sorry." Elisa Mae realized that he felt just as betrayed as she did.

"I'll never forgive them for not telling me." A tear rolled down his cheek. "I fell in love with you yesterday. That will never change. You're the most beautiful girl I've ever seen in my life." He paused for a moment. "And I'm still taking you to the drive-in, and I'm still gonna kiss ya. I just ain't figured out how yet."

They both giggled at his revelation and then fell into each other's arms and cried. After releasing their embrace Tommy kissed Elisa Mae softly on the cheek and whispered, "I will always love you."

CHAPTER TWENTY-TWO

*T*ommy was heartbroken when Elisa Mae had to leave for Tennessee; they had become very close in her short stay. They had visited the cemetery of their deceased baby sister and shared secrets that only a brother and sister could share. He told her of his hatred for Henry and Justine for keeping her from him. She begged him not to hang on to the hatred in his heart.

They wrote each other often, hiding their letters by addressing them to Mabel or Evelyn with no return address.

The summer that had started out so shocking and cruel to Elisa Mae had become one of the best summers she had ever known.

The small town of Newport was growing rapidly. New diners and shops were popping up everywhere. Downtown was becoming a small, but bustling city.

That very same summer, the Splash-A-Way pool opened for its debut. It was a large hole dug in the ground, sealed in concrete, and filled with water. A diving board was soon added to the deep end. Along with the enjoyment of swimming on hot summer days, there was a building with a concession stand and a patio next to the pool where music played loudly from a jukebox and regular sock-hops were held. At dark, when swimming was not safe, each teen would emerge from the pool and dance to the new rock and roll music.

The Splash-A-Way pool was not a place that Charles liked for Elisa Mae to be, but pressure from Evelyn to let her be a teenager kept him at bay, even though he would drive by on various occasions to check up on what Elisa Mae was doing or wearing.

Nearing the end of the summer, Elisa Mae and Lorene stood under the patio doing the jitterbug to "Rock Around the Clock" by Bill Haley and His Comets. Halfway through the song, the sound of loud, revving engines could be heard above the booming jukebox.

Four guys on motorcycles pulled into the parking lot, causing everyone to stop and stare. They all wore jeans and rugged, brown leather jackets. They stayed gathered in the parking lot for a while, seemingly checking out the scene.

After removing their helmets, Lorene nudged Elisa Mae, "That one's mine. The blond. The cute one."

This had always been their way and Elisa Mae expected no less from Lorene. She pretended to be uninterested in the boys and continued dancing, but she made sure to position herself so that she could see their every move.

The boy that Lorene had been interested in started walking in their direction. Lorene began to flip her long hair over her shoulder in an attempt to flirt. You could almost hear her puff of anger as he walked directly past her and straight to Elisa Mae. "Been watching you dance. You're good. Wanna dance with me?"

By that time, Jerry Lee Lewis's "Whole Lotta Shakin'" began to play and without a word, they danced. She smiled and laughed as they moved in perfect harmony. They buzzed around each other, he swung her around and they danced until they both felt they would fall over from exhaustion.

"Let's grab a drink," he said to her.

She had yet to speak to him. She was lost in her own world. He was older than her, much older, but she didn't care. The entire world had disappeared at the sight of him. She followed him to the concession stand where he ordered two Cokes. They worked their way through the crowd to a small table near the edge of the patio. Many people stared in their direction, but Elisa Mae didn't notice. She also didn't notice the way that Lorene stared at them. Her glare was jealous, vicious and evil.

"Where'd you learn to dance like that?" he asked.

"American Bandstand. Lorene, my friend, and I practice in my parlor when it's on," she motioned to her and waved. Lorene gave a big smile and waved back enthusiastically.

"What's your name?"

"Elisa Mae."

"Pretty name for a pretty girl."

Elisa Mae blushed instantly in spite of herself.

"Albert!" One of his friends was calling for him. "Let's blow this joint."

"I gotta run. Maybe I can come over and watch American Bandstand with you sometime."

"I'd like that a lot."

Before he stood, he kissed her. Not only was it her first kiss, it was a kiss that made her heart thump and her knees shake. He gently touched her chin as his soft lips left hers.

"I'll see you again soon, Elisa Mae."

Elisa Mae sat in a daze, staring into the darkness of the field beyond the patio. She heard the engines rev and pull out of the gravel parking lot, but she couldn't look back. She couldn't bear the thought of what had just occurred only being a dream.

"What was that all about?" Lorene's voice behind her gave her a start.

She turned to face Lorene and said, "I don't know, but wasn't he just dreamy? I mean, why me?"

"I don't know, but you two were getting awfully close and everyone was starin' at ya." She had been friends with Elisa Mae long enough to know that this was a soft spot for her. "And what about that kiss? Boy, that's sure to get some people talkin'!"

"Shut up, Lorene! I like him. He's the first boy I've ever really liked. You've been through a dozen! Why are you acting this way?"

"He's a hood."

"Because he drives a motorcycle?"

"No, he's just a hood."

"And before he talked to me, you wanted him! Ya know what? Just never mind." Elisa Mae turned and walked away from Lorene, leaving her on the patio. Lorene was yelling something as she walked away, but Elisa Mae ignored her words.

Pat and Bo were getting into their car when Elisa Mae walked to the parking lot carrying her bag. "Could y'all give me a ride home?"

"Sure!" Bo said, "Hop in!"

Pat pulled up the front seat so Elisa Mae could slide into the back of Bo's Mercury. Once she was in the backseat, Pat slid into the front and closed the door. "Do you know Albert? You ever met him before?"

"No," Elisa Mae said quietly with a blush. Maybe Lorene's accusations were merited.

Bo turned the engine and put the car into gear. "He's a great guy. I've known him a long time. It's just him and his mama. They live way, way off Cosby Highway. He can fix damn near anything. Did you see that bike he was ridin'? That was a 1940 Indian Chief he found junked and fixed it up. Looked brand new, din' it?"

Elisa Mae didn't know much about motorcycles, but it sounded impressive to her. She was soaking up any bit of information she could on him.

"He sure was smitten with ya," Bo said with a smile.

"He sure was," Pat sang back.

Elisa Mae turned her head to the side and blushed.

Elisa Mae sat in church the next day in a daze. She usually sat with Lorene, but she had chosen to sit with Evelyn and Mabel this morning.

After church, people congregated in the yard, speaking of their week and the weeks to come. Elisa Mae stood silently while the adults around her carried on their conversation. Lorene walked up to her and grabbed her arm, pulling her towards the large shade tree.

"So, did you go home with him last night?"

"That's none of your business, but you know that I didn't."

"What's gotten into you girls?" Evelyn and Mabel were walking up behind them.

"Nothing, Mama. We just had a little fight last night."

"Yeah, Elisa Mae was hanging out with a hood and she kissed him!"

"Lorene!" Elisa Mae felt like punching her in the face.

"A hood, huh? Well, I guess we better talk about that. Come on, Elisa Mae, let's get home. Have a good day, Lorene!"

Evelyn smiled to herself as Elisa Mae and Mabel got into the family sedan. Mabel started the engine while Elisa Mae started pleading with Evelyn.

Evelyn turned full around in the backseat to face Elisa Mae. "You think I don't know that girl? She's just jealous of you. She's always been the one to get the boys and she's probably just angry because this one was interested in you instead of her."

Elisa Mae smiled inside her soul at the depths of Evelyn's wisdom.

"And besides that, I'll be the one to see if he's a hood or not. When do I get to meet him?"

"Well, umm, ...I don't know. I just met him last night. Bo, Pat's boyfriend, has known him for a long time. Hopefully we can talk again soon."

Evelyn smiled and patted her hand. "I hope so, too, sweetheart."

A week later, Elisa Mae was walking down the main road to Foster and Bessie's for a visit when an old, rusted Ford step-side truck pulled up next to her.

"Wha'cha doin'?"

Elisa Mae couldn't contain her delight. "Hi, Albert! Is this your truck? I thought you had a motorcycle."

"Come on in. Let's go for a ride."

She practically jumped into the truck as he slid across the seat and swung the door open for her. They drove aimlessly down country roads with beautiful scenery all around, jumping through various conversations, as if each were yearning to know more of the other as quickly as possible.

He told her that he worked on cars, trucks, plows, you name it. Usually if the person that owned the vehicle felt that it wasn't worth fixing, they gave it to him. He would tinker with the item until he got it working again and would either sell it or keep it for a while to drive for himself. He told her of his family and home life, how it was just he and his mother. His father had left them when he was first born and they had no other family. It had been a hard life, but like so many others, they survived.

Elisa Mae told Albert all about her family and home at the farm. She told him she was adopted, but she was leery to tell him more. She told him about Charles and how everyone in town was afraid of him, including herself at times, but that he had never hurt her.

"I've heard about Charles Resenger," Albert stated. "They say he ain't one to reckon with."

"No, he isn't. That's for sure." She paused for a moment. "Speaking of which, my mama would like to meet you. Would you like to come over? I'm not sure if my daddy will be back yet. He works in Knoxville and only comes to town during crop time. He's due home any day."

"Well, I'd love to!" He had a sparkle about him. He was charismatic and charming. He was someone people were drawn to – his mysteriousness, his air of confidence, his sense of humor, his pride, his handsomeness, the way he carried himself – all of these things made him a person you wanted to be around.

They pulled into Elisa Mae's drive and saw Charles's beat up truck as well as the family sedan. Elisa Mae's heart stopped. "They're all here." You could hear the fear in her voice.

"It's alright," Albert said in his cheery way, "Come on, this will be fun!"

Elisa Mae's heart was pounding out of her chest as they walked through the gate and onto the porch. She opened the door cautiously, curiously. "Mama?" No response. "Daddy?" No response. "Mabel?" No response. Albert was poking her in the ribs the whole time, causing her to giggle uncontrollably.

"Elisa Mae?" It was Evelyn's voice calling to her. "We're out at the back house."

Elisa Mae began walking through the yard past the long line of kitchen windows. Albert walked in perfect pace with her and grabbed her hand. She almost pulled away, but the feeling of his hand in hers was like nothing she had ever felt and she couldn't let go. They walked around the side of the house and came to the back house. All three of the doors were opened and they all stood in the middle room, the canning room.

"Mama, Daddy, Mabel, this is Albert."

They all exited the small room and examined the man that stood before them.

Albert released his grip of Elisa Mae's hand and extended his right hand to Charles. "Pleased to meet you, Mr. Resenger."

Charles stuck out his hand and firmly shook Albert's, but the look of confusion was apparent on his face.

"It's so nice to meet you, Albert. I've heard a lot about you." Evelyn was genuine in her speech.

"Likewise, Mrs. Resenger." He bowed down to her slightly. "And, is it Miss or Mrs.?" he directed at Mabel.

"It's Mabel." She laughed and shook his hand lightly.

"Hi, Daddy. I'm glad you're home. Why is everyone out here?"

"It seems we have a leak," Charles stated flatly.

"I'd be happy to help you with it, Sir," Albert offered.

Charles looked at him and cocked a slight smile before walking back into the room, explaining to Albert where he thought the problem was. Albert winked at Elisa Mae before following him into the room.

"We're going to fix up some supper, and you're staying, Albert."

"Well, yes, Ma'am, I'd like that." He smiled his best smile at Evelyn and looked back at Elisa Mae one last time with the same, sweet smile.

The women walked into the kitchen and began preparing their meal.

"Well, he's a lot cuter than you told me he was."

"Mama!"

"And older," said Mabel. "How old is he?"

"He's 22." Elisa Mae spoke softly.

"And you just turned 15. Well, that's the way these things go sometimes. I mean, look at me and your daddy." Evelyn was referring to their age difference of almost 10 years. She thought for a moment. "Well, no, that's not a good example." They all giggled. "But he seems like a fine young man."

"He is, Mama. He really is."

From then on, Elisa Mae and Albert were inseparable. They would have great times and wonderful adventures. Many times he had taken her to Knoxville and each time she was fascinated. When they would go that far, they were usually with Pat and Bo, as Bo was good friends with Albert and Pat and Elisa Mae had become close due to Lorene's actions.

Albert introduced Elisa Mae to adventures unknown. They went to an all black concert in Knoxville that featured artists such as Chuck Berry, Fats Domino and Bo Diddley – greats that were not played on radio stations in the south. They had a wonderful time and danced the night away. He took her to see a wrestling match in Knoxville as well, which was something she never knew existed. It enthralled her and exhilarated her. Each time she was with him, she felt this way.

As with any man she knew, along with the good came the bad. He would sometimes disappear for two or three weeks and return as if nothing had happened. Elisa Mae's good girl ways were questioned with his outlandish behavior. After coming to a school sock-hop drunk, spiking the punch, and rushing her off on his motorcycle for a far better party, she was removed from her post as editor of the school paper.

Tommy had written to Elisa Mae and told her he was going to join the Navy. That was the last time she heard from him. He was so confused and hurt over his life being a lie that he had to leave it all behind and start again. Elisa Mae was grateful that she had Albert. As wild as he was, he kept her grounded. Many times he had pressured her to go farther with him than she cared for. When she got the letter from Tommy, she decided to tell him the entire story of her existence and why she was so hesitant to take their relationship any farther.

Evelyn surprised Elisa Mae on her 16th birthday with a party at the Splash-A-Way pool. Everyone came and it was a wonderful evening. She received her first pair of red high-heeled shoes and danced with Albert to Elvis's "Hound Dog". She thought the night couldn't be any more perfect.

Evelyn had left early and let her stay through the evening. She was with Bo, Pat and Albert and was told that her curfew was 11 o'clock. As much as she didn't want the night to end, they all knew that Charles would be furious if she were late. They all left the party, and Elisa Mae felt downhearted. Even though the lights had been turned up, the jukebox had been turned off, and the only people left were doing clean up, she didn't want this perfect evening to end.

They all climbed into Bo's Mercury and pulled into the Resenger drive around 10 minutes early for curfew. They were all still happy and elated from the party and were singing songs along to the radio and acting silly.

Albert was approaching the door with Elisa Mae when it was flung open harshly. Charles stood glaring at them with wild eyes. His hair was a mess, and his face was unshaven. He held firmly to his shotgun, which was aimed at Albert. He grabbed Elisa Mae's arm and started pulling her into the house. Elisa Mae could see Evelyn on the floor with her arms outreached, screaming her prayers to God.

"Please don't hurt her, Mr. Resenger."

"Get th' hell offa my property before I blow yer brains out, boy."

Bo and Pat were screaming for Albert to get over the fence. Elisa Mae was screaming for him to leave before Daddy hurt him. Albert was stunned and confused. He had never seen this kind of behavior in Charles, and he was dumbfounded by the events taking place. He was terrified for Elisa Mae, but when he heard the cock of the shotgun, he ran. Charles set off a blast into the air before pulling Elisa Mae inside, throwing her to the floor and slamming the door. Evelyn continued to pray her prayers with tears streaming her face.

He pulled Elisa Mae's tiny body off of the floor and had the cocked shotgun pointed directly at her face. "If you move, I'll kill you." She didn't dare move, and he turned the barrel to the side. He began to yell in her face. "Ya ain't nothin' but a whore, just like your mother, and I won't have no more bastards livin' in this family!"

"You are NOT my father and you will NOT talk to me like that!"

Blackness surrounded her.

When she woke, she thought he had shot her because of the blood and pain in the side of her face and jaw. Evelyn and JH were beside her, helping her to sit up. She looked around cautiously.

"He's gone," JH said. "For now."

"Did he shoot me?" Her words sounded strange, she couldn't form them. She touched her face and felt searing pain through her jaw.

"Nah. He hit ya. Hard. Clipped ya with his ring, too. I think you've lost a tooth."

Her face was already swelling and bruising. JH and Evelyn cleaned her up and got her to the bed. The tears that streamed down her face stung in the open wounds. She continued to let them flow as she figured she somehow deserved this because of who she was. The *tink, tink, tink* on the tin roof kept her awake. She laid on her back and watched the ceiling as the rain grew heavier and stronger. Just before daylight, he entered her room quietly. She bolted straight up.

"Get yer things."

"Where am I going?" Her voice shook when she spoke.

"To Stella's. Ya're both a couple of whores, and ya deserve each other." He had his shotgun propped on his shoulder. "Ya wake Ev, and I'll kill ya." He left the room as silently as he had come in.

A few moments later, Elisa Mae emerged carrying her suitcase stuffed with anything and everything she could find. She had her clothes, gifts from Henry and Albert, pictures, and the bible her mama had given her. There was no telling how long she would be staying. Her heart broke into pieces when she walked past Evelyn's bed. She watched her resting momentarily, but she knew better than to tempt fate.

She walked to the parlor where Charles stood with the front door open, revealing the downpour outside.

"Well?"

She grabbed her suitcase and walked slowly to the truck, not caring that the rain had soaked her to the bone. Charles jumped into the driver's seat as if they were going to a carnival and backed out of the drive and down the hill, away from the farm, away from the only thing that Elisa Mae knew.

Charles drove to the highway and stopped the truck. He handed her a one-way bus ticket to Knoxville and $5 in cash.

"The bus will be along about dawn. When ya get to the bus station in Knoxville, get a taxi cab with that money and tell 'em to take ya to Stella's."

Elisa Mae sat in the seat of the truck for a moment, unsure of what was happening.

"You want me to get out here? In the rain? You aren't taking me?"

He grabbed his shotgun and swung it in her general direction.

"Get out of my truck you filthy whore."

Elisa Mae exited the truck with her bus ticket, cash and suitcase. In an instant, he was gone, leaving her there alone on the side of the highway in the pouring rain.

Chapter Twenty-Three

*T*he bus driver came to a stop and opened the doors. He rolled his eyes as if he were staring at a dirty prostitute, beaten and on the run. "You got cash or a ticket?"

Elisa Mae held up the one way ticket in the torrential rain. He sighed, took her ticket, and exited the bus to load her luggage underneath. She stepped aboard the bus, looking for a seat, but each eye turned away from her. She could only imagine how awful she looked. She found an empty seat near the rear and slid in.

The drive to Knoxville in the rain was dark, sad, long and lonely. She allowed herself to become numb. The pain, physically and emotionally, was too much for her to bear. When they finally arrived at the bus station, she did exactly as Charles had commanded, hailed a taxicab and gave the driver Stella's address.

The rain continued to pour to the point where Elisa Mae thought, even wished, that it would create a river and wash her away.

When they arrived at the house that Stella, Burke, Rose and Catherine called home, she noticed Charles's truck parked in the street. She paid the driver and got out of the taxicab. Cautiously she walked to the long porch of the grey painted shotgun house. The house that had been the boarding home that Stella and Mabel lived in was given to Stella and Burke as a wedding gift from Burke's mother. It had been converted into a single house and was now where they called home.

Elisa Mae stood on the porch for a long time with her suitcase beside her, terrified to knock on the door.

Elisa Mae was taken aback when the door was abruptly opened. She let out the deep breath she had been holding when she saw that it was Burke.

"It's her," he said to someone inside. Directing his attention back to Elisa Mae, he said, "What are you doing just standing out here, honey? You're soaked. Let's get you inside."

Elisa Mae moved out of the shadows of the long porch and Burke gasped loudly. Stella was at the door immediately after and started screaming hysterically. She stomped back into the house and continued her rant, screaming and crying uncontrollably. "You swore you'd never lay a hand on her. You SWORE it to me and to God!"

Burke brought Elisa Mae's shivering body into the small parlor of the shotgun house. Burke quietly walked through the doorway to the back of the house. Elisa Mae stood in the corner as a wild-eyed Charles tried to defend his actions. "I done told ya what she was. She's a tramp and a whore and I told ya what she's been doin' with that boy."

Elisa Mae looked up stunned. "I haven't done anything with Albert! I promise I haven't!" She was passionate and sincere in her words, but they came out quietly, in a quivering voice.

Burke walked back into the small parlor and aimed his service revolver directly at Charles. "Get the hell out of my house and don't ever come back. You ever lay a hand on that girl again, I'll kill you myself."

Charles left the house screaming like a madman. "Ya can keep her and her whoring ways! Her and Stella belong together!"

Stella went directly to comfort Elisa Mae and try to calm her fears. Burke tended to Rose and Catherine; they were both crying from their room in the back of the house.

"He shouldn't have done this to you, Elisa Mae. I'm so sorry."

"It's not your fault, Mama." Elisa Mae had always made a point to call her mama when Charles wasn't around. She felt she owed her much more, but at least that, for bringing her into this world, however harsh it may be.

Stella remembered the pain and the terror she had borne under Charles's hand. Her heart ached for Elisa Mae and the agony she had endured. She took Elisa Mae to the bathroom, which was through the bedroom where Burke and Stella slept. Elisa Mae saw her face for the first time in the mirror and her tears began to run once more. The entire left side of her jaw was swollen, black, bloody, and bruised. Her lip was split and she already knew from her own investigation with her tongue that she had lost a molar. Her jaw and lip were too swollen to actually see which tooth was gone.

"We're going to put some peroxide on it and clean it up as best we can. There's nothing much it can do but heal," Stella stated.

"My tooth is gone."

Stella turned red, but she tried to control her words. The girls had heard enough already.

"I'd like to see Rose and Catherine, but I'm afraid I'll scare them."

"Let Burke get them settled down and you can see them in a bit. They're excited about seeing you, but you're right. It's going to break their hearts to see you this way."

"I think I'd like to get some rest anyway." Elisa Mae's exhaustion washed over her in a wave.

"You lay down on our bed and take a nap."

"I can't do that. I'll just sleep in the chair there." She pointed to a dressing chair in the corner.

"Don't be silly. We'll work out other arrangements later, but you rest up on our bed for now."

Elisa Mae was too tired to argue. She laid her head on the pillow and thought about being called a tramp and a whore. She had decided that she must be these things because she was a bastard. Somehow in her mind they became one and the same. She had been tarnished from birth and would forever carry those badges. Finally, restful sleep fell upon her.

Arrangements were made where Elisa Mae slept in Rose's bed, and Rose and Catherine slept together. In the beginning, she spent every second with them, wanting to be as close to them as she could, trying to capture each moment she had missed with them.

Soon, her face was healing, but her heart was not. She missed her mama and the mountains so much that sorrow overtook her. She became quiet and sullen. In the beginning of her stay, she talked and played with Rose and Catherine often, but as time went on, she rarely enjoyed time with the girls anymore and they had resolved to leave her alone. Even at their age, they understood that she had gone through something harsh and horrible.

Albert would come to see her often, and Stella and Burke never minded her going with him. He seemed to be the only happiness in her life. She continued to evade his advances, terrified of actually being what she was accused of.

She talked to Albert about these things and he understood. He became frustrated at times, as most men do, but he cared for her. He loved her and he would have given his life to protect her.

No matter what anyone said to Elisa Mae, she could not get the thought out of her head that she was nothing but a filthy whore. It repeated over and over again in her mind. Her anguish was torturous and apparent to all those around her.

School had been in session for about a month, but she had not enrolled in the school in Knoxville. She became so homesick and heartbroken that she cared for nothing. Albert tried to talk to her about getting married and getting a place of their own, but all Elisa Mae could think about was returning to Evelyn and the farm.

There was a knock on the door one day while the girls were at school and Burke was at work. Stella was in the very back of the house, in the kitchen. Elisa Mae answered the door to find a telegram messenger. She signed for the telegram and walked through the house to Stella.

"This just came."

Stella had just placed a roast in the oven and was wiping her hands on her apron. "Who would have sent a telegram?"

"I don't know. I was wondering the same thing."

Stella opened it up and found these words:

> Didn't seem respectful to tell you
> on the telephone Stop Poppie has
> passed away Stop Please come as
> soon as you can Stop Love Mama
> Stop

Small tears formed around Stella's eyes. "He lived a long life. It was a hard life, but he had some good times. I'm going to miss him." She laid the telegram down on the tiny counter space and walked to her bedroom.

Elisa Mae held the paper in her hand and read it again. Little Grandpa was gone. She wasn't even there to say goodbye. It was another notch of resentment in a long line that she held for Charles.

By that afternoon they were all headed back to Newport to attend Poppie's funeral.

Upon their arrival, Rose and Catherine jumped out of the sedan and ran straight to Evelyn and Mabel. "Granny! Aunt Mabel!" They sang in unison and took turns squeezing them both tight.

Elisa Mae lagged behind for a moment. When Evelyn laid eyes on her, Elisa Mae ran to her, throwing her arms around her, she buried her head in her shoulder and cried. Evelyn stroked her hair and whispered softly in her ear how much she had missed her. This only made Elisa Mae cry harder.

After she had calmed down, she stood as an adult with the other adults conversing over Poppie's death.

"We found him in the middle room of the back house. He was curled up in the back corner, squatted down with his knees pulled in. He was holding tight to his flask. His head was tucked down, and I guess he had choked on his own vomit." Evelyn replayed the events for the others.

Stella thought back to one of the worst days of her life and how she had escaped death in that exact same place. Funerals on that hill sent Stella's mind to a place she did not want to be.

While Elisa Mae was sad to see Little Grandpa go, she was relieved that her mama and JH didn't have to worry about him any more. She felt guilt from her relief, but she was somewhat happy that she was at least feeling something.

Elisa Mae was sitting on the porch thinking when Charles came and sat beside her. She had been trying to avoid him, and this was the closest they had been since she was sent to Knoxville.

"How ya farin'?"

"Fine, I guess."

"Ya're mama's been missin' ya real bad. She's been cryin' every night for ya. Maybe it's time ya think about comin' back home."

"OK."

"Good." He stood up and walked across the yard to speak with some other kin. That was that.

Elisa Mae's head spun again. He had been so nonchalant, like it had been her idea to leave in the first place. While pondering, she decided that she would not question. She wanted to come home and the only way to do that was to be on his side.

After the funeral, Charles followed them back to Knoxville. Elisa Mae gathered her things, said her goodbyes to Rose and Catherine, hugged Stella and Burke one last time, and was returned to her home in the mountains. Nothing about the series of events that had taken place was ever mentioned.

Elisa Mae was soon enrolled back in classes and was trying to make the best of her junior year of high school. Charles had banned her from seeing Albert at all, but Pat, Bo and other friends would sneak her away, saying they were going to one event or another, and would take her to see him. Her time with Albert was everything to her. They shared their hopes, their cares, and their dreams. They had both professed their love for one other eternally. She began to regret not marrying him when he had asked in Knoxville because he never mentioned it again.

Elisa Mae received letters from Henry, always disguised in a letter to Evelyn or Mabel from Marlene. He would tell her he loved her and missed her and would inform her of how Tommy was doing. She was hurt that Tommy didn't write to her personally, but she understood and forgave him.

In one such letter from Henry, he gave the news that Justine was pregnant and that Elisa Mae would soon be having another new brother or sister. She had become used to surprise in her life, so the news of yet another sibling gave her joy, but she was not elated. She knew that this child would be kept from her also, and would only be available on special occasions, if at all.

One cold, December afternoon, Charles came to Elisa Mae in her room. Evelyn and Mabel had gone to the church for a ladies luncheon. "Come with me," he stated flatly.

Elisa Mae's first reaction was one of fear, but something in the tone of his voice told her that something was wrong. She slipped on her coat and boots and followed Charles to the truck. He didn't say a word as they drove down the hillside. When they reached the highway headed to Knoxville, Elisa Mae became terrified. Mustering all of her courage, she asked him where they were going.

"That boy's been in a car accident. He was on his way home from Knoxville and hit a culvert. My friend, Danny, ya know, the ambulance driver came to tell me. He's in real bad shape, and he's askin' for ya. I'm takin' ya to the hospital in Knoxville where they got him."

Elisa Mae felt sick. Her stomach churned back and forth until she had to ask Charles to stop the truck. She opened the door, leaned out and vomited violently. She sat back in the truck, closed the door, cried, and began to pray harder than she had ever prayed before. She was pleading with God.

They arrived at the hospital, Charles guiding Elisa Mae through her maze of shock. When they arrived in the room, Mary, Albert's mother, sat alone beside Albert, holding his hand. He was hooked up to many tubes, and his face was bruised and battered all over. His right arm was in a full cast, as was his left leg that hung in a sling from the ceiling.

When Mary saw Elisa Mae, she jumped up to hug her. "I'm so glad ya're here. He's been askin' fer ya."

Elisa Mae's shock was still apparent as she stared at the love of her life, hanging onto his life by a thread.

"Elisa Mae?" She heard a faint whisper. "Is that you?"

She was by his side before he finished speaking, "Yes, I'm here, Albert." She grasped his hand and held tight.

"Was wonderin' if you was gonna make it." His voice was so soft it was barely audible.

"Daddy brought me."

"Miracles never cease." They both giggled before he coughed and gasped for air.

"You should rest," she said.

He grabbed her hand. "Don't leave me."

"Never."

For three days Albert progressively got worse, but neither Mary nor Elisa Mae ever left his side. They would cry together in anguish when they saw his pain worsen. Doctors would come in and speak to them about his condition, but the outcome was always grim. There was never any improvement - never any good news to speak of.

"I can't stand to see him hurtin' like this!" Mary cried out one day. "It's too much! He's a good boy! He shouldn't suffer this a way!"

Elisa Mae got up to comfort her, and they each broke down in the other's grip. They held tightly to one another, fearing if they let go, they may fall into an eternal darkness of gloom and despair.

Late in the evening on the third day, the sounds of the machines began to change. Elisa Mae and Mary both jolted, but before they could respond, they were surrounded by nurses telling them they would have to leave the room.

"I promised I wouldn't leave him!" Elisa Mae cried out.

"I'm sorry, Miss, but you'll have to go." She was being pushed out the door with Mary behind her. They swung a large curtain around where he lay, so while they could see through the tiny window of the hospital door, they could not see what was happening. Doctors and nurses rushed in and out of the room, none of whom spoke to Mary or Elisa Mae.

They sat in the chairs across the hall from his room, held hands, and prayed. Tears already streamed down Elisa Mae's face as she saw the doctor emerge from Albert's room and approach them. "I'm sorry. We did all we could."

Mary tilted her head back and wailed at the ceiling. The sound of pain that emanated from her at that very moment would haunt Elisa Mae forever. She had lost her only son - her only family. She was alone.

Sobs escaped Elisa Mae's throat as her continuous tears flowed. She sat back in the chair she had been seated in and covered her face. She felt nothing but darkness and pain. The world looked black and white.

It was such a bitter cold winter that the ground was too frozen to dig the grave. Elisa Mae ached at the thought of Albert alone in a dark, dank morgue. She stayed with Stella and Burke, but she could not sleep. Each time she would finally fall asleep, her dreams were filled with unspeakable horrors that caused her to wake, shaking and frightened. She would try not to fall back to sleep. She would stare at the wall, or at the girls in their peaceful dreams.

She realized she didn't know where she stood in her life. Albert had been everything to her and he was gone in the blink of an eye.

The day of the funeral, Elisa Mae's eyes were dark and sunken. She had lost so many pounds in just a few days that her cheekbones were prominent. Her dark hair was pulled up messily and she was a shell of the girl she had been a week prior.

Mary came to Elisa Mae and said, "I thought you might want this." She held up her class ring that dangled on a chain, which had hung around Albert's neck.

"Put it back on him." Elisa Mae snipped her words through the air.

"But, I thought you may...."

"I said I want to put it back on him." She grabbed the necklace from Mary and walked to the casket, re-latching the clasp around his neck.

She felt instantly sorry for the way that she had treated Mary and went to apologize.

"It's alright, dear. We're all gonna grieve our own ways."

"He's worn it for almost three years. He deserves to keep it. I'll never know anyone else like him."

"Neither will I, darlin'. Neither will I."

They embraced again and somehow made it through the hardest ceremony of their lives. After he was lowered into the ground and they were leaving the cemetery, Elisa Mae dropped shreds of her heart on the ground as she walked away.

CHAPTER TWENTY-FOUR

The long journey back to Newport passed in no time at all. Elisa Mae was surprised when they pulled into the drive between the barn and gated yard. She was so lost in her thoughts and emotions that time had slipped away. She stepped out of the truck in a trance and entered the farmhouse. She walked directly to her room and closed the door.

Reaching under her bed, she pulled out the puzzle box JH had sent her and placed it on the bed. She tediously went through the steps to open it. Once inside, she pulled out letters and photographs of Albert and examined each one carefully. She placed them in a tidy stack, stood, and walked to the back yard, to the side nearest the fields of the back house. She placed the items atop the fire pit and lit a match under the stack until it caught fire. She watched them burn – each photo, each letter, each tangible item that proved he ever existed. She didn't understand why she was possessed to do such a thing, but something told her that this was how she grieved. She cried for him. Her heart ached and broke into pieces for him. She knew she would never know anyone else like him. She knew that she had lost the greatest love of her life in him. All that she had now was his memory – and she would hold those memories dear to her forever.

❈ ❈ ❈

Elisa Mae threw herself into her schoolwork and farm chores. She had spent her summer in a trance, distracted at every corner. Her thoughts consumed her. She pushed herself in her studies her senior year of school - making very good grades, being on the annual staff, as well as the school newspaper and Beta Club - but she felt she didn't belong anywhere. She felt isolated and alone. While everyone liked her and spoke with her often, she would put up a front, smile, and play the part because she couldn't bear to be around others that were a part of Albert's group.

Pat was her only true friend. Pat, Bo, and Elisa Mae had become very close as they grieved Albert's death, and she felt that Pat was the only one that truly understood her and her feelings. She missed Albert dearly and wanted him near.

One day, early at school, Elisa Mae closed her locker door and saw James Durrell standing behind her.

"Oh, James, you scared me."

"Well, I sure didn't mean to do that. I was just wondering how you've been. Been worried about you, I guess."

It had been almost a year since Albert's death.

"I'm doing alright. Better. That's sweet of you to ask."

"Would you like to grab a Coke with me after school?"

"I, umm…." She didn't quite know how to respond.

"If you don't want to, I'll understand."

"No, it's not that. It's just that I haven't really been out since, well, since Albert."

"It's just a Coke, Elisa Mae."

She smiled at him and at herself. "You're right. I'd love to."

"Meet you out front after school."

He was gone in seconds. The bell rang, and Elisa Mae rushed to class.

Her class time was spent not concentrating on the lesson, but on James. He was a handsome boy and was very kind and tender hearted.

While she didn't know him well, she did know of him. His family was very prominent in Newport and known by all.

They went for a Coke that afternoon at Stokely's Drug Store and found a booth in the back. Stokely's was always a busy hang out after school, and many people witnessed them having a Coke, laughing, and talking in a back booth. Neither James nor Elisa Mae noticed because they were charmed with each other's company. They were both lonely and in need of one another. Sitting at the booth for hours, they connected, and for the first time in a long time, she was happy.

Word quickly spread. Most people spoke about how James could do much better than her. He had an upstanding and well respected family in Newport and Elisa Mae, no matter how rich she felt, was considered nothing more than poor mountain trash.

While she was leaving, James asked if he could give her a ride home. She had said no, not sure if Charles would be there and not wanting to face what would take place if he were.

Pat was driving her mother's sedan that day and drove Elisa Mae up to her mountainside farm. "What was that all about?"

"What do you mean?" Elisa Mae's mind shot back to Lorene's reaction to Albert.

"Well, ya know, I just. Look. I don't want to sound mean or anything, but that's James Durrell. You know how his family is and all."

"I don't know. I guess I just didn't think about it. He's a really nice guy and we had a great time."

"But, you two don't even have anything in common. I just don't understand."

"It was just a Coke, Pat."

Through the months, Elisa Mae had dreams of a different life. James wasn't reckless and daring like Albert. In fact, he was nothing like Albert at all. She could have a different life with him - a life she'd never really known before. He could take her to places unknown, places she wasn't looked down upon and where she would be respected. James adored her and made her feel special. He wrote sweet poems and letters to her and they were both soon declaring their love.

Charles seemed smitten with the fact that Elisa Mae was dating James. He was impressed with his family and felt that he himself could gain from their union.

"I'd like you to wear my ring," James stated one day while they were on a picnic by the creek. It was an unusually warm early-spring day

She smiled and said, "I'd love to."

He slipped the ring that he had placed on a chain around her neck. As he latched the clasp, all she could think of was her own class ring, buried with a man she knew she had loved like no other. She said a silent prayer, begging God not to ever let her suffer the pain she had endured again.

Elisa Mae had developed a terrible sense of loss after Albert. She felt that if she would have married him, would have stayed with him, would have given him her all, then she would not have lost him.

It was out of this fear of loss that she gave into James that day by the creek. A tear escaped her eye and rolled down past her ear, were she heard the words *Tramp* and *Whore*. But she allowed the sounds of the rushing creek to wash them away.

They remained close, they felt the love each had for the other and it continued this way. It wasn't long before she started to see the signs. She was going to have a baby.

She went to James as soon as she was certain. He promised to not leave her. They would work through this together. When they went to Charles and Evelyn and said they wanted to be married as quickly as possible, Elisa Mae's hands shook in fear. James held them to steady her.

"Well, that's jus' wonderful news!" Charles proclaimed. He put his arm around James's shoulders and walked him through the yard.

Evelyn looked at Elisa Mae knowingly. "Are you with child?"

Elisa Mae lowered her head as a tear escaped her eye. "Yes Ma'am."

"I thought better of you than that, Elisa Mae. I thought you thought better of you than that, too." She let out a sigh and walked into the house.

Elisa Mae followed her inside, pleading with her. "I'm so sorry, Mama. It just happened. I don't know what I was thinking. Please don't be mad at me."

Evelyn stopped and hugged Elisa Mae tightly. "I'm not mad at you, child. I'm mad at the situation. You've had to endure the filthy words and thoughts of others your whole life and now I'm afraid you'll be doing that forever. I'm going to help you any way I can. We'll get you hitched quick, and I will always stand beside you. I just can't help the fact that I'm disappointed."

"I know, Mama. I'm so sorry," Elisa Mae sobbed heavily into Evelyn's shoulder.

Preparations were immediately made for the ceremony. They had decided to have the wedding at Foster and Bessie's house. Stella came to visit when she first heard the news. When she arrived, she pulled Elisa Mae to the side. "You're pregnant, aren't ya?"

"Did Mama tell you?"

"Nobody had to tell me. How could you do this?" Stella's words were harsh and bitter.

"How could *I* do this? What do you mean how could I do this? What about you? At least I'm doing the right thing and not running away like you did!" Her words cut like an ax through Stella's heart. She instantly regretted saying them to her and wished she could somehow suck the words back in, but the damage was done. Without another word, Stella walked back into the house where the other women decorated and made food for the reception.

They were soon saying their *I do*'s and having their celebrations. Elisa Mae's heart was filled with joy and broken in two at the same time. She felt she had betrayed Evelyn and Stella. She was forever fearful that Charles would find out, and the horror that lie behind that knowledge was incomprehensible. If he did know or suspect, he never said a word.

Others, however, were not so nice. Several times during the reception she heard spiteful words directed at why they would rush to be married so quickly. James stayed at Elisa Mae's side and if such words were within earshot, he would take her the other direction.

Mr. and Mrs. Durrell had given them money for a down payment on a house in a quaint neighborhood in town. They moved into their tiny home and settled into their new lives as newlyweds with a baby on the way.

Elisa Mae began to write letters to Henry frequently, as this was the first time in her life that she had her own address and did not have to hide their communication. Tommy had returned home and was living near Henry in Virginia. He was married and had a child of his own with another on the way, and they began writing to each other as well. She ached for them and longed to be near them.

On a cold December day, Elisa Mae went into labor and was taken to Valentine Shultz Clinic where a tiny 5 pound baby girl was born. There were many complications, and Evelyn stayed by Elisa Mae's side the entire time. She had said early on in her pregnancy that she was going to name the baby Renee if it were a girl, but because of Evelyn's devotion, when the nurse asked what the baby's name would be, Elisa Mae plainly stated, "Evelyn. Evelyn Renee." They handed the tiny, quiet child to her and she cuddled her close, holding her tight. "We'll call her Evie."

Evelyn beamed at the new life offered to the world.

A few months after Evie's birth, Elisa Mae wrote a letter to Justine, asking if it would be alright if they came for a visit. Elisa Mae and James had been talking about a vacation, and since he had never met her true father, they felt that a vacation to Virginia would be logical. Elisa Mae made sure to address the letter she wrote to Justine because she felt that she would be intruding on her family, not Henry's.

A week or so later a return letter arrived.

> *Dear Elisa Mae,*
>
> *We would be delighted to have you and your family come and visit with us. I have always regretted that we didn't get the chance to become closer. As far as I am concerned, your family is my family.*
>
> *All my love, Justine*

It was they longest trip that either of them had been on. When they reached the James River in Virginia, they pulled off the side of the road and gazed at its glory.

"Everything's so different here. I wonder if this could be the start of something new for us, Elisa Mae?"

"I hope so, James. I truly hope so."

They were greeted by everyone with joyous hugs and tears. Henry and Tommy looked just as she remembered them. Introductions were made all around, and their visit was wonderful. Lucy, Henry and Justine's young daughter, seemed most excited out of everyone. She jumped around, hugging Elisa Mae and James over and over and begging to play with Evie.

After things had settled, Elisa Mae followed Justine into the kitchen. "Does Lucy know?"

"No. She doesn't. She still seems a little young, and I think it would confuse her."

Elisa Mae sighed a breath of relief. She didn't want Lucy to react in the same way that Tommy had. She couldn't stand to shatter that little girl's heart.

They stayed for a week, everyone trying to put a lifetime of days lost into too short a time span. Many tears were shed as they loaded up their

Bel-Aire to return to Newport. Elisa Mae shed many tears, fearful that this was the last she would ever see them.

After returning to Newport, James and Elisa Mae started talking about moving to Newport News, Virginia. Their plans were kept silent when they learned that they were expecting another child. During her pregnancy, plans were made. Henry had made it perfectly clear that he would be able to get James a position at the shipyards. Justine started looking for a place for them to stay in her spare time. Elisa Mae began to secretly pack things she knew they would not need until they had moved. The months passed quickly.

Soon, Elisa Mae gave agonizing birth to a 10 pound baby boy named James William. He quickly earned the nickname of Will. Not only to avoid confusion of being named after his father, but for his stubbornness and strong will. Evie had been a quiet, happy baby. Will was demanding and challenged Elisa Mae at every turn, but he clung to Evelyn. He was calm in her arms and soothed by her touch.

A few months after his birth, Elisa Mae had a dinner party where she invited Charles, Evelyn, Mr. and Mrs. Durrell, Mabel, Stella and Burke. During their dinner, they announced that they would be making the move from Tennessee to Virginia. The table was silent for slight moment, then erupted. Mr. Durrell was screaming just as loudly as Charles, Stella and Burke chimed in as well. They all felt that splitting their families across that far of a distance would cause too much of a strain. Mr. and Mrs. Durrell were angry that they would not be able to spend time with their grandchildren. Stella felt the same way. Charles knew that he would not have the close ties to the Durrells if his daughter were so far away, but he never mentioned that; he only fought the same fight as everyone else.

Evelyn remained quiet. She knew that there were already problems in their marriage and that the change for both James and Elisa Mae would be good. She also felt that it was a need that could not be contained for Elisa Mae to be near her father.

Elisa Mae took Evelyn to the side and asked, "How do you feel about this, Mama?"

"Well, I think it'll be good for your marriage. I just don't want you to take those babies."

"I know, Mama. I know. We'll visit as often as we can. You know they're putting in that interstate system here really soon, so that will make the trip that much shorter."

They embraced. "Don't you ever forget that you have a mama on this mountain that loves you dearly."

"I won't, Mama. I promise."

The day came for them to move, and Tommy brought a friend with a large moving truck to bring all of their things. Elisa Mae was amazed at the amount of possessions she and James had acquired in their time together. Once the truck was loaded, it was early in the night, but it was already dark out. They decided to drive through the night.

When they pulled out of the driveway, they saw Charles with his shotgun in hand, blocking the middle of the road with his farm truck.

"Ya ain't a leavin' here!"

"What in the hell?" Tommy didn't know what to think and was more frightened than anyone.

Elisa Mae stepped out of the truck fearlessly. "Daddy, stop it. You're going to scare Evie. Now this has already been decided. We're moving and that's that!"

Charles looked confused for a moment and then regained himself. "Ya ain't a goin' nowheres!"

Suddenly, police lights flashed, and a deputy stepped out of his car. "Charles? Now, come on, Charles, you're gonna have to move your truck. You can't block 'em in forever."

Charles looked around, somewhat unsure of his surroundings.

"Come on, Charles. Why don't you let me take you home?" The deputy stepped over to Charles and guided him steadily to his patrol car. He then came back and moved Charles's truck to the side of the road. "Sure am gonna miss you two and them little ones. Y'all take care, now!"

"Thank you, Hank," Elisa Mae stated. She had small tears flowing down her cheeks as she reentered the vehicle.

"Are you alright, Elisa Mae? It's not too late. We can call this whole thing off right now if you want." James tried to soothe her.

"No, I'm fine. I just hate to see him this way."

The truck went into gear, and the long journey to Virginia began.

Elisa Mae stayed with Henry and Justine until they found a small house on Gay Drive in Newport News. James had gotten work right away at the shipyards, and Elisa Mae began her first job as a waitress at the Gourmet Inn.

On Lucy's 9th birthday, they had planned a big party for her. Early in the day, Elisa Mae was in the kitchen baking cupcakes for the party when Justine said, "I'm going to tell Lucy you're her sister. She loves you so much, and she is old enough now to know the truth."

"Oh, Justine, I wish you wouldn't. I don't want her to hate me."

"She could never hate you!"

"Elisa Mae!" Henry bounded through the front door. "Come with me! I have a quick surprise for you."

Elisa Mae quickly washed up and followed Henry outside and got into his truck.

"Where are we going?"

"Well, it wouldn't be a surprise if I told you!"

He drove to a tiny airstrip where a small twin engine plane sat running. They stepped out of the truck, and Elisa Mae looked bewildered.

"This is my buddy, Chuck. He's gonna take us for a little ride!"

"In *that?*"

"C'mon! It'll be fun!"

They climbed aboard the small aircraft and were soon taking off. Elisa Mae thrilled at the plunge in her stomach as the plane left the ground. The plane flew over the city and streets, and soon Elisa Mae could see the ocean. She gasped in wonderment. It was an experience like none she had ever known.

After they landed, Elisa Mae and Henry stepped back into the truck and made their way home to the party preparations. The churning in her stomach turned from excitement to despair, frightened of what Lucy's reaction would be and wondering when and how they would tell her.

They pulled into the long driveway, and before the truck had stopped, Lucy was bounding down the front steps. Elisa Mae stepped out of the truck and faced her. Lucy looked at her for a moment then flung her arms around Elisa Mae, squeezing tight. In a soft voice she whispered, "I'm so glad you're my sister."

EPILOGUE

I remember a gentle old man sharing an ice cream cone with me on a tattered old couch. He was just as messy as I was, but he didn't care. I would gaze at the large shotgun always propped beside him and wonder what it was. I also remember climbing the stairs of what I now know to be a funeral home because I was told he was in Heaven, and I was sure that Heaven was up there. I missed him, and I wanted to see him.

I remember making the trip up that gravel road every other Sunday and every Easter. I clearly remember the Easter dress I wore the last Easter she was with us. I was 9. She was buried on Mother's Day. I feel her in my heart. I know she is there, and she always will be. She was loved by so many, and to this day, I love to hear a story told about her. Her unfailing love made my mother who she is. No one would have made it through any of it without her love, guidance and wisdom.

I lost Mabel when I was 19 years old. I had just met the man who is now my husband. He never had a chance to meet her. I wish he had. He would have loved her as much as I did and always will. My husband, who is originally from California, had just moved to Tennessee at the time of her death. He was amazed that not only did every car pull over and place their headlights on as a sign of respect, but also that the train that ran through town had stopped in its tracks to allow her funeral procession to proceed.

She had married a man of low degree when she was 72 years old. It was her first marriage. She just couldn't stand the loneliness anymore after Granny passed. She died unexpectedly during a routine surgery and left no will. Most of the land was lost, and a piece of me has never been the same.

Uncle Burr-Head passed away unexpectedly one beautiful summer day. I drove like lightning from Missouri to be there for the funeral. My brother also drove at breakneck speed from Virginia. Somehow, we both heard "Free Bird" by Lynyrd Skynyrd on different radio stations in different parts of the country on our way back to that mountain. It is a rarity to hear that song played on any station in its entirety – a rarity, just like JH. My brother and I both grieved. If there were ever a song to describe him, that would be it. He was the first person to place me upon a horse. He was also the reasoning behind my first motorcycle ride. I loved him dearly, and I regret that I didn't tell him enough. He rests upon that mountain, in Dunn's Cemetery, with so many others that lived in our line.

Grandma Stella died during the time that I was writing these words. She didn't understand much when she died. She had Alzheimer's disease, and in the end, she was reliving the words that are written here. As much as I miss her, it was a blessing when her suffering ended. She had a wonderful life after she met Burke. She had a true love and a beautiful family. To see her revert back to the torture of her younger years was too much for any of us to bear. She did the best she could with what she was given, and after everything was said and done, she won. She had made it, and she was happy. But, she always remembered him. During a moment of clarity, she asked that "Wildwood Flower" by The Carter Family be played at her funeral. Not many understood why, but I did. So did my mother. It's true what they say; you never forget your first love, however tragic it may be.

My mother escaped, but there was always a piece of her left on that mountain, for one reason or other.

After she and James married, had my sister and brother, and moved to Virginia, for the love of the mountain that he had left and the regret of leaving his family and home, James had to return. As much as he loved Elisa Mae and their children, Newport and that mountain called to him. She watched him get on a bus and ride south, back to Tennessee and the rain that it held.

She met my father when Tommy took her to see a band at The Moose Club. He was the lead singer in the band and the most handsome man she had ever seen. When he spoke, she was fascinated with his British accent. He had just arrived from England. He told her that having two names was silly, and from that day forward she was known only as Mae. They were soon married. He raised my brother and sister as his own, without question. My father also had a son from a previous marriage in England. He eventually came to live with us, and the close-knit, complicated family that I know and love was created.

I was born and at age 4, we also moved back to Tennessee. Newport was only ever a visit, though. We lived in Knoxville.

I always knew that there was an abundance of rain in Tennessee. It wasn't until I learned this story that I understood how much it truly meant.